SAFE HARBOR

K.SINKO

Copyright © 2023 by K. Sinko

All rights reserved.

Cover design by Studio Ryley

Editing by Britt Tayler

No part of this book may be reproduced in any form or by any electronic or mechanical means, including information storage and retrieval systems, without written permission from the author, except for the use of brief quotations in a book review.

This is a work of fiction. All the names, characters, businesses, places, events and incidents in this book are either the product of the author's imagination or used in a fictitious manner. Any resemblance to actual persons, living or dead, or actual events is purely coincidental.

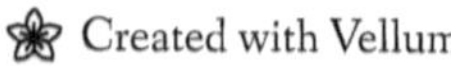 Created with Vellum

For my brothers, Mike and Bo.

I love you a stupid amount,
and I'm proud of you every day.

Chapter One

EVERYONE WAS STARING.

Melanie kept her gaze down at her black flats as she shuffled over to her locker. Students stepped to the side as she breezed past, their curious gazes and whispers causing her face to flush. But she didn't bother looking up or giving them her attention. Giving them more fuel for what would most likely be dubbed the juiciest gossip at Garrison Prep.

Thankfully, she knew no one would try talking to her. No one at the prestigious prep school ever did, unless it was necessary for a class or a project. Melanie was used to the wallflower life, to being a nobody at a school full of students hoping to be somebodies. Senators, authors, and rocket scientists were just some of the many notable graduates of Garrison Prep, all moving on to become alumni at the top ivy league schools. It was part of why Melanie never allowed anything below an A on her report cards in the past three years. If working herself to the bone gave her the chance to follow in her father's footsteps and become the next Albertson to graduate from Yale, she would do it.

The other reason had to do with why everyone had been staring at her all day.

She opened up her locker, switched out her textbooks, and sneaked a quick peek at her phone, noticing one text had come through from her mom during her last class. She anxiously tapped in her passcode and opened up the latest message.

It was a photo of a cake, slathered with a thick layer of purple frosting.

MOM

Happy birthday!!

Melanie's heart lurched at the sight of it, at how different this birthday was shaping up to be. In truth, her birthday hadn't felt normal for years now. Yet after what happened, she knew this year was going to quite literally take the cake for the worst birthday yet.

She swallowed, pushing her disappointment deep down like she always did, and sent back a single purple heart emoji. Her mother started typing almost immediately, the three little gray dots bouncing on her screen.

MOM

We're going to have a family meeting tonight with cake. Your father and I have things to discuss with you.

Another meeting. Another "Grand Plan" to fix the horror they were living in. Her stomach turned as she typed back.

MELANIE

Will he be there?

The dots began dancing again, taking an excruciatingly

long time. Melanie readjusted her headband as she waited, smoothing her carefully straightened chestnut-brown hair so it would lie perfectly flat down her back. She kept her gaze on her phone in her locker as she listened to the murmuring of students passing her by.

"I heard he was expelled," someone whispered.

"They say he was in the hospital for three days," someone else responded.

She shifted uncomfortably as she stood there waiting. Her answer was one word.

MOM

Yes.

~

SHE WAS RIGHT. The worst birthday yet.

Melanie stared down at her corner of the cake, completely speechless. She hadn't even had a chance to dig into her slice before they dropped it on her.

Mom made the same one every year—a round chocolate cake with deep purple frosting, the perfect combination of pink and blue for a shared birthday. She always cut the round circle into four giant slices as they split it amongst themselves, a tradition they kept up with since before she could even remember.

Melanie turned to her right as she silently watched her twin brother dig into his cake without saying a word. No surprise on his face, no signs of shock or anger or shame. Just a placid, serene look as he broke off a large chunk with his fork and shoveled it into his mouth.

"When?" Melanie asked softly, turning back to her parents.

Mom's shoulders were squared, her back straight, clearly looking just as uncomfortable as this conversation. Dad's eyes were drawn to his lap.

"Next Saturday, after your last day of school."

Moving.

She couldn't believe it. Duncan blew up his life completely, and now, they were leaving it. She listened patiently as her parents rambled on at first, telling her that Duncan needed a fresh start and a change of scene. How this environment was no longer working out for him, and he needed somewhere that felt new yet familiar.

"T-to Haverport?" Melanie asked, stuttering over her words.

Mom nodded her head.

"The cottage we used to rent actually happened to be for sale," Dad said calmly, carefully wading through the sentence as he explained himself. Not like he needed to worry, Melanie was never one to freak out at them. "So I bought it."

Melanie's mind flashed back to the last time she stood in that cottage, right before she and Duncan started their first year of high school. They used to rent it out for one week in August every summer, always their last "hurrah" before starting the school year. The week was always filled with long beach days, and bike rides around town. They ate fresh seafood at Pop's and then dug into massive ice cream cones every night. Melanie thought about how blissfully happy she was during those summers at the cottage, and how naive she was to the evils that would soon come to stay.

But...the cottage in Haverport was at least five times smaller than their current home. The top floor was barely a small hallway with two bedrooms and one bathroom, which Melanie and Duncan always occupied. The bottom floor had the master bedroom for her parents, another bathroom, and an open kitchen and living room. It worked well for the single week they would spend there, especially given that they mostly hung out on the beach and were barely in the cottage at all. But the thought of the four of them living in tight quarters for longer? It was hard for Melanie to even conceptualize. And now they were going to move there —*live* there. For good.

"Haverport High said they would meet with us about Duncan's education," Mom said as if she understood the look of confusion on Melanie's face. "They're going to let him go to school."

And there it was—the real reason why they had to pack up their lives and move across the state. It wasn't just a change of scenery or a fresh start, it was the fact that a school was going to let Duncan actually attend and graduate.

"Public school?" Melanie asked, her words short and tight.

Mom let out a long breath. "Yes, public."

Feeling woozy, she gripped the side of her chair to steady herself, her vision going blurry for a moment.

Years of hard work...completely gone. Night after night of choosing to stay focused, and do her school work. All to get into Yale.

Even in elementary school, Yale was always the dream. Ever since the day her father put his old Yale cap on Melanie's head and beamed down at her with pride, she knew she'd do whatever it took to see that look again. It was such a rare occurrence to see her father looking proud these days, so if getting into Yale was the answer, she would do it.

But now...without a diploma from Garrison Prep...she

felt dizzy again at the thought, her knuckles going white as she gripped her chair.

"Mel."

She looked up, noticing it was her father who spoke, a mixture of compassion and sorrow flickering in his eyes. "Colleges don't really pay much attention to senior year when you apply," he said. "They'll look at all of your work before that. I wouldn't worry too much about it."

Melanie took a deep breath through her nose, trying to steady herself. "Okay," she said softly.

"Plus, Duncan said you can choose which room you want," Mom said.

Melanie glanced over at Duncan. He'd finished his slice, his plate licked clean of frosting. He twirled his fork around in his hands, eyes on his sister. His dirty blonde hair was slightly grown out, bouncy and curly, similar to how it looked every summer. She thought of those sunny days on the beach, chasing Duncan around as they collected crabs in buckets and built elaborate castles in the sand.

She felt like her throat was closing up as she looked into those eyes, wondering if they would ever return to that kind of innocence again. Duncan had yet to speak to her since it happened, and a small part of her hoped that moving to Haverport would finally be the catalyst that could change everything between the two of them.

She smiled at him, and to her surprise, he returned it—a small smile creeping up his cheek. She almost felt like it came with an apology and an invitation, to get back to what they were.

Melanie exhaled. "When should we start packing?"

MELANIE WAS TAPING up her last box when she heard a soft knock on her door. Dad poked his head through the frame, holding the coffee pot in his hand. "Top off?"

"Yes." Melanie exhaled, looking around her room. "Although I'm not exactly sure where I left my mug."

Dad pointed at the bookshelf beside him, a sunshine yellow mug sitting on the empty top shelf. "Maybe that one?"

Melanie smiled, reaching for it and holding it out to her father, who poured the last bit of coffee out. "So, your mother and I were hoping that you could head to the cottage first."

Melanie frowned. "But won't you need help?"

Dad waved off her question. "We need someone there to let the movers in, that will honestly be the biggest help."

"No problem," she said. "Will I be taking Duncan's car?"

"You mean your car."

She didn't say anything, taking a sip of her coffee. Sure, her parents had bought it for the two of them, but Melanie never even had a chance to sit behind the wheel. Duncan was always the one driving it, the one going to lacrosse practices or out with friends. The one time she asked to use the car it turned into a screaming match between Duncan and their parents, so Melanie knew not to make that mistake again.

And yet, her father still insisted that the car was *theirs* to share.

She evaded his statement. "Which one do you want me to take?"

He reached into his pocket with his free hand, giving Melanie a set of keys. "Your mother's. It's already packed with all sorts of delicate things she thinks won't make it in the big truck."

"Sounds good." She took the keys and slipped them into the back pocket of her jeans. "What time will the movers get there?"

"If everything goes to plan, should be by three," he said, placing the empty coffee pot down on a pile of boxes beside him. "Actually"—he flipped open his wallet—"you should have some time to grab lunch, I can give you some cash."

Melanie felt her chest tighten as she watched her father reach into his wallet and start rifling through bills.

"No," she said, placing her hand gently on top of his. "Don't worry about it, I have money from babysitting."

"Well, that's for college," Dad said. "You don't need to—"

"Dad," Melanie interrupted him. "Really, it's fine."

He sighed. She couldn't help but notice the exhaustion on his face. The dark circles around his eyes just kept getting bigger, and the wrinkles streaking across his forehead seemed even more prominent these days. She didn't want to be the cause of more worry or pain. That's why she took those random babysitting gigs this year—she didn't want her parents paying for anything else when they already had so much going on.

He finally surrendered, folding the wallet back up and sliding it back into his pocket. He reached toward Melanie and placed his hands on her shoulders, rubbing them with his thumbs. "How are you doing, kid?"

She mentally browsed her current catalogue of emotions at her dad's question. Utterly exhausted after a week of taking final exams. Annoyed at trying to avoid every pitiful gaze in the halls at school. Drained from having to pack up seventeen years of memories into just a few boxes.

Sad that Duncan still wasn't talking to her. Frustrated that her parents looked at her with the same expression every day—full of regret and sorrow.

Melanie felt tears welling up in her eyes, so she quickly squeezed her hands to make them stop, digging her nails into her palms. She smiled. "I'm fine."

"Are you sure?" Dad asked. "You know you can talk to us."

She knew that. She knew her parents would be there for her if she went to them. But right now, with so much going on with Duncan, she didn't want to be another burden. No need to worry about another kid. No need to make those dark circles any bigger than they already were.

"I know," she said, reaching over to give her Dad a kiss on the cheek, hoping it would put a natural end to the conversation.

He seemed to take the hint, pulling her into a tight hug. "All right, you call us if you need anything. Remember where it is?"

She spent every summer learning the ride by heart, every sign and turn of the road etched clearly in her memory. Bringing her to a place that seemed to only know happiness.

"Of course," she said. "How could I forget?"

PULLING OFF THE HIGHWAY, Melanie took the exit that led to Haverport. She immediately rolled down the windows, letting the salty sea air swirl through her mother's car. She followed the familiar route to Sandy Cove—a left down Franklin, then a right on Boston Ave, which eventually led to Main Street at the end of the road.

She turned slowly, marveling at how the little town looked exactly the same. All of the same shops were there—the movie theater, the boutiques, the bookstore. A line was snaking out of Grampy's Bakery as always; Melanie wondered if customers still queued up for a slice of that heavenly blueberry coffee cake.

She drove slowly through the town, her eyes continually glancing toward the shiny blue ocean beyond Main Street on her left, glimmering under the early summer sun. She took a deep, solemn breath. After months of rocky shores and sleepless nights, she felt thankful for the calm sea and the cozy familiarity.

Melanie reached the end of the main drag, greeted by the massive sign for Scoops By The Sea. She turned the corner, peering out her window as she gazed at the ice cream shop. She wondered how many ice cream cones she consumed with Duncan at that shop over the years, sitting at those picnic tables. Dozens? Maybe hundreds? There was that one summer when Duncan was determined to try all 32 flavors at the shop, ranking every flavor in a small notebook he carried in his back-pack. He finished every single one...except Rum Raisin. Said it wasn't worth massacring his taste buds for something so vile. She chuckled thinking of the venomous way Duncan had said *vile*, then immediately yearned for those simpler days.

The thought of his determination to finish every flavor that summer had Melanie flicking on the blinker of the car and pulling into the Scoops parking lot. Deep down, she wanted to stand in front of the shop again, wondering if a piece of Duncan was hidden somewhere in this special place.

She parked and pressed the button to kill the ignition, reaching to unbuckle her seatbelt. A movement at the shop window caught her eye through the side-view mirror as she watched a guy slide it open. Melanie froze, clenching her seatbelt as she watched him pull a small paperback novel out of his back pocket, leaning against the counter as he flipped it open. His hair was buzzed short, almost military-like, and the sleeves of his Scoops T-shirt were rolled up to reveal a set of toned arms that made her stomach do a summersault.

Okay, this was a dumb idea, she thought to herself. *He won't notice if I just go. Too engrossed in his book.*

But her stomach growled like it had other plans. It seemed packing that morning had distracted her from actually eating breakfast, and after consuming copious amounts of coffee, she knew it was probably smart for her to eat something.

She looked back through the mirror and noticed the guy now glancing toward her car, probably wondering what was taking so long. She squeezed her eyes shut, fully aware that if she left now, it would just be awkward.

Melanie unbuckled her seatbelt slowly and opened her wallet to grab some cash. She took a deep breath and opened the door, the heat from the sun blazing down on her pasty white arms. She made her way to the counter, watching as the guy continued to read his beaten-up copy of *Oliver Twist.*

Melanie watched him for a moment as he read, wondering what exactly she should do with her hands, which were now dripping with sweat. She crossed her arms tightly around her chest, glancing up at the menu.

Just like the rest of Haverport, the menu at Scoops didn't seem to have changed at all—still 32 flavors. Still an option to make it into a hot fudge sundae or a milkshake.

Still the three options to dip the cones in chocolate, strawberry, or butterscotch.

"Welcome to Scoops," drawled a deep voice from the counter. "What can I get you?"

Melanie glanced down at the guy, who was now staring up at her with a pair of eyes so strikingly blue, she instantly felt her face flush. She quickly looked back up at the menu, but all of her attention was on the small smirk on his face as he stared up at her. He closed his book.

"Uh—um," she said, her voice cracking slightly. "What's your favorite?"

"Oreo," he said confidently.

"Mmm," Melanie said, wincing internally. Why was she so awkward?

She glanced at him, noticing he was now standing upright, his arms crossed along his chest. He was much taller than she anticipated, definitely more than Duncan. Maybe six feet or so? She wasn't sure why she was hyper-focusing on his height when she *should* have been focusing on which flavor to order so she could get the hell out of there.

"Um, I'll have strawberry," she said quietly. "Two scoops."

He nodded. "Sugar, cake, or waffle?"

"Huh?"

"Cone? Which cone do you want?"

"Oh, uh, waffle, I guess."

He nodded, opening up a case next to him and grabbing what looked like a homemade waffle cone. Melanie watched as he reached for a clean ice cream scoop in a small bucket, noticing the way his arm flexed as he flicked the warm water from it. She turned toward the car, hoping he wouldn't notice how flushed her face was when he approached the window again.

Her phone buzzed in her hand.

MOM

Movers are en route!

Her stomach tightened. That gave her about thirty minutes to get to the cottage and open it up for the movers, and to also finish consuming what looked like the largest ice cream ever that was now coming toward her.

The guy held out her cone, a napkin wrapped tightly around the bottom. Melanie reached for it, her fingers grazing his hand, making her whole body zing. She pulled away immediately. "Thanks," she mumbled.

The guy smirked. "New to town?"

"That obvious?"

"Your headband and your polo sort of gave it away."

Melanie's face fell. "What's that supposed to mean?"

He shrugged. "Just that you look like the usual summer people we get."

"Summer people?"

"You know," he said, leaning back against the counter. "People with money who come for the summer. They rent all the pretty houses down the shore and essentially pay businesses in town enough to last them the rest of the year."

"And you can tell I'm one of them from my shirt?"

He shrugged, that smirk plastered on his face still. "Mostly the headband."

"What's wrong with my headband?"

"Girls here don't really wear them," he said.

"Great," she said sourly, turning away from the guy and very much feeling ready to get away from him. Not only was she new in town, but her wardrobe was going to make her stand out like a sore thumb. And it wasn't like she had any idea what to even wear to her new school.

"Hey, wait," he called out.

Melanie turned back toward him, feeling irritated.

"It's $3.75."

"Oh," she said. "Right, sorry." She reached into her pocket and pulled out a five.

The guy opened up the cash register and started counting coins at an excruciatingly slow pace, almost like he was doing it on purpose, his eyes roaming toward her.

"Keep it," Melanie said, feeling flustered. She had to somehow finish this cone and get to the house before the movers did.

"Thanks." He closed the register and tossed the change into a jar in front of him. "See ya, headband."

She rolled her eyes, wondering if she could balance her now-melting ice cream cone without getting it all over her mother's car.

Chapter Two

She couldn't.

Melanie had to pull over once she drove down the hill, the ice cream cone now melting down her hand and onto her lap. She turned the car carefully into Hillside Park. The gate was currently open, and no one sat at the small stand guarding the entrance. It was the first time she'd ever seen the stand boarded up and the park open to the public. She slowed the car down to read the sign that was nailed to the stand's door.

Summer season:
Memorial Day to Labor Day.
Get your passes!

Melanie only ever saw this place in August, when the parking lot was like a giant jigsaw puzzle, cars jam-packed in a long line trying to find an open spot. The streets were always lined with parked cars, some beachgoers even brave enough to park at the dirt lot up the hill as they climbed down with their beach chairs and umbrellas to avoid it altogether. Melanie's parents never bothered getting a beach pass for Hillside when they stayed in Haverport; it wasn't worth paying for a non-resident pass when they had easy access to Sandy Cove's private beaches whenever they wanted.

Melanie sat in her car and licked her ice cream as she watched a mom and a toddler by the water, the mom holding the baby's hands as he stomped his little feet in the wet sand. She wondered if maybe some families would need a babysitter this summer—it could help her make a little more money while keeping her away from what was going on at home.

She looked down at her cone, amazed at how she barely scratched the surface. Melanie wondered if that guy did it on purpose, or if the scoops really were supposed to be *that* big. She thought about the slight smirk on his face as he handed her the cone, his blue eyes twinkling deviously at her. Her stomach flip-flopped again at the thought of him, which frustrated her. She did *not* want to be thinking of him after he so clearly made assumptions about her based on her outfit.

Melanie looked at her phone, realizing she now only had ten minutes until the movers were set to arrive. She sighed, turning on the car and pulling out of the empty lot. As she inched toward the gate, she saw a trash can at the entrance and tossed the rest of her half-eaten cone into it.

She followed the windy road down the coastline, away from Hillside Park and down to the private beach communities. The houses were much smaller than the sprawling mansions she became accustomed to in Garrison, yet bursting with so much charm. Hydrangea bushes lined white picket fences in front of the cottages, blooming in soft pinks, purples, whites, and blues. She watched as Haverport came to life, joggers out on a run, neighbors greeting one another as they watered and pruned their hydrangeas as others grabbed the mail.

Melanie finally came to that familiar sign, the one that she and Duncan fervently looked for every summer as soon as Dad veered his car off the highway.

Sandy Cove.

Her eyes began to water as she pulled onto the sandy road and drove slowly down the row of cottages that had become so familiar to her. Spending a week in Sandy Cove every summer was her favorite part of the year. More than Christmas. More than her birthday. It meant she could relax and not have to worry about school or her grades. It meant she had time with Duncan without any lacrosse practices or friends interrupting them.

Eventually, those things became more important. The summer before their freshman year at Garrison, everything was about Duncan's lacrosse. Summer camps and travel games dominated their schedule, and practices for Garrison's team began an entire month before school started. Their week in Haverport soon became something of the past.

Melanie counted down the numbers on the cottages like they always did before reaching their summer home. *Nine, Eight, Seven, Six...*

And there was cottage five. Cedar shingles, baby blue shutters, white trimming, and a sweeping front porch. It looked exactly the same as it did when they left it three years ago. Like it was waiting for them to finally come home.

Melanie turned the car into the gravel driveway and cut the ignition, sliding out of her seat. The tiny rocks and seashells crunched underneath her Converse as she climbed up the creaky wooden steps. The porch swing was still there, swaying softly in the breeze. She dug into her pocket for her mother's keys and unlocked the front door.

Melanie expected the usual setup: the wicker couch and the lamps covered in seashells, the turquoise kitchen table with chipped paint, the pictures of Haverport lining the walls. But the stark emptiness of it startled her, how different it seemed on the inside. She made her way up the small staircase to the second floor, peeking into both rooms. Melanie and Duncan never really declared a room in summers past; they always shared the one, alternating which to stay in. One year they attempted to split into separate rooms, but Duncan gave up on the first night, slowly sneaking into Melanie's and tucking in next to her.

Each was empty except for a set of old curtains that still hung on her right, blanketing the space with darkness. The room on her left was full of streaks of light like they were beckoning her to enter. She stepped inside and gazed at the bay window in front of her, the bright sun beaming through. She sat down on the small wooden bench beneath the window, watching the afternoon light dancing on the waves at the beach across the street. The image of it all seemed so pure, so untouched and unaware of the anger and disappointment tainting Melanie's heart, that it finally made her cry. Tears streamed down her face willingly as she sat in the cottage staring out at the sea, wishing she could protect this special place from what was to come, wishing it would retain only her happy memories.

MELANIE HEADED down the stairs fully expecting to greet the movers but found two people in tie-dye standing near the front door instead.

She felt her shoulders drop away from her ears as she flew right into Jan Fletcher's arms.

"It's been too long, girlie," Jan said, giving her a tight squeeze. "We missed you."

"I missed you too," Melanie mumbled.

Jan gave her one more squeeze before pulling away, leaving her hands firmly planted on Melanie's arms, her face full of concern. "How are you doing?"

She shrugged. "As good as I can, I guess."

"Your mother told us everything. I'm so sorry. I can't imagine how you're feeling."

She simply shrugged again as she watched Dan Fletcher place a massive basket filled with different jam jars on the kitchen counter. The Fletchers lived in the cottage next door where they operated a jam-making business aptly named Fletcher Fam Jam. Jan said she started making jam after she retired because it gave her something to do, but when her friends convinced her to set up a small stand at the Haverport Farmer's Market, it was "game over" as Dan always said. The jam sold out every week in a matter of minutes.

She smiled at the basket, peeking into it. Strawberry Rhubarb. Blackberry. Peach. All of her favorites. Melanie remembered summers in cottage four, stirring big pots of jam with Duncan as the Fletchers blasted the Grateful Dead over the speakers, the entire inside of their cottage a homage to their favorite band.

"How long has it been now?" Dan asked.

"Three years," Melanie said quietly.

"Too long, if you ask me," Jan said. "Have you eaten anything?"

"I got a cone at Scoops," she responded, thinking of the other half of her massive ice cream cone now probably melted at the bottom of the trash can at Hillside.

Her neighbor's face lit up. "Oh, we love that place! Was Calvin working?"

Melanie's stomach twisted. "Uh—"

"He always opens Saturdays, so I'm sure you saw him."

Melanie thought about the way his arms flexed as he scooped her ice cream. She quickly brushed off the thought as a flash of orange outside the window alerted her to the moving truck pulling up in front of the cottage.

"Oh, looks like you're getting started, we'll get out of your hair," Jan said. She pulled Melanie into one more hug, whispering softly into her ear. "If you need anything, you come find us, okay?"

Melanie nodded, her face flushed. She wondered how much her mother actually told the Fletchers about what happened. Did they know the entire story or just the small bits Mom *wanted* people to know? She didn't have the energy to ask.

She waved the Fletchers off, watching as the two of them said hello to the movers, offering them free jars of jam when they finished. Melanie shook her head, a smile creeping up on her face. It was good to be back.

～

"No. I am not going."

Melanie woke up to shouting. She blinked her eyes open, her boxes neatly stacked in the corner of her bedroom coming into view. After two days of helping her parents unpack most of the downstairs, she didn't have the energy to unpack her own things. So she just grabbed a blanket and plopped down on her unmade bed each night.

But now she was jolted awake, listening to the arguing that seemed to be the constant melody of the Albertson household.

"Duncan, you have to," Melanie heard her mother say. "They are giving you a *chance*. The least you can do is meet the principal and hear what he has to say."

"And have someone else tell me how much of a fuck up I am?" Duncan shouted back. "No thanks, I'll pass."

Melanie pulled open her door, glancing downstairs. Duncan and Mom were facing each other at the bottom of the stairs as Dad sipped on a cup of coffee at the kitchen table, the table surface still covered in bubble-wrapped glasses and plates.

"It's not our fault you put yourself in this position," Mom said sharply. "Maybe if you actually—"

"Alice," Dad said coolly, cutting her off. "Don't."

Silence swept through the house. Mom was fuming.

Dad set down his coffee mug, looking at his son. "You will get dressed and go with us to Haverport High," he said rather calmly. "You will be polite to the principal and hear what he has to say. We will make a plan for your next year. There is no negotiation here."

Duncan rolled his eyes as he turned toward the steps, slamming his feet down so hard, Melanie thought the creaky stairs would plummet. She winced with each step, shrinking into her doorway to make a clear path for the wrath of Duncan.

After he pointedly slammed his door, she noticed her parents now looking at her, both of their faces an unspoken apology.

"Sweetheart," Dad said softly. "Come here for a minute."

Melanie obeyed, walking down the steps quietly toward her parents.

Dad put his arm around her. "We have a surprise for you," he said sweetly.

Melanie's eyes widened as they darted between both of her parents. Mom's arms were crossed firmly around her chest, and on her lips was a tight, forced smile. Melanie was familiar with that stance—the one Mom always took after a fight with Duncan.

Before Melanie could respond, Dad was leading her out the door of the kitchen, which led to a shed and an outdoor shower. It was a well-known rule that you *always* showered off after the beach—one that Melanie and Duncan used to conveniently forget.

Leaning against the shed was a brand-new bike. It had a white frame with white taped handlebars and a big red bow tied into a small wicker basket.

"If I remember correctly, you used to love biking around Haverport every summer," Dad said.

Melanie turned toward her father, tears welling up in her eyes. She didn't bother swatting them away this time. Yes, she loved biking around town, but she was never alone. Her brother was always with her. Two peas in a pod.

"I'm not dumb," Dad said softly, as if he didn't want a particular person in the house to hear. "I know it hasn't been easy sharing a car with him." He leaned closer, a smirk on his face. "Truthfully, I wanted to buy you a car."

"Harold," Mom's voice came from behind them.

Dad chuckled. "We just...don't exactly have the funds for it right now, kid. The hospital...the—"

"It's perfect," Melanie interrupted, flinging her arms around his middle. "Thank you."

He hugged back as Mom revealed a matching pearly white helmet. "Safety first."

"*All right*, I'm ready," Duncan boomed from inside. "Are we doing this or what?"

Dad sighed. "You going to be okay by yourself for a few hours?"

Melanie nodded. "Yep," she responded, surprising herself with her latest revelation. "I'm gonna go look for a job."

MELANIE KNEW she didn't want to hang around the house hearing them yell at each other all summer. She needed out —some kind of escape to get her through the next few months before she could drown herself in school assignments again. Maybe something she would actually enjoy doing. Something that could save what looked to be a bleak summer ahead.

After rifling through her boxes and slipping on a pair of jeans and a light blue polo, she carefully guided her bike along the lawn to avoid the harsh gravel driveway, remembering she popped both of her bike tires on it one summer. When she reached the sandy drive she mounted it, feeling excitement bubble in her chest. Dad was right—she always loved riding around town, seeing Haverport at different times of the day. Watching beachgoers as they lazily left the beach, or sailboats bobbing in the bay.

She rode through the curvy roads of Haverport, taking her time, enjoying the view of the sun glittering on the ocean, the mid-May heat warming her skin yet still not hot enough to make her sweat. As she eventually neared Hill-side Park, she noticed someone tinkering with the small stand at the entrance, wearing a bright white T-shirt that said *Haverport Parks & Rec.*

Melanie turned her bike into the entrance and slowed, watching as the man nailed another sign underneath the first one.

Summer season: 12 days!

She leaned her bike against the fence and unhooked her helmet, smoothing out her hair, then walking over to him. "Um, excuse me."

"Beach is open to the public," the man huffed. "No need for a pass yet."

"Actually, I was wondering if you, um, were hiring this summer?"

He turned to face Melanie, looking down at her polo, then back up at her face. "Why aren't you in school?"

"Oh, um. I just moved here, my school gets out the first week of May."

The man huffed. "Well, sorry kid, but we have no openings. We filled these positions back in March."

Melanie nodded. "Okay, no worries, thank you."

The man turned back to his work, finishing up nailing his sign. Melanie wondered if he truly would be coming back every day to paint the next number for the countdown until the summer season. *He probably will*, she thought. From what she was gathering, summer was a *big* deal in these parts. So much so that a simple job at a beach stand wasn't even available.

With so many businesses on the main drag, she figured Main Street was likely her best bet for finding some kind of job, so she made her way there next. Curving down the same road she drove two days ago, she came right back to Scoops By The Sea at the corner. And there, by the window, she spotted him. *Again.* With a new book.

For a brief moment, she wondered if she should ask him. Scooping ice cream cones for the summer could be a fun job, and the place would definitely be air-conditioned. But then she thought back to his comments about her clothes, the assumptions he made about her being a "summer person." Her face tightened as she pressed her lips into a firm line. No, she didn't want to deal with him. She sped up on her bike and turned the corner, eyeing the different businesses on that main strip, before her heart sank.

Everything was *closed.* It was one o'clock on a Monday afternoon, and Melanie was shocked that the town looked like a ghost land. Sea Breeze Cafe, Penny's Pizzeria, Haverport Cinemas, Pop's Seafood, Bayview Antiques—all closed. Even Grampy's was dark. No line for magical blueberry coffee cake, no scents of butter and cinnamon and sugar.

Melanie sighed as she turned to head back up Main, making a mental note to come out here first thing tomorrow and try again. When she finally made it back near Scoops, a small line had formed. She watched the guy who was likely Calvin hand a customer a hot fudge sundae with a bright red cherry on top.

She squeezed her handlebars. She may not like him, but if he was connected in town, he might know who was hiring, which could save Melanie a lot of time going into each business and embarrassing herself tomorrow.

She hopped off her bike and pushed it toward Scoops, leaning it against the brick wall. As she unhooked her helmet and walked toward the front, she immediately saw him through the glass. He was mixing some kind of milkshake. He carefully finished, turning to grab a lid for the cup, and locked eyes with Melanie through the window. The smirk that sprouted on his face was knowing—like he expected her to come back.

She nervously swung her helmet by her side while she waited for him to finish his orders before approaching the window herself.

"Where's the headband today?"

Melanie rolled her eyes. "Doesn't fit well underneath my helmet."

Calvin pointed toward her bike. "Nice bike. New?"

"Yeah," Melanie said quietly, the confidence quickly draining from her body.

"The red bow sort of gives it away," he said.

Melanie turned and noticed the red bow from her dad still tied to the basket. She silently cursed herself.

"Back for more ice cream, headband?"

Melanie rolled her eyes again as she faced him. "No, actually. I'm looking for a job."

Calvin's eyes widened slightly. "Here? At Scoops?"

"Um, yes," she said. "But also, if you know anywhere in town..."

"No," he said sharply. "Everyone's all booked up. Summer jobs are coveted around here. Every shop in town is fully staffed by March or April."

She exhaled loudly, feeling frustrated. "And here?"

"Here as well," Calvin said. "Although Ron hires back the same people every summer. Positions only open up when someone leaves for good."

"And what happens when a position opens up?" Melanie asked.

"Well, he goes through his applications, I guess," he said. "But he never touches them, no need."

"I'll take one."

Calvin's eyebrows furrowed. "Didn't you just hear me, we're boo—"

"I don't care," she snipped, surprising herself by the frustrated tone in her voice. "I'd still like to apply."

Calvin sighed, pressing his arms up from the counter, his tricep muscles flexing. She swallowed hard, averting her gaze. "Fine," he said dryly. "Wait here."

She waited for what felt like an eternity, wondering if he was taking his sweet time on purpose, probably hoping she would just eventually give up and leave. But it made Melanie all the more stubborn as she waited. She crossed her arms tightly around her chest.

He finally came back up the front, sliding a paper application on the counter. He tossed a pen her way and pointed to the counter at the other end of the shop. "Fill it out there while I take these customers."

She looked behind her, noticing a small line had formed. She nodded, grabbing the application and heading for the other counter, meticulously filling it out. After writing down the obvious things—name, age, phone number —she came to a set of open-ended questions.

What's your favorite ice cream flavor, and why?

The question seemed like a silly filler, but at a place like Scoops, it probably meant a great deal to have a favorite. She scanned the menu, thinking back to the countless times she would bike here with Duncan, remembering how she would always order the same thing as Duncan made his way through the Scoops menu.

Strawberry. It's underrated.

She filled out a few other questions, trying to think of something witty or smart to say with each answer.

Until she hit the final one.

Why do you want to work at Scoops?

Melanie paused, tapping the pen on the counter for a few beats before hunching over her paper.

Because I need a fresh start.

She clicked the pen and walked back to the counter as Calvin handed out a cone to the last customer. She stepped up and carefully slid him her application and the pen.

He glanced at it before looking back up at her. "Don't expect a call."

Melanie huffed. "Is no one in town really hiring?"

Calvin shook his head. "And don't bother trying today, it's Monday."

Melanie stared at him for a beat, waiting for him to explain. Like it made sense that things were closed on a weekday.

He sighed, sounding audibly frustrated. "Weekends are big for business here, so most businesses take a 'weekend' on Monday. Some drop the day off during the summer, but during the off-season, the town is shut down on Mondays."

"Then why are you open?"

"Scoops is only open between March and October, so Ron keeps it open every day."

"And school?" Melanie asked, surprising herself with such an invasive question.

Calvin's eyebrows raised as he crossed his arms. "Senior dismissal," he said. "I get out at noon."

She nodded and glanced toward her bike, not sure what else to say, aware that those bright blue eyes were on her. "Okay well, I should go."

"Again, don't expect a call."

She rolled her eyes. "I get it, Calvin."

His eyes widened. "How'd you know my name?"

Melanie's face flushed as she quickly clipped her helmet on her head, grabbing her bike. *Shit.*

"Headband! Who told you my name!?"

Melanie ignored him, mounting her bike and speeding off, hoping he didn't get a glance at her cheeks which were certainly brighter than the color of her favorite ice cream.

Chapter Three

THE DOOR to Melanie's room creaked open. It was *early*. Or late? The sun hadn't even touched the horizon yet so Melanie assumed it was the middle of the night as she blinked her eyes open and watched Duncan tip-toe his way inside. He smiled shyly, taking a seat at the corner of her bed as she sat up, crisscrossing her legs.

"Hey," Duncan whispered.

He did it. He spoke to her.

"Hey back," Melanie said, her voice catching in her throat.

The two of them sat there in silence for a moment. Melanie watched as Duncan played with his hands, his long dirty blonde curls shifting in front of his face. She was always jealous of his bright curls, wondering why he was the one blessed with those genes when her hair was darker, frizzier, and always out of place. She needed a large dollop of hair product and a good half hour with her straightener to get it looking halfway decent.

She shifted awkwardly, waiting for her brother to speak first. She hated seeing such anguish on his face, but he was *here*. In her room. Talking to her. It was a long time since he had approached her like this. Almost three years now.

Duncan huffed, and she could immediately smell it on his breath. Some kind of cheap whiskey. Her back went rigid. How did he already have access to booze?

"They're making me repeat junior year," Duncan finally revealed, his face half hidden as he continued to play with his hands.

Melanie exhaled, stunned into silence. That meant they wouldn't graduate together. They wouldn't sit side by side and receive their diplomas, take a picture with Mom and Dad, wearing dark green robes with white ribbons and threads. Or...whatever the Haverport High school colors were.

She wasn't sure what to say at first. She tried reaching for his hand, but he pulled away from her. It was like the tiny spell that broke the magic in her room. He sat up from her bed and started for her door.

"Duncan, wait," Melanie whispered, flinging her quilt off of her to get up herself. "Talk to me."

But he was already out of her bedroom, heading for his own. Melanie watched as he swiftly shut the door, locking it with a muffled click.

She crawled back into her bed even though sleep had completely escaped her. She leaned against her headboard and watched as the sun slowly started to rise above the water, a mix of burnt orange and purple painting the sky.

She thought through the last time he came into her room like this, the memory she played over and over in her head. She always wondered if she should have done something different, wondered if there was something she could have said to change it all.

It was the summer before their freshman year, two

weeks after their week in Haverport. They had to go a bit earlier that summer, to make room for Duncan's lacrosse tryouts. Garrison's lacrosse teams were continually ranked the best in the entire state of Connecticut, so they started everything early.

Duncan was one of two freshmen who made Junior Varsity. When he got the email, he screamed. Melanie remembered hugging her brother tightly as their parents tackled them in a group hug. Mom made a big platter of tacos for dinner that night—Duncan's favorite. Dad pulled out the leftover ice cream cake they saved from Scoops as the four of them demolished the rest of it with spoons in hand, no plates necessary.

But what was meant to be one of the happiest memories soon became a nightmare.

Duncan was invited to hang with the team later that night, a Garrison lacrosse tradition. Mom gave him a quick hug before he left and told him she was so proud of him. Dad leaned over and whispered something about being safe and making smart choices, from what Melanie could make out.

Duncan nodded, a gleam in his eye. The same one he had when he slowly opened her door four hours later before sloppily plopping down on her bed.

"Mel, wake up," he whispered to her. He reached out his hand and started shaking her elbow. "Get up, stupid."

"Why are you in here, weirdo?" She let out a big yawn.

"Mel, guess what."

She rolled her eyes. "It better be worth waking me up or I'm going to strangle you."

Duncan looked back at the door as if to make sure no one was listening before leaning closer to her. "Mel, I had a *beer*."

She could smell it. His breath was pungent and sour. She froze.

"Actually, I had a *few* beers," he said, giggling to himself. "I always thought it was gross, but turns out, I kind of like it."

"You drank?" Melanie said, still in shock. She knew this would likely happen someday, that one of them would try alcohol at some point. But she figured it wouldn't be so soon. They weren't even freshmen in high school yet.

"Yeah, but it was totally chill," Duncan said confidently. "You should come next time."

Melanie's face fell. "To a lacrosse team party?"

"It wasn't really just the lacrosse team," Duncan explained. "There were a few girls there, some from the girl's team, others were friends or girlfriends or whatever."

Melanie shifted uncomfortably in her bed, not sure how to respond. *Drinking?* He wanted her to drink?

Duncan looked at her like he could read her mind. He was always good at that, looking at her face and pretty much knowing instantly how she felt. He joked that it was the "twin thing," even though Melanie wasn't as intuitive as he was. She could never figure out what was going on in that head under all of those bright, bouncy curls.

He reached for one of her hands and squeezed. She relaxed a little at his touch. "Mel Mel, it's really fun. And you have nothing to worry about. I'll be there."

When Melanie thought back on this moment, she thought of her response to his statement. Should she have said something different? Was there a different string of words that could have changed his fate?

But her response was short and evasive. "I don't know," she said back to him. "I'm not sure."

He patted her hands like he was an old man. He

laughed at the gesture, clearly tipsy. "I'll tell you when the next one is," he said quietly. "You think about it."

Melanie slowly watched the sun rise above Haverport's bay, pulling her out of the memory. How much he'd wanted her to go to the next party and drink with him. She thought about his reaction earlier, how different it was. How he wouldn't even let her touch his hand, how he wouldn't even stay in the room to hear her response. Like she burned him in some way, and the wound left a scar that was too damaged to heal.

The sky shifted into bright yellows and pinks and then gave way to blazing orange light, the seagulls soaring across the ocean and diving into the water hopeful for breakfast. Melanie lay there unmoving, unsure of what to do next. She wanted something to hope for as well. She wished everything could have been different.

MELANIE SAT at the kitchen table later that morning, nibbling on a piece of toast with peanut butter as Mom busied herself with cooking scrambled eggs.

"Are you sure that's all you want, sweetie?" Mom asked.

Melanie shot her a small smile. "Positive." She didn't feel like her stomach could handle more than the toast in front of her at the moment. She still felt unsettled after that morning, how Duncan couldn't even look her in the eye when he spoke the words. She opened her door hours later, hoping to get another chance to talk to him about it, but he was gone.

"Well, if you get hungry, we could always grab you something at the market," Mom responded, walking over with a skillet and sliding eggs onto Dad's plate. "Jan said the bagel shop still has that stand where they make all of those fresh breakfast sandwiches."

Every Saturday during the summer season, Haverport's elementary school parking lot transformed into a vibrant farmer's market. Fresh produce and local vendors, small craft stands, lots of freshly baked goodies, and hot sandwiches. And of course, a particular stand decked in tie-dye and filled to the brim with jars of jam.

Today was the first one before the summer season officially started, and Melanie found herself agreeing to go as she pressed her slice of bread into the toaster.

"How's the job hunt going?" Dad asked.

Melanie huffed. *Not great*, she thought. Unfortunately, Calvin was right. No one in town was hiring. Everyone already had enough workers booked up for the summer and had no need for an extra person—especially someone without any work experience or skills beyond a few babysitting gigs and the ability to make a mean deck of flash cards. But it didn't stop her from going into every business on Main Street, asking for an application anyway, just in case something fell through. With no success, Melanie was seriously considering searching for babysitting gigs again. If so many "summer people" came into town, surely some parents would look for a babysitter every now and then?

Dad caught onto Melanie's silence, reaching over to pat her hand. "You'll find something. Maybe one of the vendors at the market will be looking?"

"Maybe," Melanie mumbled, biting into her toast.

The front screen door swung open as Duncan charged in. He was drenched in sweat from an early morning run, his curls pushed back with a sweatband. He immediately went for the sink, filled a glass of water, and chugged it down. He looked down at the empty greasy skillet and frowned. "Do you have any more food?"

Mom forced her mouth into a smile. "Well, I could cook you something, or—" She hesitated, glancing at Dad first. "We're about to head to the farmer's market in town if you want to join. They still have those breakfast sandwiches if you want one of those instead."

He placed the glass in the sink. "Uh, sure, just need to shower."

"Great!" Mom said a little too brightly as Duncan moved toward the stairs, taking them two at a time. The three of them listened in silence as he closed the bathroom door and turned on the water.

Melanie watched as her parents glanced at each other, both looking a bit too happy at how well that conversation went. She rolled her eyes, knowing they were likely feeling hopeful that their new Grand Plan to get Duncan's life on track seemed to be working. She ignored them and finished up her toast, bringing her plate to the sink. "I'm going to go get changed."

Dad reached for her hand as she walked toward the stairs. "Mel, we have to tell you something."

Melanie looked at her father's face, aware of what he was likely about to say. "He told me," she said softly.

"Ah," Dad said, squeezing her hand. "And how do you feel about it?"

She watched as her mom busied herself again, taking the empty dishes in front of them and charging for the sink.

"I don't know," Melanie admitted, practically in a whisper. Because she didn't. She couldn't wrap her head around it yet. It seemed weird, Duncan not graduating with her. They reached every milestone together, every little life moment, like learning how to ride a bike or going to their first school dance. The thought of not having her twin brother by her side as she finished high school had knots forming in her stomach. The entire situation felt so out of place, it almost didn't seem real.

Dishes were now clanking in the sink as Mom vigorously scrubbed at their plates.

"If you want to talk about it, you know where to find us," Dad replied calmly.

Melanie nodded, slipping her hand out of her father's palm and heading up the stairs. She knew she could turn to them if she wanted to, she knew her father would be careful with his words and her mother would try to pretend not to be upset that this was all happening to them. But she also didn't want to put them through any more pain. The last thing Melanie wanted to give them was more things to worry about.

As she changed into a pair of faded jean shorts and an old T-shirt, she decided she would make some flyers that night to see if anyone needed a babysitter.

THE MARKET WAS a lot busier than Melanie remembered. Cars snaked out of the side parking lot onto the field next to the playground as people streamed into Haverport Elementary. But despite the crowds, Melanie noticed how familiar and friendly each person was with each other—like they were all part of one big family. Melanie soon realized that *this*—the first farmer's market of the year—was for the locals. For the people of Haverport to support their friends before the frenzied summer season ahead.

The line for bagel sandwiches was long, but the four of them waited patiently for Duncan to get a sandwich that he finished in five bites. Now they were wandering through the market, admiring the produce stands with mounds of lettuce and containers of fresh berries, bakers with pastries and fresh loaves of sourdough, and artists with local paintings and crafts.

"Oooh, isn't this pretty!" Mom said, reaching her hand over to squeeze a throw pillow, billowing waves at a beach stitched in the center.

Melanie walked around the inside of the small tent, admiring the other set of pillows and framed art; a mixture of pencil drawings and watercolor prints of local spots in town. After a beat, she turned toward Duncan who was also admiring something inside the tent—but not exactly at the art. His eyes kept glancing at the girl behind the counter with silky blonde hair and bright hazel eyes.

Mom looped an arm around Melanie. "Come on, let's find the Fletchers before all the jam is gone."

As they stepped out of the tent, Melanie looked back to find Duncan slowly trailing behind them, his gaze still fixed on the pretty girl in the tent. But soon he followed with his head down, hands deep into the pockets of his athletic shorts.

The four of them finally found the tie-dye tent, the colors even more vibrant than Melanie could remember. Such a stark contrast compared to the white and burlap-colored tents at the market, just like the vibrant people who sold jam. When they finally turned the corner toward the tent, they came to a line that was so long, it was almost comical.

"Wow," Dad breathed. "They weren't kidding."

Mom's face was bright with pride for her friends. "Come on! Let's get on the line."

"Don't we still have a basket full of jam at home?" Melanie asked.

"It's not really about getting jam sweetie," Mom said, pulling Melanie into the line next to her. "It's about supporting our friends' dreams."

So they waited patiently as the line slowly crept forward. At one point they reached another craft tent that had Mom squealing with glee.

Melanie felt a soft tap on her shoulder. She turned to find Duncan looking right at her. "Mel Mel, do me a favor."

She swallowed, fearful of what he was about to ask of her, yet elated that he was talking to her again. Looking at her.

She nodded at him.

"Think you could cover for me for a few minutes? I want to go back and check out those, uh"—Duncan looked back toward the craft tent with the hazel-eyed beauty—"uh, those throw pillows."

Melanie smiled. "Sure sure, *throw pillows.*"

Duncan chuckled, starting to back up in that direction. "Tell them I went to the bathroom?"

A funny feeling sat in the pit of her stomach as she watched him go, wondering to herself if this was yet another situation she was getting all wrong.

"Where did Duncan go?" Mom asked as she came back.

"Uh, bathroom." The three of them just about reached the entrance of the tent when Melanie's phone buzzed in her pocket. She grabbed it and looked at the screen at an unknown number.

"Who's calling you?" Mom asked.

She shrugged as she swiped open the screen to answer the call. "Um, hello?"

"Melanie Albertson!?" someone said on the other end in a panic.

"Yes, that's me," she said, her heart hammering in her chest. *A job*, she thought buoyantly. *Maybe someone does need another worker.*

"Oh, thank god," said the frantic man. "Daria just *had* to get into that fancy music camp in Hartford this summer and won't be around to work now, which makes *me* desperate."

She couldn't help the smile that now burst from her face. Her parents watched her expectantly, letting the people behind them move around them through the line.

"It's a commitment, a lot of work," he said. "Probably five or so days a week. But you'll make good money."

"A job?" Mom mouthed in front of her.

Melanie nodded and watched her silently whoop with glee. Dad reached over and patted Melanie's back with pride.

"So, do you want it?" the man on the phone asked impatiently.

"Wait," Melanie said. "Sorry, but who is this? My phone didn't show the caller ID."

"Oh, got ahead of myself, classic," he said. "I'm Ron, from Scoops By The Sea."

Her stomach dropped. *No.*

That would mean five days a week...with *him*. Calvin. The one who abrasively told her she would never possibly work there. How would he treat her five days a week?

But...it was five whole days a week out of the house. Even if Duncan was starting to slowly talk to her again, she couldn't handle the way things were. She needed the distraction, and if it meant scooping ice cream and dealing with a guy who, for whatever weird reason, seemed to love making fun of her headbands, she would do it.

"I need someone, like, immediately," Ron said. "Your application was at the top of my stack so if you can't do it, I'm just going to start calling through the list."

"No no, I can do it," Melanie hastily replied.

"Good, how soon can you get here?"

Melanie's eyes went wide. "Oh, you meant, like, *immediately* immediately?"

"That is what the word means," he said. "Yes, I need you now. I'm one short for this shift. Can you get here in fifteen minutes? Thirty at most?"

Melanie eyed the road that went up to Main Street. She could see the corner of the Scoops sign behind a bushy oak tree.

"Fifteen," she said. She looked down at her clothes. "But I'm not sure if I'm exactly dressed for it."

"It's fine, we have what you'll need here," Ron said in a rush. "See you in fifteen."

He hung up. Melanie looked at her phone screen in a daze before glancing up at her parents, who now looked beyond confused.

"I got a job at the ice cream shop."

"That's amazing sweetie!" Mom said, pulling her into a tight hug. "When do you start?"

"Um, right now."

Mom pushed back slightly. "Wait, seriously?"

She nodded. "Says he's one short for the shift and he's desperate."

"Well, we better get going then," Dad said, pulling his car keys out of his pocket.

She glanced over at the line of cars slowly creeping in and out of the school's playground, the line moving at a snail's pace.

"No, stay here, I'll walk," she said. "It's just up the hill."

"Okay, call us when you're done and we can pick you up. Do you know what time?"

Melanie shook her head. She had no idea how long she would be there. She didn't even know how much money she was going to be making. All questions she probably should have asked Ron before blindly accepting a job.

But it was a job.

Melanie said goodbye to her parents and left the market, following the sidewalk up toward Main. Despite whatever faced her this summer, she was ready for it. That small bead of hope in her chest made her smile as she neared the bubblegum pink sign.

Chapter Four

THE LINES at Scoops were already massively long, trailing back from the shop and pooling out onto the sidewalk. Melanie inched toward one of the windows where a girl slightly shorter than her was working, a ponytail with thick brown hair tucked into a ball cap that said *Scoops* on her head. She opened the window and handed a perfectly scooped chocolate ice cream cone to a small boy at the counter who looked like he just won the lottery.

"Now don't drop this one, Jonny, or your mom is going to kill me," the girl said.

A wide grin spread on little Jonny's face. "Promise!" He ran off with his cone, the girl now shaking her head like she knew he definitely wouldn't be keeping that promise.

"Hey, Ron called. Where should I—?"

"Back door," she said without even glancing up, then moving on to the next customer.

Melanie walked around the small brick building. She knocked on the metal door and waited for a beat, but no one answered. She reached for the doorknob, nervous energy coursing her entire body as she twisted it open.

"CAKE!"

Melanie jumped as she saw someone charging toward her, holding up an ice cream cake box so massive, it almost looked bigger than the tiny young woman holding it. Melanie quickly stepped aside, stumbling on a small set of stairs behind her as the woman brushed past, handing a cake to a customer that appeared outside the back door. Melanie pushed herself from the stairs and took a peek through the plastic at the top of the box. The cake had gorgeous trimmings of navy blue and white, with a curly script that said *Happy Graduation, Sam!* The edges of the cake were decorated in glittering blue sprinkles.

"Wow," Melanie said in awe as the tiny woman closed the door. "That was beautiful."

The woman, with wispy blonde bangs and round glasses that took up half her face, nodded slightly, looking pleased with the compliment before her face hardened and she went back to work. She opened up a massive industrial fridge next to them full of blank round and rectangular ice cream cakes ready for decorating. She took out a medium-sized round one and closed the fridge door with her foot before walking further into the shop.

Melanie trailed behind her until they ended up at a tragically messy desk, order slips and receipts sprinkled everywhere. But there was only one sheet of paper that seemed to have a stocky middle-aged man unraveling in his seat. He looked down at the paper like it was the hardest test he'd ever had to take, his hands buried in the few hairs left on his scalp. She figured this must be Ron.

Melanie took a small breath. "Um, hi."

The man looked up from the paper, which she glanced at quickly. It was the shift schedule for the week, penciled arrows pointing haphazardly in different directions with names under specific days and times.

"Oh, thank god," Ron said, standing up from his desk. "It's chaos. Pure chaos. I don't know what to do."

She nodded, not sure how exactly to respond to that. But Ron didn't seem to notice as he brushed past her, beckoning her to follow him to the back of the shop where a small bathroom was located. He pointed to a set of shelves at the side. "You can place your stuff in a cubby there and be sure to wash up before starting your shift," he said, gesturing to a sink and a small mirror with a sticker obnoxiously placed in the center that said *Scoopers must always wash their hands!*

"What shirt size are you?" Ron asked.

"Medium," she answered, watching as Ron stepped around her to charge up that small set of stairs, coming down a beat later with a few teal-colored T-shirts and a matching hat.

He handed it to her. "Uniform is a T-shirt and a pair of khaki shorts or pants, but your shorts are fine for this one shift," he said. "Ball caps must be worn at all times, state law."

Melanie nodded.

"CAKE!"

Ron took a step to the side as the woman charged past them again, this time with a cake that said *Happy Birthday, Georgie!*

Ron waited a moment as she handed off the cake before continuing. "That's Jess, she's our cake designer," he said, walking back toward his desk. Melanie dutifully followed, still awkwardly holding her stack of T-shirts. "I usually would have her train you but she's swamped because of graduation season."

Almost immediately, a guy with perfectly bronzed skin slinked through the doorway that led to the ice cream shop out front, holding a metal cup in one hand. His smirk was devious as he leaned against the doorway and winked at Melanie. "Don't worry, Ronny, I can train her."

Ron rolled his eyes. "Fat chance, Jay."

Jay reached out his free hand. "Pleasure to meet you, Melanie Albertson. It seems you're our hero of the day."

Melanie shyly reached out her hand and placed it in Jay's, but he didn't shake it, instead he just slowly rubbed his thumb against her hand.

"Wow, such soft skin," he said. "You sure you want to ruin those gorgeous hands at this hell hole?"

The girl with the thick brown ponytail came bursting through the doorway, shoving Jay slightly with her shoulder as she brushed past them.

"Ow, Rory, what was that for?!"

"Quit flirting and get back to work," said a familiar voice. Melanie watched as Calvin came into view, holding out a bright teal paper cup toward Jay. "Line two also wants a double scoop of Caramel Pecan."

His body straightened, holding his hand to his forehead in salute like a soldier. "Sir, yes, sir!"

He shoved the cup at Jay's chest, who took it as his cue to escape to the front.

"Anyway, Calvin will train you," Ron said.

Melanie let her eyes travel over to Calvin. Gone was the small smirk and the twinkling eyes from before. His face was all straight lines and resolute, like this truly was the military and she was about to enter basic training.

She could feel the small bead of hope squash in her chest. *What have I gotten myself into*, she thought. Clearly, he was displeased that she was here, looking like the thought of training her was the absolute last thing in the world he wanted to be doing.

Calvin crossed his arms in front of his chest. "Hat."

Melanie's brows furrowed. "Huh?"

"Hat, put it on."

"Oh," she said, feeling her face flush. She placed her stack of T-shirts down and put the hat on, taking note that he was the only one who didn't have a hat covering his head. Though there wasn't much to cover anyway, with how short his buzzcut was.

A small hand reached in front of her, holding a black hair tie. Melanie looked over and noticed Jess holding it out to her as she continued piping red frosting around the edges of a cake with the other.

"Thanks."

"CAKE!" she screamed again.

Melanie winced, pausing as she fastened her hair up. "Why—"

"Cake disaster last year, the frosting stained the rugs for weeks," Ron answered, like he didn't have any more time to explain. He turned to Calvin. "Have her stock and clean today, she can learn to scoop on a day when it's not so busy. I'm going to try to figure out this schedule."

Calvin placed a hand on Ron's shoulder. "I can handle it. It's Saturday, you shouldn't even be here."

Ron sighed, relaxing a little as he turned back toward Melanie. "This guy," he said, pointing a thumb toward Calvin. "He's the best."

Melanie nodded as she glanced up at Calvin. His intense eyes were on her, the rest of his face practically expressionless. She wondered where that guy went, the one she met her first day here, the one who'd teased her with a smirk. Instead, this guy was all rigid and serious, his arms now crossed tightly across his chest as he stared down at her, almost like he was evaluating if she was worthy enough to even be here.

"So, Melanie, no aspirations to become a famous musician and flee to a camp in Hartford?" Ron inquired. "No summer internships? No boyfriends trying to steal away your time?"

Melanie swallowed uncomfortably, aware of Calvin's eyes beating down on her. "Nope, none of that."

"Good, then welcome to Scoops."

CALVIN CAME BACK from the upstairs storage space with another box, smacking it down in front of her at the desk. Unfortunately, she already knew what was inside of it. She unfolded the top of the box to reveal hundreds of plastic cotton candy-colored spoons.

"Do you really go through this many spoons in one shift?" Melanie groaned.

"Yes," he answered without hesitation. He reached for the empty metal cups next to the sink, which Melanie already washed and dried, placing them on the desk next to the box. "It's the weekend, so we end up filling these at least twice a day. On weekdays we can usually get away with filling just once."

Melanie let out a weary breath. She swiveled her arms side to side, trying to stretch her aching back.

Calvin put the last set of metal cups on the desk. "When you're finished, fill up the toppings out front. Dry ingredients are in the containers behind you, and wet ingredients are in the walk-in," he said, heading toward a large fridge behind him with a sealed metal door. He opened it up and pointed to the handle. "It locks when you close it, so if you get stuck, just press this button when you pull the handle."

Melanie nodded, glancing behind her to find large containers of toppings with faded labels—chocolate chips, Oreos, M&M's, peanut butter cups, pecans, peanuts, and...

"Rainbow jimmies?" Melanie asked. "What are those?"

Calvin frowned at her. "They're jimmies."

"That doesn't exactly answer my question."

"They're sprinkles," Jess said, not looking up from the cake she was decorating.

"We call them jimmies," Calvin said defiantly. "They go in a metal box near the counter."

"And do me a favor darling," Jay said, popping his head through the door frame as he winked at her. "Start with those jimmies. We're running low."

Melanie nodded as she reached for the container. Her arms were already screaming at her, and it had only been two hours. As soon as Ron left, a massive ice cream shipment arrived, so she carried tub after tub of ice cream back and forth from the truck into the freezers, her hands and arms burning from the cold as sweat pooled down the center of her back. Soon after, Calvin had her cleaning all of the dishes, making waffle cones (which she burnt her elbow while trying to seal up a cone), and filling the dispensers out front with napkins, cups, cones, spoons, and now, toppings.

Calvin watched as Melanie flinched bringing the container down, her arms already feeling sore. "Still want to work here, headband?"

Melanie gritted her teeth before pressing them into a fake grin. "Yep, happy to be here."

He shook his head as he walked out front, but if

Melanie wasn't mistaken, she caught a hint of a smirk as he left. She wondered if he found amusement in torturing her.

So she slowly filled all of the toppings, shocked at how low everything was after just a few hours. She filled the jimmies first, which Jay praised her for like she was the queen of England, then all of the containers of fruits, nuts, and candies.

"Okay," she said to Calvin, who was currently scooping a small bowl of Mint Chocolate Chip. "I think I got it all."

"No, you didn't," he automatically said, not looking up from his scooping job, like he *knew* she was going to fail.

Melanie took a deep breath, suppressing the urge to slap him across the face. The feeling surprised her, how much he irked her. Even after years of dealing with Duncan's irrational behavior and the mountain of expectations that came with being one of Garrison's top students, she never felt this frustrated and angry. But there was something about Calvin that made her want to scream and throw things.

She squeezed her hands into fists to let out some of that anger before taking a few deep breaths and asking, "What did I miss?"

He looked up and pointed to a row of syrup bottles in front of them. Then he turned behind him and pointed with his scooper at the line of steel pumps for the fudges and sauces.

Melanie sighed. "Where can I find those?"

Calvin finished scooping his ice cream and went to the counter, handing it to the woman behind it. "That will be $3.75."

She noticed that he didn't need to calculate it at the register—he just knew the price automatically. He moved with such practiced ease, like he clearly did this hundreds of times before. The woman handed him four bucks as Calvin punched it in, opening up the register and sliding a quarter back to her. He then gestured for Melanie to follow him to the back of the shop—which Melanie learned the Scoopers called "The War Room"—and pointed to a long line of boxes next to the topping containers. Without saying another word, he left, heading back to his line at the counter.

Melanie sighed, reaching for yet another box.

"THE SIDEWALKS NEED washing before you go," Calvin said, serving the last customer in his line.

The shop hit an afternoon lull, which according to Jay, was completely normal. "Dinner time," he told her when Melanie asked. Quietly, of course, so Calvin wouldn't notice—she didn't want to give him more fuel for his hate-burning fire. "We don't see many people between five and seven, then things start getting absolutely wild."

"Wilder than this?" Melanie asked, looking around the shop. Despite her efforts to keep things clean and stocked up, the shop was a mess. Candy toppings and jimmies were sprinkled all over the counters. Dollops of fudge dripped from the spouts. Wayward cups and spoons scattered the floor from the last rush, brushed underneath the counter quickly with shoes to get them out of the way. The wet rags in buckets resembled a completely different color than at the start of the shift, stained with sauces and ice cream.

"Oh yeah, this is nothing," he said before Calvin approached her with his last request of the shift. One that seemed even more nuts than the container of wet nuts she had to fill—a concoction of walnuts doused in maple syrup that was so messy, Melanie was pretty sure she'd have maple syrup stuck underneath her fingernails for the rest of the summer.

"How do I do that?" She hoped the irritation she felt didn't seep through her tone. She didn't want him to think she was some summer person complaining about hard work, or whatever other assumption he'd made about her. She would continue to work with a smile on her face and show him that she *was* capable of being here—and more than happy to do it.

Calvin gestured to the back, so Melanie followed him through The War Room and out the back door. He reached for a grubby-looking broom and a bucket, handing it to her without a word and disappearing back inside.

Melanie looked down at the broom and the bucket and just started to laugh. Exhaustion consumed her—all she could think about was eating something and going to bed. Maybe a greasy cheeseburger. Or a few tacos from Taco-port, the place in town that Jay couldn't seem to shut up about.

The back door burst open and Melanie jumped, fidgeting with the broom like she knew what to do with it, but relaxed when she saw it was Rory coming through the back with a massive black garbage bag. Rory was short but built like an athlete. Her bushy black hair was half falling out of her ponytail as she swung the garbage bag into the dumpster out back.

She sighed. "God, that shit is nasty," she said, approaching Melanie. Her smile was bright and welcoming, her eyes a unique shade of sea foam green. "Well, I would hug you, but I was just touching garbage, and your shirt has seen better days."

She looked down at her Scoops shirt and noticed it was

covered in streaks of sauces and fudge. Rory's shirt was pristine like it just came out of the laundry.

"Don't worry, it'll get better," Rory said as if she was reading her mind. "Pretty sure my shirt needed to be burned after my first shift."

"That's if I'm still alive after today. I'm not sure I'll be able to get out of bed tomorrow."

"Hop in the ocean after work," Rory said confidently. "Sounds strange, but the salt in the sea always seems to help my muscles. Then eat a cheeseburger."

Melanie chuckled, a big grin on her face. "Are you a mind reader?"

Rory laughed. "No, just remembering how I felt after my first week here."

"When did you start?"

"Last summer," Rory responded. "I was the newbie until Blake joined a few months ago. But I guess you're the newbie now."

Melanie nodded, looking down at the broom and bucket in front of her, feeling every facet of her body ache. She noticed Rory slowly reach for the bucket, each of her fingernails painted in a different bright color. She thought about how she would never see something like that at Garrison—all the girls wore the same pale pink polish or French tips. Never any bright colors, never the idea that painting nails could actually be *fun*.

"Come on, I'll help you with this," Rory said. She held the bucket to a waterspout near them that Melanie had failed to notice and started filling it up.

"Are you sure? He'll probably be mad at me for it."

"Calvin?" she asked, turning off the faucet and grabbing the handle of the bucket. "Tough shit. He can bite me."

Melanie chuckled again, following her to the sidewalk

that wrapped around the shop. Rory slowly poured water on the surface as Melanie trailed behind her, sweeping the sidewalk clean. It was surprisingly messy, covered in drips of ice cream and jimmies from customers taking greedy first bites as they waited to pay.

"So, are you here for the summer?" asked Rory.

Melanie shook her head. "Just moved here, actually."

"Wait," Rory said, standing up straight. "Like, moved here, moved here?"

She nodded.

"Holy shit." Rory placed the bucket down on the sidewalk, her eyes wide with—delight, perhaps? "This is *huge*!"

"Is it?" Melanie asked reluctantly.

"Oh yeah, new people in town is practically front page news in the Port," Rory responded excitedly, her hands moving with her expressively. "Small town, and all."

"Right," she said, feeling a bit embarrassed. She wondered if she would always feel this way—the newbie at the shop, the newbie in town.

"So does this mean you'll be going to Haverport High?" Rory asked.

"Yeah." Her and Duncan. In different grades. Her stomach churned thinking about what next year was going to be like for them.

Her expression must have changed enough for Rory to notice, because now she was stepping toward her, placing a hand on her shoulder like she actually was a mind reader. "Don't stress, you'll totally be fine, you have us now."

Her eyes went wide with surprise at how willing Rory was to loop her into *us*. Into the group. Even after just one shift.

"Well, you have me, maybe stay away from Jay," she teased.

"Are we paying you two to gab, or to work?" Calvin called out from the window at the counter.

Rory flicked him off before picking up the bucket. They finished up on the sidewalk, placing the empty bucket and broom back near the faucet.

"We just leave it here?" Melanie asked.

"I mean, if someone wants to steal that nasty thing, by all means."

Melanie smiled. She liked Rory and her bright-colored fingers and the way she talked with her hands. How warm and inviting she was. She already felt like she could spill her secrets from just these few moments talking to her.

Again, like a mind reader, Rory reached out her hand. "Give me your phone."

She obliged, watching as Rory added her contact info, then texted herself from Melanie's number. "Let's hang. We can go to the beach and get tacos and I'll tell you all about Haverport. We can gossip about Scoops and how much Jay sucks."

"You mean how much Calvin sucks," she mumbled, shocking herself with how easily that confession slipped from her lips.

Rory smiled. "Nah, he's harmless, just a little protective of this place," she said. "Jay, on the other hand, will always and forever be a douchebag."

Melanie took her phone back from Rory, wondering how on earth someone could prefer Calvin over Jay, who was nothing but kind to her the entire shift. Or...maybe a little too kind, she thought, as she remembered back to his winking and the way he brushed her hand.

Okay, maybe Rory wasn't completely wrong.

"Now," she said. "Ready for the best part about working here?"

"Please don't tell me it involves rainbow jimmies or wet nuts."

Rory threw her head back and cackled in delight. She looped her arm with Melanie's as she pulled her back into The War Room. Melanie followed her to the desk where the others were gathered, watching as Calvin slowly counted a fluffy stack of bills.

"Come on, man, we don't have all day," Jay said.

"Chill," Calvin snipped. "You also know you can't leave until the others get here."

"What's this?" she whispered to Rory.

Rory's eyes sparkled. "Tip money."

Her eyes practically bulged out of her head as she looked at the stack of bills. Not just ones, but fives, tens, and even a few twenties.

"People really tip twenty bucks for a four-dollar ice cream?" she asked.

"Sugar makes people do crazy things," said Rory.

After counting it all up, Calvin split the stack into five piles, then handed them out. He handed Melanie the last one, holding on briefly and looking her in the eyes. "Be here at noon on Monday. I'll text you the rest of your schedule for the week."

Melanie nodded as she took the money, looking down at the pile in her hand. She quickly counted out $37.

"Is it like this every shift?" Melanie asked, flabbergasted.

"Nah, this is a mediocre day," Jay said. "Wait till you work a night shift."

As if on cue, she watched the back door swing open as two guys stepped through. One with mocha-colored skin and arm muscles bulging out of a sleeveless workout tee, and another the stark opposite—short, pale, covered in freckles, with a bushy set of red curls.

Jay raised his arms. "His first night shift!"

"Don't," said the scrawny red-head. "I feel like I'm going to throw up."

"You're going to be fine," Calvin said calmly. "Tyler will take window two and we'll work together at window one."

"Just think of the money, Blakey-boy," Jay said. "*The money.*"

Blake rolled his eyes, then realized Melanie was standing there and burst into a huge grin. "Oh my god, a newbie?!"

"Yes," Calvin said with a dramatic exhale. "This is Melanie, she's Daria's replacement."

"Holy crap," Blake said, holding his fists above his head in triumph. "I'm not the newbie anymore!"

"You'll always be the newbie," Tyler teased, tossing Blake's hair before cramming into the small bathroom and closing the door.

Chapter Five

She called it the lion and the lamb.

It's the first thing that came to Melanie's head when she started experiencing Duncan's temperamental behaviors. The first time his rage came in full force, it was like a storm. Dark and ominous, with thundering booms and lightning strikes, his storm was unrelenting and left disaster in its wake.

It was Thanksgiving weekend. In the four months after he visited Melanie's room after his lacrosse party, he'd transformed into a whole new person. The boy who was once bubbly and loved to make sand castles for crabs had completely vanished, like a shell that was left empty by the creeping critters of the sea. He was quiet and secretive, always drawn to the text threads on his phone, and less motivated to look up at the three people above his screen. Melanie tried talking to him, knocking on his bedroom door to see if he would want to hang out or play Mario Kart. But each attempt broke her heart as Duncan told her to stop bugging him and leave him alone.

They were about to sit down for Thanksgiving dinner when Mom told Duncan to put his phone away.

"Why?" Duncan asked sharply.

"Because we're going to spend time together as a family is why," Mom said cheerfully, placing down the carved turkey on the table.

Duncan rolled his eyes. "Great, you mean bore my brains out."

"Duncan Albertson," Mom said, eyes wide as she took a step back. "Since when do you hate hanging out with your family? It's like you went to high school and want nothing to do with us anymore."

"That's because I realized how boring and dull you all are," Duncan snipped.

Melanie inhaled, holding her breath, watching Mom who stood frozen in place. Dad was sitting in his seat, his brows furrowed like he was trying to figure out some kind of solution for what was going on.

"That was incredibly mean, you apologize," she said, holding out her hand. "And give me your phone, now."

"No."

"Duncan, listen to your mother," Dad said coolly.

"No."

"If you don't give me your phone right now, young man, you are grounded."

"Does that mean I don't have to sit here and eat this shitty dinner with all of you then?"

Mom looked at Duncan like he'd just slapped her across the face. She walked around the table and forced his phone out of his hand. "Get out of my sight."

"Fine by me," Duncan said, turning from her and storming out of the dining room. A door slammed a short distance away.

The three of them ate in silence. Mom had made all of their favorites—the sweet potatoes with mini marshmallows on top, big fluffy dinner rolls, gravy so thick it worked well as a dip for the crispy potatoes Mom always made instead of mashed potatoes because Duncan hated mashed.

But the meal just felt like ash in her mouth as she slowly chewed, glancing every so often at the empty chair next to her, wondering what had gotten into her twin brother.

After washing up the dishes, she asked if she could at least bring Duncan a slice of pie. Mom sighed. "Fine, but no whipped cream for him."

Melanie nodded, sneaking a dollop of whipped cream anyway before heading for his room. But, his room was empty. She walked down the halls of their house and found the slammed door wasn't from his bedroom, but Dad's office.

She balanced the plates in one hand as she opened the door, only to find Duncan on the ground. He had a bottle of liquor in his hand, and by the sloppy way he was splayed out on the floor, he certainly drank some of it. Or a lot of it.

"What are you doing?!" Melanie whispered.

"Having fun," Duncan said rather loudly, clearly not picking up on her cues to keep quiet. "Did Mel Mel bring me piiiiie?"

She froze, hearing footsteps coming their way. Mom shoved open the door.

"Duncan Albertson, what have you done," Mom said breathily, like the wind was kicked out of her. She charged into the room and snatched the bottle from him. "Harold, your office, now!"

Melanie stepped aside, still holding two plates as the whipped cream slowly slid off the tops of their slices. Dad came in and looked at his bottle of liquor in Mom's hand, then back at Duncan, shaking his head. He grabbed Duncan's arm and pulled him up aggressively.

"Owie, that hurts," Duncan said, giggling.

"You are officially grounded young man, for the rest of this year," Mom said tightly, placing the bottle down on Dad's desk.

"No, no, no, you can't do that," Duncan said. "I have the lacrosse Christmas party, the fundraiser, the—"

"Well, you should have thought about that before you decided to help yourself to your father's bar," Mom said. "No party, no fundraiser, no phone. We will pick you up from school at three on the dot. You will do homework on the counter until it is finished. All technology will be stripped from your room and the basement."

"Wow, you'd even take away stupid Mario Kart from my boring sister?" Duncan asked, his tone vicious.

It was the first bolt of lightning, striking Melanie right in the heart. She stood there completely shell-shocked, looking at her brother who seemed to not care an ounce about her anymore.

"Harold, go get his computer out of his room, now."

This was the moment when the lion finally roared, when the storm came down on their house brutally and relentlessly. As Dad left the office, Duncan started screaming at him, following closely at his heels. As they went through the kitchen, Duncan picked up the leftover pie dish and threw it on the floor, pumpkin and pie crust and glass smashing everywhere. He walked right over the pieces as he continued his verbal torment...until he reached the knives. Melanie watched in horror as he started reaching for one, but Dad caught him just in time. He scooped him up like a sack of flour and gripped his legs hard as he climbed the stairs, Duncan screaming about how much he hated them.

Melanie remembered the lurching in her stomach, and the quiet stillness after as the three of them cleaned the mess. The extra squeeze Mom gave her that night before going to bed.

But the next day, it's as if the storm had ceased. Duncan was calm and quiet. He read books and magazines on the couch. He smiled. He even asked Melanie to play cards.

She lay in bed after that horrible weekend and the poem she once recited in school came to her. "In like a lion, out like a lamb."

The lion made a more frequent appearance over the years, like a storm that felt like an earthquake and a hurricane all at once. Now, as Melanie lay in her bed after her first shift at Scoops, it seemed they were in the season of the lamb. For how long, Melanie wasn't certain. The changing seasons were never predictable.

Melanie was *exhausted*. Every muscle in her body ached. She couldn't even find the strength to lift her head in the shower to wash her hair, letting the hot water pour down on her head. She stared down at her feet, amazed at the sight of a few rogue rainbow jimmies circling the drain. A green one lodged between the metal and her foot, and she wondered if she, too, was bound to feel stuck in a place where she didn't truly belong.

She reached for her phone on her nightstand, moaning as her arms ached with every stretch. Thank god she had an extra day to recuperate before her shift on Monday, because this felt like torture. She cursed herself for hyper-focusing on schoolwork all the time instead of trying to lift a dumbbell.

Her phone dinged in her hand as a new text message

came through from a number she didn't recognize. She tapped it open and noticed it was a picture of that same white piece of paper that almost had Ron pulling out the few hairs left on his head.

Melanie zoomed in on her name to see when she was working, then groaned.

She may have tomorrow off, but he had her on the schedule for every single day after that—Monday to Friday, 12 to 6. Then Saturday for her inaugural night shift, 6 to 10.

Another text message came in from the same number.

See you Monday, headband.

She glanced at when Calvin was working, noticing that he scheduled himself at the same time every single day that week.

She rolled her eyes, tossing her phone to the other side of her bed, the motion making her arms scream in utter agony. How was she going to survive an entire six days in a row when her body couldn't even handle one shift? Let alone an entire summer?

Melanie switched off her lamp and stuffed her face in her pillows as she willingly let her exhaustion consume her.

"YOUR SCOOPS ARE STILL TOO SMALL," Calvin said, looking at the cone Melanie just handed him.

She had been scooping ice cream for over an hour now. She worried that her back would never be properly straight again after leaning over the ice cream freezer in front of her, her shirt frozen against her skin as she scooped. Calvin showed her countless times how to properly scoop and made it look impossibly easy, while her cones always came out lopsided.

Melanie frowned. "Show me again."

He scooped off the top of her cone and dropped the ice cream back down in the tub of Raspberry Truffle. "Okay, think of it this way. How do you make the ball on a snowman bigger?"

"Add more snow?"

Calvin pointed the scooper at Melanie. "Exactly." He turned back to the tub. "Shave off some of the ice cream and pack it in like a snowman until you make a scoop about the size of your fist."

She watched as he swiftly lifted the new-and-improved scoop, packing it back on the cone. He handed it to her, motioning for her to continue. Melanie flipped open the stainless steel lid for the hot dip. She rolled the cone in chocolate and waited for it to harden before flipping it up and handing it to the customer at the counter.

"Napkins," Calvin mumbled.

"Crap." She grabbed a few napkins from the dispenser, which you were supposed to wrap around the bottom of the cone to avoid dripping. She handed them to her customer. "Um, that will be $3.75."

The prices were actually not hard to learn—they always added up to the same amount after tax. A single was $2.50, a double $3.75, and a triple was $4.25. Added fudges, candy, dips, and nuts were 50 cents each. It made it a lot faster to rattle off amounts to customers when the orders were small and the lines were long.

The woman behind the counter handed Melanie a five as she punched it into the cash register. She opened up the drawer and froze, completely forgetting what he taught her.

"Start with the coins and count up," Calvin said patiently, without her having to ask.

Right. She grabbed a quarter to round it up to four, then a dollar bill to make it five. She handed the change to the woman who just plopped it right back into the tip jar. "You're doing a great job, sweetheart, keep it up!"

Melanie's face brightened as she closed the register, looking over at Calvin. To her surprise, he was actually smiling at her—or at least in the best way he could, with a small smirk that curled up the side of his mouth. She hadn't seen that smirk since their first conversation at Scoops, when her cheeks turned strawberry pink.

But Melanie realized that smirk wasn't out of pride for doing a good job, but the fact that she probably forgot something. "What?" she asked, feeling annoyed.

He reached over to the hot dip containers, flipping the lid closed. "You have to close this after you use it, straight away."

"Oh," she said, her chest deflating. How was she going to remember all of these mundane details?

"Otherwise the little buggies will find it!" Jay boomed from The War Room.

Melanie frowned. "Huh?"

Calvin pointed to the open window at the counter, which he closed. "If you leave the window open, bugs fly in, and the first sweet thing they smell is..."

Melanie looked down at the dips, realizing what he was saying. "That's absolutely disgusting."

"Which is why you always close the lid," Calvin said, reaching over Melanie to grab the tip jar. "And why you should never order the dip."

Melanie felt her throat tighten slightly as his arm brushed her shoulder. She followed him back toward The

War Room, watching him dump the rest of the tips on the desk as Jay counted. "Slow," Jay said. "Just $23 today. Really glad tomorrow is payday."

Melanie thanked him softly as Jay handed her a stack of bills. "Um, how much do we get paid?"

Jay and Calvin looked at her like she had three extra heads jutting out of her shoulders.

"You took a summer job without knowing what you would be paid?" Calvin asked.

"He sort of forgot to mention it," Melanie mumbled. "And I didn't have many options."

Calvin shook his head, his smirk completely gone, disappointment painted all over his face yet again. He turned to the sheet behind him and signed off for the end of his shift. "You get paid hourly based on how old you are," he said.

"So if you're seventeen, that's seventeen an hour, eighteen get's eighteen an hour," Jay said. "Ron's always worried people won't come back, so he hopes the raise each year is enough of an incentive."

"Well, clearly it works," Melanie said to him, almost as a tease. Jay was easy to get along with, and during a grueling shift at Scoops, she found herself enjoying his company over the tyrannical reign of Calvin Ball.

"Because we pay well," Calvin said defiantly.

"Sure sure, but the movie theater pays twenty-five an hour," Jay said, looking at Melanie and winking at her deviously.

"They don't do tips," Calvin said flatly. "And if you want to work at the movie theater so badly, be my guest."

"Oh, army boy," Jay said, slapping Calvin's back as he stood up. "How could I do that when I love working with you so much?"

Calvin brushed him off, looking down at Melanie. "Same time tomorrow?"

Melanie nodded. She now only had two more days until her first night shift. Two more days to perfect ice cream cones and count change correctly and remember to close the lid on the dip containers and somehow not finish a shift with her shirt looking like a Rorschach painting. They kept saying that night shifts were completely chaotic—it seemed everyone in town wanted to end the day with a scoop at Scoops. Plus, she was working on Saturday, historically the busiest day of the week at the shop...and the first official Saturday of Haverport's summer season.

MELANIE TRUDGED up the front porch steps to find her parents and the Fletchers sitting around their outdoor table, the four of them deep in thought as they chewed on something.

"Maybe spicier?" Mom asked.

"No, it's already too spicy," replied Dan. "People in town hated it when we tried a hot pepper jam, so many complaints that year."

"Yeah, but the sweetness of the raspberry tones it down a bit," Jan countered. "And it all helps if you pair it with the cream cheese."

"Not everyone will though," Dad mumbled, his mouth full of whatever they were eating.

Melanie walked up to the table and noticed a particularly unappetizing block of cream cheese topped with a gooey magenta jam, a sleeve of crackers next to it. "What's going on?"

Mom turned her way, her face lighting up at the sight of

her. "Hey sweetie, the Fletchers wanted us to try a new jam they're thinking of adding to their collection this season."

"It's a hot raspberry preserve," Jan clarified.

"Served with cream cheese?" Melanie asked.

"Don't knock it till you try it," Dad said, spreading a large hunk of it on a cracker and flicking it into his mouth.

Even if the appetizer was, well, a bit off-putting, she was starving. She always packed a peanut butter and jelly sandwich to eat during her 15-minute break, but it never seemed to hold her over, every shift feeling more exhausting than the last.

She plopped down into the chair next to her Mom and reached for the knife, sliding the smallest amount of the jammy cream cheese onto a cracker and taking a skeptical bite. And somehow...it was magical. The sweet and spicy jam mixed with the creamy cheese paired with the crunchy, salty cracker made her stomach growl.

"Wow," she said, her voice sounding a little winded. "This is incredible."

"Did you hear that dear? *Incredible*," Dan said, nudging his wife.

"Too spicy, honey?" Jan asked.

Melanie was already shoveling another cracker into her mouth, this time with a greedy slathering of cream cheese and jam on top. "Nope," she said, not caring if her mouth was full and the crumbles of her cracker dribbled down onto her dirty khaki shorts. "It's perfect."

"Well then, it seems we finally have a winning batch," Jan said, looking pleased. "Maybe we should name it after Mel."

She looked up at Jan in surprise, pulling her out of her jammy cream cheese daze. "Huh?"

"We'll call it Mel's Hot Raspberry Preserves," Jan said.

"It has a nice ring to it," Mom said, with a smirk.

"I-I don't—" Melanie sputtered.

"Our jams sell faster when we put a name in the title, too," Dan commented. "Remember that batch of Barry's Blueberry Jam we made?"

"Our entire stock sold out in a week," Jan responded, looking up at the bright blue sky as she reminisced.

"Who's Barry?" Dad asked.

"Oh, he was this guy that came to fix our downstairs toilet when it was broken a few summers ago. We gave him a piece of toast with the new jam and he about had the same reaction."

"You named your jam after your plumber?" Mom chuckled, completely amused.

"Have to name it somehow," Jan said, turning to Melanie. "So, what do you think sweetheart?"

"Uh, I don't—uh—but I didn't really do anything," she said, stumbling over her words.

"Well, why don't you come over one day and make a few batches with us to make it official." Jan winked at her. "You know, like the old days."

But not really like the old days, Melanie thought to herself. She remembered late nights with the Fletchers in their kitchen, a massive tie-dye tapestry plastered on the wall behind the table where she sat with Duncan as they smashed berries, sealed jars, and tied labels with *Fletcher Fam Jam* to the lids with thick strands of twine.

"That's if you aren't too busy, of course," Dan said. "Your Mom and Dad say you've been working at Scoops every day this week."

Melanie exhaled, feeling the exhaustion deep into her bones. "For now. I have no idea what my schedule will be this summer."

"Honey, why are you doing this?" Mom asked, concern etched all over her face. "You know you don't have to worry about money."

"We have college covered," Dad added.

"It's not that," she said quickly, feeling flustered by their worried gazes. "It's just something fun to do, I'm meeting new people."

It wasn't totally a lie. She was meeting new people, and there were parts of working at Scoops that felt somewhat fun. Jay was the complete opposite of Calvin—always joking around and finding ways to make someone laugh, never too serious about anything. And Rory was like her personal instructional manual to Haverport, telling her every detail she needed to know about living there—like how you could easily sneak into the movie theater if you entered through the back door. Or how to snag a hot slice of Grampy's coveted blueberry coffee cake by knocking on the bakery's back door three times before 7 a.m.

They didn't need to know the other things—that she didn't want to be in the house, that she needed some kind of distraction now that she wasn't graduating from Garrison Prep. Even if they were in the season of the lamb, even if Duncan seemed to be behaving himself...despite the small slip-up when Melanie could smell the whiskey on his breath. Because deep down, she knew the season wouldn't last. At some point, the lion would make an appearance. It always did, and Melanie wanted to limit her chances of being around during the first crackling roar.

She looked down at the block of cream cheese in front of her, realizing she consumed at least half of it by this point. She took a deep breath, calming herself, wondering if she needed to start packing herself a heartier lunch.

The gravel on the driveway crinkled as Duncan's car

slowly pulled in. He stepped out wearing his Ray-Ban sunglasses, a big grin plastered on his face.

"Well, isn't that something," Dad said rather quietly to the group. Melanie eyed her parents, taking note of their hopeful faces. The sight of them made her stomach turn with unease.

Duncan walked up the porch, looking at the five of them sitting around the table. "Did I miss the party invite?" he joked.

"Just testing a new jam for the Fletchers," Mom responded, clearly not bothering to explain it further to him while getting to the heart of what she *really* wanted to know. "Where did you just come from?"

Duncan shrugged, that smile making the dimples on his cheeks even more prominent. "Somewhere."

"Somewhere?" Melanie asked him, feeling almost confident that this very happy shift in his behavior had to do with a particular blonde-haired, hazel-eyed artist.

Duncan looked down at her and winked. "Somewhere."

Maybe she actually did have "the twin thing" after all.

Chapter Six

Melanie walked through the back door of Scoops at 5:45 and noticed everyone was crowded around Ron's desk.

"Melanie, good, that makes all of us," Ron said as she approached the circle.

She leaned close to Rory. "What's going on?" she whispered.

"Staff meeting," she whispered back.

"Okay everyone, we have a few things to discuss before the Haverport season officially kicks off," Ron said. "First things first, we'll be adding a new ice cream as a special for this summer. It's called Blue Bombshell."

"What's the flavor?" Jess asked, her face stern, like her mind was already calculating all the cake possibilities.

"It's a blue ice cream with flavors of vanilla and mixed berries," Ron said. "A friend of mine at Cherrywood Dairy up north has been playing around with some new flavors. I recently went up there to try some and told him I would test this one out in our shop this summer."

"So it's bad," Jess said flatly. Melanie noticed her

looking over at Calvin, the two of them having some kind of silent exchange.

"No, it's not bad, I think it's rather good, but you'll have to see for yourself. The first tubs arrive in a few weeks," Ron said. "Now, starting Monday, we officially move to summer hours. We'll be opening at 11 a.m. closing at 10 p.m. This means the morning shift should be here at 10:45 and the night shift should be out of here before eleven. Please let me know now if there are days you cannot work during the week. I know Calvin doesn't do Sundays. Jess, what about you?"

"Wednesdays," she said.

"Okay," Ron said, scribbling that down on a paper in front of him. "Jay."

"Can't do mornings, too busy," Jay said.

"Sleeping in doesn't count as busy, out of the question," Ron said. "Rory."

Ron continued around the circle, jotting down each Scooper and their schedule. When he finally reached her, she shrugged.

"Um, nothing."

"No schedule conflicts this summer?"

"No," she said, feeling her cheeks flush with embarrassment, knowing how pathetic she must sound for having absolutely nothing planned but this all summer long.

Ron smiled, pointing his pencil at Melanie. "I knew I hired you for a reason."

"Wasn't just for her good looks?" Jay teased, winking at her. Calvin bristled at Jay's comment, crossing his arms tight around his chest. Rory rolled her eyes and kicked Jay in the shin.

"That's inappropriate, Mr. Sanchez," Ron said. "Now

onto our final point of business. This year the summer festival—"

As soon as the word "festival" left Ron's lips, almost everyone in the shop brought a finger up to their nose. The only ones who didn't were Blake, Calvin, and herself.

Ron sighed. "I really wish we could go about this in a civilized manner, but it seems you guys always decide this for me."

"What's going on?" Blake asked, looking confused. And maybe a bit nauseous.

"The three of you will be working the festival shift," Ron said, jotting it down on his paper.

"But—but—" Blake sputtered.

"It's tradition, Blakey-boy," Jay said. "It's always the newbies. And Calvin."

"Someone has to volunteer," Calvin said coolly.

"Yeah but not *every year*," Rory teased him. "That's lunacy."

He didn't respond, just keeping his eyes on his shoes, his arms still crossed against his chest.

"Sorry, but," Melanie said, already regretting the fact that she was going to ask this. "What's the festival?"

"It's called Haverfest, the day we celebrate the town's founding," Rory replied. "They close down Main Street and we basically have a big town party. All these vendors come and there are fireworks—"

"A Ferris wheel," Blake said wistfully.

"Kettle corn, cotton candy," Rory continued.

Ron let out a satisfied exhale, like he too was dreaming about Ferris wheels and cotton candy. "All right, I think that's it. Melanie, good luck on your first night shift."

To her surprise, they all cheered loudly. She felt her face flush again as she smiled, glimpsing briefly over at

Calvin, who wasn't cheering. Instead, his stern gaze was focused on her, making the knots in her stomach tighter as she signed in and embarked on her first Saturday night working behind the Scoops window.

~

IT WAS BEYOND CHAOS. It was madness. Complete mayhem.

"We're out of Cookie Dough, and I think the hot fudge needs to be refilled soon," Jay said as he sprinkled rainbow jimmies into a waffle cone, moving at breakneck speed. "And I'm pretty sure we only have a couple of waffle cones left."

Rory finished up her order and reached into the ice cream freezer, lifting an empty tub and charging for the back. "Got the Cookie Dough!"

Melanie placed a scoop of Chocolate Chip into a bowl, pressing it down with her scooper. In the time she did that, Calvin was able to reach around her, grab a medium-sized cup, and already have a perfect scoop of Blueberry Cobbler ready to press in.

"God, I'm so slow," she mumbled, turning to the hot fudge dispenser. She pushed the lever down hard, hot fudge sputtering at her, already forgetting Jay had said it was practically empty.

"Take your time," Calvin reassured her, the calming tone of his voice surprising her. "They've already waited in line, they're not going anywhere."

Melanie nodded, walking the cups she just scooped to the counter she was working at with Calvin. "One scoop of Death By Chocolate, two scoops of Chocolate Chip with hot fudge."

"Oh, I think I ordered Black Cherry Chunk," the woman said.

Melanie grimaced. "Right, sorry."

Calvin was already finished ringing up his order. He handed her a lid. "I'll scoop it."

She nodded, clicking the lid onto the cup and bringing it to the back freezer with the extra tubs of ice cream. Unfortunately, she already knew what to do with the mess-up orders—this was her third one of the night. She dropped it down next to an upside-down Vanilla cone dipped in chocolate smashed into a cup (was supposed to be butterscotch), and a cup of Caramel Pecan with hot caramel sauce (was supposed to be Pistachio).

She trudged back up to her counter, wondering how many more mess ups of hers would accumulate at the bottom of the fridge by the end of the night. She was only an hour and a half in.

Calvin finished ringing up his customer and gestured for her to take the next order.

Melanie forced her lips into a smile. "Hi, welcome to Scoops!"

"Okay, we've got a *big* order here," the customer said, a whistle dangling around his neck. Melanie took in the brood of miniature soccer players standing around him, all with grubby cleats and grass-stained socks.

Calvin pushed a writing pad and pen in front of her. She sighed, wondering if he thought she wasn't capable of remembering orders (okay, maybe she wasn't). She begrudgingly took them and started writing everything down.

She was halfway through the list, checking off each order as she scooped, when it was time to make a Chocolate Peanut Butter Swirl milkshake. She filled a 16-ounce cup halfway with ice cream, then filled the bottom third with milk just like Calvin taught her. She went over to the machine, pushed the cup into the drink mixer, and pressed down on the petal below the counter.

An explosion of ice cream and milk spewed everywhere. Melanie's eyes slowly blinked open, assessing the damage. It was all over her shirt and down the front of her shorts. The back wall was covered in streaks like an abstract painting. The inside of the machine was dripping milk, and a rogue scoop of ice cream slid on the counter next to her and plopped down on the floor.

She felt a hand on her back. "It's okay, breathe," Calvin said softly. "It's just ice cream."

Tears welled up in her eyes. This was not what she needed right now—for Calvin to see her crying over an exploded milkshake. Yet the feeling of his warm hand on her back calmed her instantly.

Calvin reached into the machine and pried the messy cup from her hands. "Go wash up in the back, take a breather. I got this."

"But the order," Melanie said. "And the line, it's so long."

"People who come to Scoops know the line is going to be long, it's part of the experience," he said reassuringly. "If you really want to, why don't you fill the fudges and candy that are running low?"

"Okay," Melanie muttered, embarrassment creeping up her neck at the milkshake casualty that was splattered across the side of the shop. She stepped into the back and took a long, calming breath before wiping down her shirt and shorts, then started pulling boxes off the shelves. By the time she was back up front filling the hot fudge, the side of the shop was already spotless, and Calvin was finishing up the soccer team's order.

"My first explosion was my third week in," Jay said as he scooped a cone. "RIP to the 16-ounce Banana Cream Pie milkshake."

"Pretty sure you had more than one explosion," Calvin mumbled, which only Melanie could hear. She smiled to herself.

"At least it wasn't an entire cake," Rory said. "I whacked into Jess, causing her to drop the cake she was holding. Then Tyler stepped on it right away and the frosting smeared all over the rug."

"God that rug reeked for weeks no matter how much we cleaned it, so glad Ron decided to replace it," Jay laughed, poking Rory in her side. Melanie noticed her flush slightly before turning toward the front counter and squirting a generous serving of marshmallow sauce into a cup. "How about you, army boy?" Jay asked. "Ever have some kind of monumental fuck up?"

"Language," Calvin said flatly, sprinkling a small scoop of M&M's into a bowl of Rocky Road. Ron made it clear to all Scoopers—no swearing when customers were in the window. *This is a family establishment,* he said. *I don't want to be the cause of Billy Bob's first F-word.*

Jay rolled his eyes. "Come on, man, be human for a moment. Did you ever mess up?"

"No," he said sharply, trying his best to end the conversation abruptly with one word. "Get back on the line."

Jay shook his head, looking defeated. But his look quickly turned into a smirk when he saw who was at his counter. Two tall females leaned against the counter to read the menu board, their loose shirts dipping low, revealing a bit more cleavage than they probably realized.

"Well, hello, ladies," Jay said, his smirk growing wider and wider. "How's it going?"

Jay teased and charmed these two girls as they completely fawned over him, poking his hands, and laughing at his jokes. Melanie filled up the rainbow jimmies and looked over at Rory. Her face was stern as she ignored what was happening, keeping her eyes on the cup of Strawberry Cheesecake she was scooping. But her ears were a dark shade of pink.

Jay kept teasing them as he scooped their cones, handing each one to them slowly, brushing their hands as he did so. "On me, ladies."

"Oh my gosh, *free?*" the brunette asked, her eyes sparkling.

"You bet," Jay said, his teeth gleaming. "Come back any time."

The girls giggled as they left. Melanie was now onto filling up the candy containers along the side wall.

"Wait, employees can give out free ice cream?" said a familiar voice behind the counter.

"If you know someone, maybe," Jay said.

"Well, good thing I do," the voice said. "Isn't that right, Mel Mel?"

She swiveled toward the counter as her eyes met Duncan's. He was smiling wide, his arm around the shoulders of the familiar blonde.

"Duncan," Melanie said, feeling a little shocked that he was here in front of her. She knew at some point her family would come see her in action. She just never thought Duncan would be the first.

He leaned against the counter as blondie stroked his back with her hand. "Can we have free cones, Mel Mel?"

"Who's we?" Melanie asked, her tone sounding way more aggressive than she intended.

Duncan slid an arm around the girl's waist. "This is Leila. Leila, this is my twin sister."

"You're a *twin?*" Jay asked, sounding exasperated. "Dude, you literally can't tell."

"Fraternal," Melanie said flatly as if it wasn't already obvious.

"Come on, Mel Mel, a little treat to celebrate," Duncan said, squeezing Leila's side.

"Um, I—" Melanie started, looking over at Calvin. She knew he could hear this entire conversation, but he was pretending not to, serving the customers at the counter she should be at. Despite how much she felt Calvin didn't like her being here, Melanie knew she shouldn't do it. Even if Calvin willingly let Jay give away two free cones, that didn't mean she should continue to stay on his bad side as well.

Because deep down, despite how much she despised him in return, she didn't want to be on his bad side anymore. She didn't want to admit to herself that her mind drifted to the thought of him often. The way his arms flexed carrying heavy boxes down from the attic storage. The way he always had a tiny paperback novel tucked in his back pocket. The way his hand felt on her back after the milk-shake explosion, like a soothing warm blanket in an ice-cold storm.

Melanie turned back toward Duncan, taking a deep breath. "Sorry, I can't."

His face fell. "What? Why not? He literally just did," he said, pointing to Jay.

"He's not supposed to," Melanie said confidently, even though she didn't have a clue what the rules behind free ice cream were at all.

"Come on, this is stupid," Duncan said, the volume of

his voice increasing. "I'm your *brother*, doesn't that count for something? Family discount?"

"You heard her," said Calvin, coming up to stand directly behind her. "She said no."

Duncan looked at him like he wanted to reach through the counter and punch him in the throat. "Who made you prince of the ice cream shop?" Duncan spit at him.

"Literally Ron did," Jay mumbled. Melanie heard Rory chuckle softly as she scooped.

"Would you like to order, or should we take the customer behind you?" Calvin asked. "You're holding up the line."

"Jesus, Melanie, who is this guy?"

A chill trickled down her spine. He said *Melanie*, not Mel Mel. She needed to stop this or the lion was going to make an appearance. Except, she had no idea how to diffuse the situation.

"Her boss," Calvin responded.

"Who willingly let an employee give free ice cream to some chicks?!"

"It will come out of his paycheck," Calvin said. "Now, order something, or please leave."

He huffed, grabbing Leila's hand. Melanie noticed her demeanor change, watching Duncan in a shocked daze. She felt the sudden urge to jump over that counter, gather her up in her arms, and tell her to run. But Duncan was already pulling Leila away to his car, his eyes dark and his shoulders tight.

The customers in line were completely silent as Duncan got into his car and slammed the door.

"Are those cones really going to come out of my paycheck?" Jay whispered to Calvin nervously.

"No," Calvin said.

Jay exhaled, looking relieved. "Thank God."

Calvin ignored him, turning to Melanie, his face relaxed and unfazed by what just happened. It was the same expression she always saw when he was discussing something with Ron, his demeanor soft and soothing. He gestured for their counter. "Ready for round two?"

She nodded, following him to their window, and started taking orders, feeling thankful she had something to distract her from the thoughts now swirling in her head about waking up the lion...and what might be waiting for her when she got home.

"THAT'S THE LAST ONE, shut it down," Calvin said.

Melanie handed a double scoop of Raspberry Truffle to a young couple behind the counter with two spoons as Calvin flipped the sign at the front window. Officially closed for the night.

Surprisingly, the rest of her shift went smoothly. Maybe it was the fact that he wasn't acting so tough and abrasive as he had the rest of the week, or how Jay and Rory kept trying to make her laugh. She knew the three of them probably pitied her after what happened.

Calvin held two small buckets of warm soapy water with rags, handing one to Melanie. A stereo blared in the back as Jay turned up the music, and the four of them fell into a steady rhythm. She started wiping down surfaces at one end of the ice cream shop, Calvin at the other. Rory bounced around filling the candy, fudges, sauces, and sleeves of cups and cones. Jay washed dishes in the back, shamelessly singing along to his music, his voice very much off-key.

Eventually, Melanie and Calvin met in the middle, the two of them wiping around the edges of candy containers and the shelves of extra spoons and napkin dispensers below.

Jay sang a particularly high note, completely out of his range, his voice cracking as he belted it out.

"You'd think he would get better after all this time," Calvin mumbled quietly to Melanie. "But I think it's getting worse."

Melanie smirked. "Did you just make a joke?"

"Not a very good one if you're not laughing."

"I don't laugh easy," Melanie said, dipping her rag into the now grayish water in her bucket, squeezing the excess water out. "You'll just have to try harder, I guess."

"Yet you seem to always laugh easily at Jay," he said, his eyes intent on wiping around the hot fudge canister.

Did he look...jealous? Melanie couldn't help but notice the way Calvin's jaw tightened, wondering why it bothered him so much that Jay flirted with her. Jay was definitely a charmer, but Melanie wasn't one to ever find that kind of confidence attractive. She tended to like...quiet types. Those who always looked like they were deep in thought. Who kept small paperback novels in their back pocket.

Melanie slapped the rag down on the counter and furiously started scrubbing at a hardened smear of caramel sauce. She knew she was getting ahead of herself. Calvin was certainly acting nicer to her tonight, but it was probably out of pity for what he witnessed, she thought again. Even if she felt a tiny twinge in her heart each time he looked at her, he clearly was not interested—his behavior toward her all week was proof enough. Besides, after tonight, he would probably just go back to being moody and broody.

They fell back into silence as they worked, listening to

Jay's painfully bad singing voice ring through the shop. Rory came around and tied up the garbage bags, hauling them over her shoulder. Calvin reached for two new bags in a box underneath the counter. He pointed to the tip jars before replacing the bags in the bins. "Count the tip money?"

"Oh!" She hadn't been asked to count the tips at the end of a shift yet.

The jars were stuffed to the brim, and they were *heavy*. She sat down at the desk and dumped out the jars, completely in awe of the pile of bills and the absurd number of coins that plopped down in front of her.

She counted a hundred, but still had a pile to go.

Another hundred.

"Jesus," she muttered, not noticing the others now huddled around her.

She kept counting. Fifty seven.

Then, the coins. Another thirteen.

"Two hundred seventy bucks," Melanie said, bewildered.

She looked up and noticed Rory was snapping a photo of her. She blushed as Rory flipped her phone to show Melanie's reaction—eyes bugging out of her head as she held a massive pile of money in her hands. They all started laughing at the photo—Calvin included.

"That's sixty-seven each," Calvin said, helping her divvy up the money. "The last two dollars go in the tip jar for tomorrow."

"Why?" Melanie asked.

"A courtesy for those who open," Rory said. "Plus, people don't tip an empty jar. They tip when they see other people have tipped."

The logic didn't make any sense to Melanie, but she just nodded, holding a very fat stack of bills in her hand.

"All right, I'm starving," Jay called. "I'm out."

The four of them gathered up their things, turning off lights as they left the shop. Melanie watched as Calvin swiftly shut the door, locking it with a key attached to a carabiner clipped on a loop of his khakis.

She waved goodbye to Jay and Rory as they took off, heading for the bike rack behind the shop. She clipped on her helmet but then groaned at the sight of a very deflated-looking back tire.

"Everything okay?"

She turned toward Calvin, pointing to her bike. "Looks like I have a flat."

"Well shit."

"Language," Melanie teased.

That got a chuckle out of him. A *chuckle*. Deep and leathery. She couldn't help it—she wanted to hear it again immediately.

"I can text my buddy at the bike shop if you want. See if he's available tomorrow to fix it."

Melanie nodded. "Uh, yeah, that would be great. Which shop?"

Calvin smirked. "There's only one in town."

"Of course," she said. "Small town, how could I forget."

He chuckled again. She felt weak in the knees.

"Need a lift?"

She hesitated, looking down at her phone. She'd texted her mom earlier during her break to check-in. Mostly to see if everything was okay...wondering if Duncan ended up home after his fit at the counter.

She never responded. It was never a good sign when she didn't respond.

She knew she could call them. But if they were in the middle of a battle with Duncan, she didn't want to create more problems.

She exhaled audibly. "Yeah, sure. Thanks."

Melanie unlocked her bike and pushed it toward Calvin's car—a beat-up, forest-green Chevy pickup that had seen better days. Calvin popped the bed and lifted her bike into it.

"Where do you live?" he asked, pushing the trunk door closed.

"Sandy Cove."

"Near the Fletchers?" he asked, walking toward the driver's side of the car.

"Um, yeah." Of course he knew where they lived—everyone seemed to know everyone in Haverport. She opened up the creaky passenger side door and slid in, the interior of the car surprisingly clean. "Right next door, actually."

They rode in silence down the winding, calm roads of Haverport, past sleepy Hillside Park, and into the beach communities. Melanie couldn't help but stare down at Calvin's right hand, placed loosely on his lap. When he looked over at her, she felt her face flush as she quickly turned her head toward the rolled-down window, the cool early summer breeze chilling her arms. She tucked her hands underneath her thighs.

Calvin turned the truck onto the sandy roads of the Cove, parking in front of cottage five.

Yelling could be heard from where they sat.

It was explosive. Duncan was screaming at them. Melanie could hear Dad's voice through it all, calming but stern, trying to make him see reason. The sound of Mom's voice was shrill above them both. But Duncan wasn't listening. He was a swirling hurricane with a torrential downpour of terror. She couldn't make out what he was saying, but Melanie knew that his words were causing disaster. She heard her parents' silence as he kept at it.

She turned to Calvin, but couldn't look him directly in the face. She kept her eyes on his hands again, both of them grasping his steering wheel, his knuckles white.

"Is everything oka—"

"It's fine," Melanie said, interrupting him. "All good."

Calvin's phone dinged. He fumbled for it and read his screen. "Um, Kevin says he can take a look at your bike tomorrow morning at ten."

"Awesome." She reached for her belt buckle, desperately wanting to get out of his truck. Get him away *now* before Duncan discovered who was outside. "Thanks."

"Do you need a ride to the bike shop tomorrow?"

"Nope, I've got it," she said, slamming his car door a little too forcefully, making him wince. She ignored the clear look of pity all over his face as she went for her bike in the back, hoping to get to it before he could even get out of the truck.

"Great job tonight," she heard him call out.

She lifted her arm up with a quick wave, too embarrassed to look back at him. "Thanks for the lift."

She walked around the back, leaning her bike in the usual spot against the fence, listening for the truck's ignition to kick in. He seemed to hesitate for a beat, then two, before turning it on. Relief flooded Melanie's body as she finally heard the truck slowly roll away.

Chapter Seven

At the time, Melanie hoped the storm of Thanksgiving was a one-time thing. But the fighting—and the drinking—got progressively worse.

After one month of being exiled into grounded prison, Mom and Dad decided to loosen the reins a bit for New Year's. Duncan said he was just going to a friend's place. "Just video games and pizza," he said. "Garrett's parents will be there the whole time."

They were skeptical at first, but eventually, Duncan wore them down, and they allowed him to go. Melanie watched from her bedroom window as he slung his duffel bag into the back seat of Garrett's car before jumping in the front, the two of them blasting music as they sped down the road.

She sighed, sitting down at her desk as she stared at the mountain of homework in front of her. Two essays, one biology lab report, and flashcards for her next World History test. She was already swimming in schoolwork but found the work a delightful diversion from the constant ache that sat at her chest, right beneath her throat. It was like her heart was slowly breaking with each passing day, and she had no idea how to make the aching stop. Her schoolwork seemed to be the only thing that dulled the sensation when she was knee-deep in equations and literature.

She heard the door creak open. "More school work?" Mom asked.

"It never ends," she moaned. "I have to finish all of this by Tuesday."

Mom placed a warm hand on Melanie's shoulder, her shoulders relaxing at the soothing touch.

"Come on, we have a fire going, and Dad bought that sparkling apple cider you love." She jostled her shoulder lightly. "Yale can wait."

She looked up and caught a small gleam in her eye as Mom looked down at her. Her parents knew how important it was for her to go to Yale, how much she wanted it. But now, with this impossible amount of homework in front of her, she wondered if it was even worth going down that road at all. She was already worn out, and she was only four months into her high school career.

She let herself follow her Mom to the sofa and wrapped herself beneath a blanket. The three of them watched Ryan Seacrest flash his glistening smile to the camera as he shuf-fled through the excited crowd in Times Square all bundled up in warm scarves and hats and bright hope that every-thing would change after the ball dropped. That this next year would be *different*.

Melanie liked the idea of a fresh start as she watched the ball drop. She wondered if there would be a fresh start for her family—if that one incident at Thanksgiving would be the start and end of whatever was going on with her twin brother.

But that small whisper of hope in her heart was completely flattened just 30 minutes later.

She was half asleep when her phone started buzzing, a call from Duncan.

"Mel Mellll," he whispered, his words slurring. "I need help."

Melanie sat up straight. "What's going on?"

"Cops," he whispered. "They broke up the party. I ran. I'm behind a bush. Or a tree. I don't know."

There was no pizza or video games. He went to a party. He was drinking.

"Oh shit," he said, before she heard him pull the phone away to hurl. Melanie clenched her eyes closed as she listened to her brother puking his guts out, waiting for him to finish.

"Where are you?"

"Uhhh, Rolling Hills," he whispered. "Party was at Jake's."

"The senior lacrosse player?"

"Yeah, he got BUSTED. But the rest of the team was able to get away."

Even in a time of such stupidity, it seemed the lacrosse team still had one goal: to protect the players at all costs. Even if that meant leaving someone behind and potentially ruining his life.

It didn't take long for Duncan to fully immerse himself into their culture. He changed his everyday attire from jeans and tees to baggy athletic shorts and sleeveless tanks. His sentences now always started with "dude" or "bro." And when he wasn't texting in the team chat or at practice, he was in his room lifting weights, his arm muscles getting freakishly larger each day.

And now, apparently, he partied like them.

"Can you come get meee?" he whispered.

"Uh, I can't...drive?"

"No one will pull you over," he said confidently. "You know how to drive."

"But isn't the scene crawling with cops?"

"I'm far enough away, I think," he whispered. But Melanie wasn't so confident. She could hear muffled sirens through the phone.

"Duncan, I—"

"Mel, it's fiiiine," he said. "Just get the keys from the basket, take Mom's car."

Melanie pinched the bridge of her nose. "Okay."

"Mel Mel you're the bestttt, I lovee youu," he said.

"Send me your location," she said flatly and hung up the phone.

She rushed out of bed and quickly slid on a pair of leggings and a sweatshirt, stuffing her feet into an old pair of boots.

Steal Mom's car? Drive illegally? It was all insane. She felt anger slowly simmering in her chest as she tip-toed downstairs. How could he make her do this? It was all completely out of her comfort zone...and for what? So he could have a few beers?

When she reached the bottom of the stairs, she ran right into her mom, wrapped in her bathrobe.

Her brows furrowed. "Where are you going?"

"Um." She wasn't sure what to say. "I—"

Then she wept, and it all came tumbling out. When she finished explaining what happened, she felt hollow. She knew she'd just failed her brother. But she couldn't lie, that's not who she was. She couldn't sneak out and keep secrets from her parents. She also knew she had it lucky, that she had a set of parents invested in her life and who cared deeply about her. So why would she choose to disobey them and go behind their back?

And why was Duncan so quick to do it without a second thought?

Mom looked angry, but not at her. At the fact that Duncan so easily defied them yet again, and that he pulled Melanie into it so she could cover up his tracks.

She watched as Mom bolted out of the house in her robe, her car screeching out of the driveway. Sitting on that bottom step, she waited, until she heard the soft footsteps of her Dad's slippers padding down the steps. He sat down and put his arm around her, rubbing his thumb against her shoulder. They didn't say a word, but Melanie sensed it— Mom must have called him and told him what happened.

When they finally arrived home, there was screaming. Melanie jumped up as the front door swung open and Duncan came charging in, his face purple with such anger, it had her stumbling back into the wall behind her.

"You RAT!" he screamed. "You went right to Mom?! HOW COULD YOU!"

"I—" Melanie sputtered.

"Do *not* bring her into this, Duncan Albertson," Mom said, voice stern as she slammed the front door closed. "She was scared for you and did the right thing."

"Scared? HA!" screeched Duncan. "God forbid your perfect angel daughter ever breaks the rules!"

"Duncan," Melanie whispered, her heart sinking lower and lower.

"Shut the fuck up," he snapped, pointing his finger so close to her face, she flinched. "You clearly don't care at

ALL about me! It's all about being the perfect kid, right? Well congratulations, Melanie. You finally got it."

Melanie was speechless at his words. Perfect kid? How could he say that? The thought that they were somehow in competition for Mom and Dad's favorite child had never once crossed her mind.

"Oh, don't look at me like you didn't know," Duncan spewed, spit landing on her face as he spoke. "It's always been about you and Yale and being the smart one. And then there's me," he said, thumping his chest. "But I know how to have a life and friends, while you just float around school like a sad, lonely ghost."

Melanie felt the whoosh of wind against her face as Mom slapped him hard across his cheek. He stumbled back, but without missing a beat, he moved toward Mom and reached two hands up.

To choke her.

Dad flew in, grabbing one of his arms and twisting it back, pulling him away from her. He shoved Duncan at the stairs and told him to climb.

Slightly winded by Dad's quick maneuver, he climbed up the steps like a ragged old dog.

Mom looked over at Melanie, tears streaking both of their faces.

"Go to bed, Melanie," Mom said sternly.

She obeyed. When she got to her room she closed the door. Then locked it.

Never in her life had she needed to lock her door. But after that night, it felt reckless not to.

Melanie slept with her door locked every night after, up until the night they received another devastating phone call. When their worlds all drastically changed.

They were still yelling at each other when Melanie slid

into the back door of cottage five. She shuffled through the kitchen, hearing bits and pieces of the fight. Duncan was screaming at them with such venom, about how angry he was they made him move to this horrid place. Mom tried yelling over his booming voice, reminding him that he was the one who chose this—he was the one who said he needed to get out of Garrison. But Duncan interrupted, his words like knives as he blamed them for everything.

No one seemed to notice her as she slipped past them and went up the stairs, turning the knob of her bedroom door so no one could hear the muffled click. She exhaled as the fighting continued, her head pounding, her body exhausted from her shift.

And then she locked her door.

MELANIE WOKE up with the bright morning sun glaring down on her face. She covered her eyes as she sat up, a bit shocked at how she was able to pass out immediately last night despite the scene she'd come home to. Maybe she should have gotten an exhausting job sooner.

But then it came back to her—the look of worry on Calvin's face as they pulled up to the house, the way his knuckles turned white as he gripped the steering wheel. Melanie felt a deep shame that he had to witness even a glimpse of it. She wondered what he thought of her now.

She tried shoving thoughts of Calvin out of her mind as she slipped out of bed and pushed her feet into a ratty pair of slippers. The smell of coffee pulled her downstairs like a magnet. She snatched her yellow sunshine mug from the cupboard and poured herself a large cup.

"Hey kiddo," Dad said, reaching behind her for a mug as well. "I see you beat me to the coffee."

Melanie smiled shyly, taking a sip and leaning against the counter to give him some room. He took a large slurp like he always did with his first sip. "So, how was your first night shift?"

"Chaos," Melanie admitted. "But we each made sixty-seven in tips."

Dad's eyes went wide. "That's insane. I still can't believe people tip that much."

"Me neither," Melanie said. "Although, a lot of it I think will have to go toward my bike."

"Uh oh, what happened?"

Melanie sighed. "Flat tire."

"Oh, that shouldn't cost you too much," Dad said, waving his arm.

"Actually, do you think you could take me to the bike shop in town?" Melanie asked. "You can just drop me off and then I can ride it home."

"I can wait with you. Maybe we could go to the café for breakfast while we wait, just you and me?"

Melanie grinned. "That would be—"

"Harold, you almost ready?" Mom said, rushing into the kitchen. "We have to be there in fifteen."

"Where?" Dad said, his eyebrows furrowed.

"The Sandy Cove breakfast, remember? We're being introduced to the association?"

Melanie's heart sank a little.

"Oh shoot." He snatched his car keys from the little hook near the door. "Sorry, kiddo, want to just take my car?"

"Sure," she mumbled, taking the keys from him.

He hesitated as he looked at his daughter. Melanie

cursed herself for showing her disappointment and forced a smile on her face. She was okay. It really wasn't a big deal.

But her expression must have done enough damage, because next thing she knew he was reaching into his pocket for his wallet, pulling out a twenty. "Grab yourself something from the café anyway."

"Dad, it's okay, I have tip money," she said, refusing to take it.

He pressed the bill into her hand. "I know you do, but let me treat you, please?"

Melanie sighed, holding onto the bill as she watched her parents exit the cottage, large travel tumblers full of steaming coffee in tow.

"Shouldn't take me long," Kevin said to Melanie. He already had half the tire peeled off her bike wheel. "Fifteen minutes."

"Wow, great, thanks," Melanie answered. She took a few steps around Port Wheels, looking at the bikes lined up next to each other, like plates stacked neatly in a dishwasher. Another parallel row of bikes was perched up on the ceiling. There must have been at least a hundred bikes in the tiny shop, maybe more.

"So, how do you know Calvin?" Kevin called out from the back.

Melanie felt her cheeks flush. "Um, we work together."

"Ah, the late-night text makes sense now," Kevin responded. "Work the night shift?"

"Yeah, found my flat tire after."

"Bummer. How do you like working there?"

"Cool, I guess. This was my first week."

"Damn, lucky you," Kevin said. "Everyone wants that job."

"Really?" Melanie walked back to Kevin, shocked that he was almost done with her bike as he finished pressing a brand new tire into her wheel.

"Yeah, the most coveted job in the Port," he said. "Are the tips really that good?"

Melanie smiled, nodding her head.

Kevin whistled. "Must be nice. And Jess...she giving you a hard time?"

"Jess?" Melanie asked. "How can she give me a hard time? She hardly talks."

Kevin smiled to himself as he finished up pressing in the tire as if the thought of Jess amused him. "That means she likes you. And if you got that job, Calvin must really like you, too."

Melanie frowned. "I don't think Calvin had anything to do with it. Ron called me."

Kevin pumped some air into her new tire before wheeling it over to Melanie. "Nah, that place wouldn't run without him. Even if Ron called, it was probably orchestrated by Calvin."

Melanie stood there for a beat, her thoughts wandering. Ron said that her application was on the top of the pile, which was why he called her. But was it a pile that Calvin had put together? Did he make sure she was at the top?

And if so, why would he do that when he clearly didn't want her to have the job?

Or maybe he did, Melanie thought. Maybe he...

"You good?" Kevin asked.

Melanie shook her head. "Yeah, sorry, how much?"

"Ten."

Melanie balked. "What, seriously, that's it?"

Kevin smiled. "Consider it a family discount. Calvin's a good buddy."

"Wow, okay, thanks," she said, reaching for the money in her back pocket. She stared at the twenty from her Dad for a moment, then handed it to Kevin.

"Hold on, let me get change," Kevin said, turning toward his desk.

"No, keep it," Melanie said, grabbing her bike and wheeling it toward the door.

"For real?!" Kevin said, looking at her like she was an angel sent from above.

Melanie smiled. "Consider it a Scoops-level tip."

MELANIE SAT on the outdoor patio of Seabreeze Café with a Sandy Cove latte and their last warm slice of blueberry coffee cake, which she was miraculously able to snag. Seabreeze had a latte named after every neighborhood in town. Sandy Cove was a toasted hazelnut latte with caramel drizzle, which, embarrassing as it was, made Melanie moan after her first sip. She was on her phone looking at Haverport High's website, scrolling through the list of classes they offered, mentally trying to prepare for what she would sign up for in the fall. The school did offer a few AP classes, but all ones she'd taken before—English, U.S. History, Latin, Chem. She noticed the school offered other AP-level courses through a nearby community college and was about to take a look through her options when a familiar head with a buzz-cut breezed past her.

Melanie tipped her baseball cap low hoping Calvin wouldn't recognize her as he walked past, his arms looped with a woman Melanie presumed to be his grandmother.

He held open the door for her as she shuffled inside. She wore a button-down white cardigan, her tiny feet pressed into a classic pair of loafers, and her head covered with the poofiest set of gray curls. But it was Calvin's outfit that had Melanie's gaze lingering. A white button-down shirt and a pair of black slacks, perfectly fitted around his waist and falling down neatly to his ankles, and a shiny pair of white leather sneakers on his feet.

Melanie couldn't help but stare at him through the glass door, watching the way he looked as he moved around the café. He grabbed a tray of coffee and sandwiches before holding the door open again for his grandmother and following her to a picnic table on the patio.

She wondered if she should make a run for it. She was in no mood to see him right now, especially in a grubby T-shirt and an old pair of jean shorts, her hair unwashed and still greasy from the night before.

Calvin was holding out a seat for his grandmother as Melanie snatched her latte and stood up, quickly making a break for it.

"You can't leave a half-eaten slice of blueberry coffee cake, that's sacrilege."

Melanie turned to face a smirking Calvin heading toward her. The top two buttons of his shirt were undone, revealing a patch of smooth tan skin, a silver chain peeking out from underneath.

Melanie felt her throat go dry. She swallowed. "You finish it then."

"Already put it on my table," Calvin responded. "Did you get your bike fixed?"

She nodded. "Yeah, he was nice. Gave me a discount."

"Sounds like Kevin," he said. "I told him if he keeps doing that he will definitely go out of business."

Melanie crossed her arms. "Do you, like, know everyone in town?"

He smirked again. "Sort of."

Melanie's heart fluttered at the sight of that smirk. God, why was she being like this? Every time she tried pushing away those feelings, they automatically came back to her... sometimes even stronger than before. Like a scoop of ice cream that kept getting bigger and bigger.

"And everything all right at home?" he asked, his voice quiet and serious.

"Oh, yeah, all good," Melanie said tightly. She fumbled with the keys as she tried to unlock the door. "See you tomorrow?"

Calvin's face was still full of concern when she hopped into the front seat of her car. "Uh, yeah, second night shift," he said. "You ready for it?"

Melanie thought about the chaos of last night's shift, how it took her mind off everything else, how she was able to easily crash when she got home and sleep soundly.

"Oh yeah. More than ready."

Melanie walked into Scoops the next night to the sound of sniggering in The War Room. Jay and Rory were standing by the walk-in fridge, failing to look casual as she signed in for her shift. "What's going on?"

"MELANIE! Is that you?"

It was Blake. But the sound of his voice was coming from inside the walk-in.

She stepped toward them, looking suspiciously at Jay and Rory. The two of them couldn't seem to hold it in any longer and burst out laughing.

"Blake?" Melanie asked.

"Melanie, please help me! They locked me in here!"

She scowled at them. "Why would you do that?"

"Tradition," Rory said, trying and failing to hold in her fits of giggles.

"Seriously? That seems cruel."

"It *is* cruel, now get me OUT!" Blake yelled, his voice cracking. It sounded like he was starting to cry.

The two of them burst out laughing again as Melanie frowned, stepping closer to the door. "Blake, there is a small button underneath the door handle, can you feel for it?"

Melanie heard fumbling on the other side, then the sound of a pulsing button.

"Yes, but it's not working!" He was panicking, and Melanie could hear a muffled sob.

"Press that button at the same time as you pull the door handle," Melanie said. "It'll unlock and let you out."

Now Rory and Jay were the ones frowning as Blake stepped back into The War Room, his face blotchy and red. He beelined for the bathroom and slammed the door, causing the shop to rattle.

"You're no fun," Jay said. "And how did you know how to do that?"

"Calvin taught me on my first day," she said. "Just in case I got locked in."

"Or in case *someone* locked you in," Rory said, rolling her eyes. "No fair, he told us not to even try with you."

"What do you mean?" Melanie asked.

"He told us if we tried locking you in the walk-in, we were...how did he put it?" Jay asked, holding his hand to his chin like he was pretending to remember. "Oh right, 'deader than dead meat.'"

Melanie stood there for a moment, bewildered. Why was he treating her differently?

At that moment, Calvin walked into Scoops, the silence causing him to pause at the door. "We all good?"

She nodded, pulling her ponytail through her Scoops cap before heading toward the front of the shop, ready to bury herself in ice cream orders and avoid the annoyingly worrisome gaze of Calvin Ball.

Chapter Eight

SHE CLIMBED the front porch steps of the cottage, glancing down at her shirt. It wasn't nearly as messy as her first week, but after three weeks of working at Scoops, she hoped she would be at the point where she could come home and not have to scrub stains out of her uniform. She sighed, flicking off her Converse that the shop had officially destroyed, and stepped into the house.

Mom and Dad were dressed up and looking like they were ready to leave. Dad was holding tightly to whatever was bulging inside his jacket. Melanie lifted her eyebrows at him, wondering what he was hiding. He then reached into his jacket and pulled out a bottle of red wine. Melanie nodded. She understood.

She pulled off her Scoops hat and placed it down on the counter. "Where are you guys off to now?"

"Sandy Cove beach association meeting," Mom said, picking up a tray of what looked like freshly baked brownies.

Melanie frowned as she saw her Mom wrap them up. "They seem to always have meetings."

"That was just our initiation, this is the real meeting they have once a month," he said, pointing to his jacket, "Except with the amount of, well, you know, that everyone brings, I doubt they get anything done at these things."

"He's all the way out on the beach, Harold, he can't hear you."

Melanie glanced out the window and noticed Duncan out on Sandy Cove beach. He was lying down on a beach blanket, shirt off, sunglasses on, and a speaker next to him as he lay there scrolling on his phone.

"Food, huh?" Melanie said, turning back toward her parents. "Am I allowed to come?"

"Sorry honey, owners only," Mom said, touching Melanie's cheek. "There's money on the counter if you guys want to order something for dinner."

She looked down again at the tray of brownies in Mom's hands, frowning obnoxiously.

Mom chuckled. "There's a container above the microwave."

Melanie leaned in, kissing her on the cheek. "Thanks, you're the best."

"No," Mom said, lifting a finger and playfully poking Melanie's nose. "*You're* the best."

She felt elated by her mother's words as she watched her parents leave, walking down the sandy road and over to cottage two. But the feeling slowly died as she looked out at Duncan, now feeling nauseous. She didn't want to be the best. It wasn't supposed to be a competition.

Or...was it? Melanie always tried hard to be everything her parents wanted—a no-problem child with good grades and hopefully bound for Yale. She always told herself she was doing it because her parents deserved it, because they worked so hard to give her what she had. But as she thought of her twin brother on the beach, she wondered if there was another more sinister reason. If the real motivation behind all of it was to push her way to the top, like she did at Garrison. Maybe she was the one to blame for everything that was happening. Maybe she was the one causing the pain, the one who led him to who he was today.

Without really thinking, Melanie charged out of the cottage and down to the beach, listening to Duncan's music get louder and louder as she approached him. When she finally reached his towel, he glanced up.

The words were on the tip of her tongue. She wanted to say it, wanted to tell him she was sorry. She wanted to tell him how much she missed him.

But before she could get a word out, Duncan grinned at her. Teeth and all. Like the fight weeks ago never happened.

"Mel Mel, come join me," he said, shifting on his beach blanket to make room for her.

She took a timid seat next to him as he slightly lowered his music. She noticed he had half a bottle of beer open next to him as he reached for the canvas bag at his feet, pulling out another one. He held it up to Melanie, and lifted his eyebrows.

An invitation. He wanted her to have a drink with him.

She knew she shouldn't. They'd never had a drink together before—Melanie set that boundary long ago. She didn't want anything to do with that part of his life, hoping that it would just eventually fade away.

But his eyes were full of expectation and hope, a bouncy dirty blonde curl falling in front of his face.

What if she was just taking the wrong approach? Maybe if she actually said yes, if she casually had a drink with him, he would see that it really wasn't a big deal. That this partying phase he was in was just that—a phase—and it didn't have to consume his life.

She nodded. Duncan whooped with glee as he popped off the top, handing it to her. He lifted his own beer and they clinked glasses. Melanie placed the bottle to her lips as she watched Duncan down the rest of his beer, tossing the empty bottle on to the sand.

Duncan watched her enthusiastically as Melanie finally tipped back her beer, taking her first pull.

It tasted sour, like a piece of bread that went bad, and it was uncomfortably warm from sitting in Duncan's bag. The fizzing from the beer made her throat catch. She coughed roughly, some of it coming out of her nose.

Duncan laughed heartily.

"Th—that tastes like piss," Melanie said, wiping her face with the bottom of her filthy Scoops shirt.

"Oh, it gets better with time," Duncan said, a huge toothy grin still plastered on his face.

Doubt it, she thought. "Maybe if it wasn't so warm," Melanie mumbled, glaring at the bottle.

"Well, what was I supposed to do, chill it in the fridge?" Duncan joked, gesturing back toward the cottage.

Melanie wondered how in the world he got alcohol in the first place. Did he have a fake ID, or was someone buying it for him? Where was he hiding it? Thinking about the particulars had her feeling even more nauseous, so she tried to avoid her nagging thoughts as she took another pull of her beer, which was still just as awful the second time around. Why did people like this so much? At least she was able to swallow it down this time without coughing.

The two of them sat there for a beat, watching seagulls swoop down from the skies into the bay. One ballsy seagull tried walking up to the two of them, probably looking for food, but flew away soon enough.

"So," Duncan said, twisting open another bottle. "How's the new job?"

Melanie exhaled. "Tiring."

"Dad says you're making bank," Duncan said.

Melanie chuckled. "I am, it's wild. Who knew people loved sugar so much."

"Who would have thought," Duncan joked.

"How's, um, Leila?"

Duncan grinned again, sliding his sunglasses back onto his face. "She's really cool. Just finished up her freshman year at this fancy art college in Baybrook. She's also a girl boss like you. Makes bank selling her stuff on Etsy."

Melanie smiled, feeling happiness bubbling in her chest. They were talking, *connecting*. When was the last time they actually did this? Before that first lacrosse party? Maybe the last summer they were here in Haverport?

Was taking a single sip of beer really all it took for her to get here?

"She jokes about being a cougar and dating a younger guy," Duncan said. "Even though I'm not even two years younger than her. The whole 'I'm still a junior' thing threw her off a bit."

"Oh," Melanie said, feeling a bit shocked that Duncan actually told her. "Does she—"

"She doesn't know the particulars," Duncan said, cutting her off. "I just told her I got into some trouble which landed me here."

Melanie nodded. "Got it."

Duncan smirked, bringing his beer up to his mouth. God, how was he doing that? Didn't he know it tasted like absolute garbage?

"So, what's going on with you and that sergeant?"

"Excuse me?"

Duncan sat up. *"Would you like to order?"* he mocked, trying to act like Calvin with his back straight and rigid. *"You're holding up the line!"*

Melanie couldn't help but laugh as Duncan slumped back down onto the blanket, laughing as well.

"Please don't tell me you like that anal piece of shit," Duncan teased, shoving Melanie's thigh.

Melanie's throat tightened. "He's anal, perhaps," she said, thinking about the particular way Calvin told her to count how many spoonfuls of candy should go in each size ice cream bowl, or how to perfectly squirt the hot fudge so it wouldn't overflow with the spoon. But then she thought of how relaxed Calvin looked driving her home, his fingers tapping playfully on his thigh. Or how he opened the door for his grandmother at the cafe, holding a patio chair out for her and gently sliding her into the table. "But maybe not a piece of shit."

Duncan rolled his eyes. "Whatever, he's got an attitude."

"Says the king of attitude," Melanie quipped, immediately regretting her words. Did she take it too far? Was he going to scream at her?

But instead, he belly laughed, rolling his head back onto the sand. Melanie chuckled along with him, enjoying the sound of his raucous laughter. God, she missed seeing him like this. She wondered, briefly, if she was just in a hazy Haverport dream, and if she would soon wake up to the nightmare that left her in Garrison. She pinched her wrist just in case, but she was still here, and he was still laughing.

Duncan sat up, reaching into his bag again. "Want another?"

Melanie panicked briefly, her beer practically untouched in her hand. "Actually, maybe we should have dinner?"

Duncan tapped his stomach, like he just realized how hungry he was. "What's Mom making?"

"They're at that beach association meeting," Melanie said. "We're on our own."

"Like, cooking? That sounds like a very bad idea. You and I can't cook for shit."

"Okay, I will have you know that I can make a mean milkshake now," Melanie bantered. "Sometimes so mean it just explodes everywhere."

He chuckled. "Milkshakes are cool, but I definitely need meat. And cheese."

Melanie thought about it for a moment. "Tacos?"

Duncan stuck his tongue out like a dog, panting. They were his favorite food, after all. "Tacos! Tacos!"

"There's a place my coworkers won't shut up about."

"Does that mean you're taking me out to dinner, moneybags?"

"Mom left us money, but sure, you can tell all of your friends I took you out to dinner and how much of a nice sister I am," she teased.

Duncan reached over, ruffling Melanie's head, her ponytail falling loose behind her. "You are a nice sister, Mel Mel."

She felt like her heart was going to explode as they started collecting his things. He picked up the canvas bags, empty bottles clinking as he stood up, slightly swaying as he did so. She stared at his bag, wondering how many empty bottles were in there, how much alcohol he had before she even came out here to join him.

She knew he shouldn't get behind the wheel. Her throat

caught in her chest as she quickly evaluated her options, but she kept coming back to the same conclusion.

"Hey, Dee?"

She rarely called him Dee. It was only when they were playing around, when they weren't around Mom and Dad. She hoped the use of his nickname after so many years would soften the blow. Would make him see her as his nice sister for a little while longer.

"Mmm?"

"Could I drive?" she asked, trying to make the tone of her voice seem as casual as possible. "I never get to, I'm always on the bike."

For a moment, Melanie thought she'd really blown it as they stood there. This was it, the brief season of the lamb was over. The lion was going to come roaring like it did the last time they had this conversation. She hadn't asked to drive their car in two years.

But to her utter shock, he reached into the pocket of his shorts and tossed her the keys. "Sure, Mel Mel. I would love to judge your terrible driving skills."

Melanie smiled, relief flooding every crevice of her body. She followed him away from the beach, looking down at her almost full beer. She slowed, making sure Duncan wasn't looking before dumping the rest of the bottle into the beachgrass behind her.

"So THAT's a medium Banana Cream Pie milkshake, a hot fudge sundae with Rocky Road, and a Neapolitan double scoop with rainbow jimmies."

The customer looked flustered. "Jimmies?"

Melanie chuckled. "Sprinkles," she said, ringing up the order. "That will be $10.25."

The customer handed her fifteen. "Keep it!"

Melanie grinned, dropping the rest of the change in the bulging tip jar. It wasn't even a night shift yet the jar was completely full, and she just went through her first full shift without making a mistake.

"What's got you all happy?" Rory asked, leaning against the counter.

"The fact that maybe I don't suck at this too much," Melanie answered, a grin still plastered on her face.

"Well, clearly, look at that tip jar," she said. "Tell me, are you flirting with the customers like Jay does? No shame in the game."

"Ha! No way, I'm a terrible flirt."

"Hmm, I doubt that," Rory said with a wicked grin. "Hey, what are you doing Sunday? I saw you had the day off."

She always had the day off on Sundays. Same as Calvin. She wondered if she should ask him why he kept doing that, but decided against it. A day off was a day off, after all.

"No plans, why?"

"Want to go to the beach? I don't have to be here until the night shift."

"Oh, sure!" Melanie said, sounding a little too eager. She reined it in.

Rory didn't seem to notice her overenthusiasm. "Awesome, let's hit Hillside in the morning before it gets packed. Want to meet at like, I don't know, ten or so?"

"I don't have a beach pass for Hillside."

"Melanie, come on," Rory said, pointing to herself. "Who do you think I am?"

She laughed as Jay came charging up to the front. "What are you laughing about, cutie?"

Rory's face flushed. "Your horrible haircut."

Jay feigned looking upset, like Rory just sent a dagger to his heart. "Hurtful, Gilmore."

"Oh for the love of..." Rory didn't finish her sentence, grabbing a spoon and flinging herself at Jay, who was already armed and ready with his own spoon. The two of them started sword fighting with them.

"Um," Melanie said, standing back watching them. "I—uh—does someone want to explain to me what's going on?"

Rory swiveled to the right, sticking her spoon into Jay's ribs. He pretended to wince, holding his chest like a fallen knight as he dramatically hit the floor. "My mom named me after Rory Gilmore," she said. "And for some reason, I'm the only person on this planet who thinks that show is completely stupid."

Jay stood back up as if he resurrected from the place he just died. The two began sword fighting again.

"Do you children want to keep fooling around, or are you going to come try this flavor?" Calvin yelled out from The War Room.

Jay froze. "Oh, right, forgot to tell you, the new flavor is here."

The three of them rushed to the back where Calvin and Jess were standing above a tub of fluorescent blue ice cream. Everyone took a small spoonful and held it up.

"God, it just smells terrible," Jay said.

"It smells like ice cream," Calvin snipped

"Yeah, but Jay's not wrong," Jess admitted. "The smell is kind of off-putting, and you know Ron doesn't have a great track record when it comes to new flavors."

"There have been others?" Melanie asked, thinking

about the same 32 flavors that have been on the menu since her first summer at Haverport.

"He's attempted," Jess answered. "But they've always sucked, never lasted a summer."

"For a guy who runs an ice cream shop, he—uh"—Rory glanced at Calvin before finishing her sentence—"has horrible taste."

Calvin shrugged, enough of an agreement from him as any. "Shall we?"

The five of them took a bite. The taste was...overwhelming. Melanie knew she was supposed to be tasting vanilla and berries. But for some reason, all she could taste was bubble gum.

"Why does this taste like marshmallow?" Jay asked.

"Seriously, I'm getting almond," Rory said. "Like...the expired extract my grandmother puts in her cookies."

"All I taste is blue dye," Calvin said.

"I'm getting cotton candy...or bubble gum?" Jess asked.

"Same," Melanie said. "Isn't this supposed to be like a type of vanilla?"

"Jesus, this is bad," Jess admitted.

"Well, we only have three tubs, hopefully it will go slowly," Calvin said. "He wanted to order ten, but I told him to hold off and see how it goes."

"Smart," Jess said.

Jay patted Melanie's back. "Hey, maybe this is the flavor you should give your brother for free!"

"I'm not that mean."

"Do you even have the capacity to be mean?" Rory teased, sliding her ponytail into her Scoops hat.

Melanie looked up at Calvin, who was staring down at her, that same infuriating smirk on his face, almost as if he was about to tease her for something.

She frowned as Jess finished up the cake in front of her and the others got ready for their shift. "What is it?"

Calvin pointed to her shirt. She looked down and realized there wasn't a single spot on it. It was completely clean —like she'd just taken it out of the laundry.

Her heart swelled. She spent a lot of her life studying for tests and trying to get good grades, yet for some reason, this particular moment felt like her greatest accomplishment.

"Good shift?" Calvin asked her.

She nodded, looking back up at him, the twinkling blues of his eyes making her heart skip.

"Great shift."

Chapter Nine

"So sweetheart, how do you like working at Scoops?"

Melanie took a sip of her coffee as she sat in between Mom and Jan. Jan had a habit of stopping over each morning for coffee with Mom, the two of them gossiping about what was going on within the beach association. Melanie had an hour before she had to leave and sign in for her afternoon shift, giving her enough time to enjoy a slice of toast with blackberry jam.

"It's fun," Melanie said, thankful that working a shift no longer made every muscle of her body scream. It really did feel like fun now, to the point where she actually looked *forward* to her shifts—hanging with her coworkers, handing cones to smiling customers at the counter.

"Well, of course it is," Jan replied, taking a big bite of her toast. "Who wouldn't love working there? Especially if you're working with Calvin, such a nice young man."

Mom's eyebrows raised. "Calvin, who's Calvin?"

Melanie felt like someone sucker punched her in the gut. "Um, just a friend."

A friend? Would she actually consider him a friend? He

clearly told Duncan that he was *her boss*. Not a friend. Not...anything else, for that matter.

"Oh shit, here she comes," Jan mumbled, shifting lower in her seat.

Mrs. Pearson was walking down the sandy road, a foofy Pomeranian tucked underneath her arm.

"Does she know that walking the dog means actually letting the dog *walk*?" Mom teased softly.

Jan snorted as Mrs. Pearson approached the porch, not bothering to step any close—just a few yards from the steps. "Alice," she said steely. "Jan."

"Mrs. Pearson," Mom replied, trying her best to sound cheery.

Jan smiled, but Melanie could tell it was forced. She chuckled, Jan kicking her playfully underneath the table.

"Are you good for beach duty tonight?"

"Beach duty?" Mom asked, sounding flustered and looking over at Jan. She raised her eyebrows as if to communicate that she *should* know about beach duty. "Oh, yes!" Mom replied. "Beach duty, of course. We're on it."

Mrs. Pearson didn't seem convinced, but she nodded. "Good. No bonfires, we don't want a repeat of last year."

"Of course, no repeats," Mom said. Mrs. Pearson lifted her hand as a goodbye, not making an effort to even wave, just walking down the street toward cottage two, the little Pomeranian panting in her arm.

Mom swiveled over toward Jan. "Beach duty?"

"Just walk out to the beach tonight around midnight," Jan explained. "Make sure there are no trespassers, check for teenagers drinking."

Mom looked at her briefly before turning back to Jan. "And last year?"

She grinned mischievously. "Oh, just a little mishap during the Fourth of July bonfire."

Mom's eyebrows raised. "Does that mean the bonfire this year isn't happening?"

Jan cackled. "Are you kidding? Do you think she can stop me?"

Mom shook her head, her eyes now drawn to Duncan who'd abruptly stepped out of the cottage, heading for his car. "Where do you think you're going?"

He turned to face her, looking irritated. "Downtown."

"And what's downtown?"

"An art show," Duncan said, his eyes shifting toward Melanie when he said it. "Thought I would check it out."

"An...art show?" Mom asked.

But Duncan didn't respond, jogging down the steps and toward the car.

She turned to Melanie after he left, her expression expectant. "Care to explain?"

"No," Melanie said flatly, taking a big slice of her toast.

Mom's eyebrows raised as Jan leaned against the table, both of them staring at Melanie so acutely, she finally broke underneath their gazes. She really, truly was incapable of keeping a secret.

Melanie glanced at the time on her phone. She now had twenty minutes until she needed to be at Scoops.

"God, there are so many tents," Mom said. "I wonder if they have a map somewhere."

Melanie had no idea if Leila had a tent set up at the Haverport Art Show in town over the weekend, or if Duncan and Leila were simply perusing the show together.

But that detail didn't stop Mom and Dad from pushing Melanie into the car and driving over.

"Guys, come on, this is creepy," Melanie pleaded. "He'll introduce you when he's ready."

"No, he won't," Mom said, turning her head back and forth, evaluating which way to go next. "Besides, there's nothing wrong with glancing from a distance."

"And if he sees us?"

"We tell him the art show sounded really intriguing, and we decided to go ourselves."

She rolled her eyes. If Duncan saw them he would figure it out. He would know she spilled the beans and told them.

"Is this how you're going to act when I'm seeing someone?" Melanie asked. "Sneaking around, trying to catch a glimpse?"

Mom paused. "Why, are you seeing someone?"

Dad coughed.

Melanie's face flushed. "No, just trying to make a point."

"Well, the difference is, you would actually *tell* us," Mom said. "No need to sneak around if there is the chance of meeting someone."

"I see them," Dad said, leaning into the two of them. He pointed down a few tents on the left.

The three of them watched as Duncan appeared from the tent, holding a stack of large watercolor prints. He placed them down where Leila directed him, then curled his arm around her waist and pulled her in for a brief kiss on the lips.

"Oh my god," Mom whispered, like she needed to keep quiet at a fifty-foot distance so as not to disturb the moment. "She is *gorgeous.*"

"How in the world did they meet?" Dad wondered. "It's not like we've been here long."

"She had a stand at the farmer's market we went to," Melanie admitted. "Duncan snuck off to meet her."

"Oh this is wonderful," Mom said, a not-so-subtle grin plastered on her face. Like this new girl was the perfect addition to the Grand Plan. "Maybe she's just what he needs."

"Don't tell me she's going to change him or something," Melanie deadpanned, feeling rather annoyed at how hopeful they seemed about the situation.

"No, no, but it could be good motivation for him," Dad said. "Help him clean up his act a little bit."

"Headband."

Melanie twisted around so quickly, she felt slightly dizzy as she glanced up at Calvin standing behind her. He was next to his grandmother, her bushy gray hair tucked into a wide-brim straw hat. Calvin was wearing his usual work attire, probably also killing time before heading to their shift.

"Why do you look so suspicious?" Calvin asked. "I feel like I just caught you in the act."

"Because they're being creepy," Melanie said flatly.

"Not creepy, just curious," Mom said, her and Dad finally turning to face Calvin as well. "Just wanted a glimpse of Duncan's new girlfriend."

"We don't even know if she's his girlfriend yet," she said.

"Your generation is so confusing," Dad said. "You don't kiss someone like *that* unless that's your girlfriend."

"I bet you Duncan would beg to differ," Melanie mumbled.

Calvin chuckled softly to himself. "Gram," he said, patting his grandmother's shoulder. "This is Melanie."

"Oh, I've heard so many good things," she said, reaching over to pull Melanie into a big hug. "Congrats on having your first no-mess-up shift."

Melanie fell awkwardly into Gram's arms, then patted her back as she glared at Calvin. He'd told her that?

Gram pulled away. "How do you like Scoops? My grandson isn't being too hard on you, yes?"

"Um, well, now you mention it," she teased, making Gram laugh out loud, the sound ringing in the air like beautiful silver bells. Melanie noticed Calvin grinning at the sound of it—his actual *teeth* showing with his smile.

"Mel, honey," Mom said sweetly behind her. "Introduce us?"

"Oh, sorry," she said. "Um, Mom, Dad, this is Calvin. We work together at Scoops. He helped train me."

Calvin held out his hand first to Dad, shaking it. "Nice to meet you, sir. Melanie's doing a great job."

Dad coughed a laugh. "Sir? I am definitely not a *sir*."

Melanie gave Calvin the side-eye. *Great job, huh?*

If Melanie wasn't mistaken, she thought she saw Calvin smirk at her as he held out his hand to shake Mom's as well.

"I admit, Melanie hasn't mentioned you yet," Mom lied, looping an arm through Melanie's, her grin looking just as devious as it did a few moments ago. "Actually, she hasn't talked about any of her new friends at Scoops."

"You haven't come to visit," Melanie admitted, realizing that simple fact did sting a little. She'd worked there for almost a month now. Why hadn't they tried to visit her while she was working, yet they were so eager to jump in a car mere seconds after finding out Duncan was seeing someone?

"Didn't want to overwhelm you," Dad said. "But we'll come tonight. Any tips from the pros on what to order?"

"Not the Blue Bombshell," Calvin and Melanie both said in unison. They chuckled, eyeing each other awkwardly.

"Okay, whatever that is, not that," Mom said.

"The best time to come is the first hour of my shift before it gets busy," Melanie explained. "So maybe come grab a cone before you head home?"

Dad put his arm around Melanie. "We'll be there."

Her heart swelled. She had to admit, having her parents like this all to herself was nice. *Really* nice. The lack of Duncan-shaped problems in front of them, just the three of them bonding. Meeting her friends. Or...whatever Calvin was.

"Well, we have to finish making our rounds before I take Gram home," Calvin said. "See you in a few?"

Melanie nodded before being pulled into another tight hug by Gram. "So nice to finally meet you," Gram said softly in her ear. She noticed Calvin rolling his eyes as she pulled away from Gram's arms, waving goodbye.

"So you're *not* seeing someone right?" Mom teased.

"Maybe Mel does have a few secrets up her sleeves," Dad taunted.

"Definitely not," Melanie snipped.

"Sure sure," Mom said. "Because that's definitely how *friends* look at each other."

THE SKY WAS DEPRESSINGLY GRAY. Thick clouds blocked the sun and a bitter cold wind swept through the beach, causing Melanie to shiver. She reached for her sweatshirt and pulled it over her bathing suit. "When you invited me to go to the beach, I wasn't exactly picturing this."

Rory smiled, placing her sunglasses on her face like it was still the brightest day. "This is the best type of day to go—no summer people."

Melanie looked around Hillside Park, realizing Rory wasn't wrong. There weren't many people here, besides a mom with her kids, and two couples perched up on the beach just like Rory in wicker hats and sunglasses, sipping on cold beverages like it was a hot, summer day.

"Did you put sunscreen on?" Rory asked.

"Do I need to? It's freezing."

Rory reached into her bag and tossed her a tube. "Rookie mistake, you can still get sunburnt on a cloudy day."

She rolled her eyes but obliged, applying some to her legs.

"So, do you miss Garrison? I bet your life was a lot more glitzy than living like a Haverport beach bum."

Melanie sighed. Did she miss Garrison? Truthfully, she hadn't thought about it much in the past few weeks. She plunged herself into work, willingly letting her mind be occupied by perfecting the size of her scoops and not exploding milkshakes all over the shop.

"Honestly? I don't know," she admitted. "There wasn't much for me in Garrison anyway."

Rory sat up straight. "Really? No cool rich kid parties in mansions, or as Taylor Swift once said, hot boys with fancy cars?"

"Not at all. But I had a lot of hot dates with my textbooks. Cup of coffee, my desk, lots of long nights."

Rory groaned. "So you're a smarty?"

"I guess you could say that." She curled her lips into a small smile.

"No boys to keep you company?"

Melanie shook her head.

"Wait, so you've never had a boyfriend?"

"Nope. Haven't even been kissed, actually."

"Oh damn," Rory said. "Well, that's depressing."

"Thanks for the reminder," Melanie quipped. "How about you, Gilmore, have you been kissed?"

Rory picked up a handful of sand and tossed it at her, making her shriek. "Do not call me that or we can't be friends!"

Melanie laughed. *Friends.* She liked the sound of that, and how easy it was to hang out with Rory and talk to her. She didn't realize until this moment how desperately she needed an actual friend.

"Yes, I have," Rory said, lying back down on her beach towel. "Wade Harley, sixth grade, school playground. It was terrible. He did not know what to do with his tongue."

"Yikes, gross."

"Tell me about it. Then there was Nick Vasquez, freshman year. We went out for a bit. But then he decided he preferred guys and broke up with me."

"Oh," Melanie said, not sure how to respond to that.

"Oh, it's all fine, we're actually good friends now," Rory said. "I'm proud of him."

Melanie smiled, leaving room for silence, waiting for her to continue. But the silence grew longer and more awkward, so she decided to just ask what she was thinking all along. "And Jay? Have you kissed him?"

"That brat, no," Rory said. "Complete and utter dirt. Totally a disgusting man-whore."

Melanie lay back as well, glancing over at her. "A man-whore that you, um, like?"

Rory grabbed fistfuls of sand, holding on tensely before letting go. Melanie watched as she took a beat to respond, the silence confirming what she'd already figured out her first week at Scoops. "Does he know?" she asked softly.

"God, no," Rory said. "It would just make things awkward. And he's so infuriating."

"Then why do you like him?"

Rory sighed. "Because...because, I don't know, he's just fun, I guess. Makes my life feel a little less boring. He makes me laugh a lot and I enjoy being around him. When he's not drooling all over some female, of course."

Rory took off her sunglasses, looking over at Melanie with her wide, sea foam-green eyes. "Plus, his taste in women is so specific. They're all tall and skinny without an ounce of fat or muscle on them, each of them with long blonde manes. And I'm just"—she looked down at her body, pointing to it—"not that."

Melanie frowned. "Well, at least with you there's actually something to look at. Those other chicks are all skin and bones and nothing else."

"But somehow with great tits."

"Probably fake," Melanie deadpanned.

Rory chuckled. "Yeah, you're probably right."

Melanie wasn't sure why she felt so bold to do it, but she reached for Rory's hand, squeezing her palm. "You are so beautiful."

She saw tears well up in Rory's eyes as she squeezed her hand tight, not taking her gaze off the gray cloudy sky above her.

"Really...never been kissed?" joked Rory.

She jabbed Rory's ribs, making her laugh out loud.

"But seriously, we need to find you a boy to kiss this summer," she said. "Unless, of course, we've already found one."

Melanie felt her face flush. "Who?"

Rory rolled her eyes, shoving her sunglasses back on her face. "Don't give me that look, Mel. You know who I'm talking about."

Melanie scowled. "No, I really don't."

She tipped her sunglasses down to her nose. "Super short hair, tall, acts like he's in the army."

Melanie shook her head, lifting the hood of her sweatshirt over her face so Rory couldn't see her blushing.

"Sure, sure, deny it all you want. But I know it when I see it."

"Are you the relationship whisperer or something?"

"Relationship?!" Rory scoffed. "Girl, we aren't looking for a *relationship*. We're just looking for a steamy first kiss. And from what I see, there's a whole lot of chemistry there that needs to be dealt with."

Melanie exhaled. "Or he just hates me."

"Oh, come on, Mel," she mused. "Haven't you heard of a good ol' enemies to lovers trope?"

Melanie rolled her eyes. "I thought you just said a kiss. Now we're lovers?"

Rory winked. "We'll see how the kiss goes first."

Chapter Ten

JUNE CAME AND WENT, and somehow, things felt eerily normal. Melanie kept up with her usual schedule at Scoops, five or six days of the week, finishing almost all of them with a clean shirt by the end. On the foggier days when she and Rory weren't working, they spent time at the beach—Rory giving Melanie all the details about Haverport High and what she should expect come September. She even begrudgingly followed Rory to Lacey's after admitting she had no idea what to wear to school and was able to pick out a few things she liked at the boutique, replacing her polos with breezy tops and loose cotton tees.

But it was her home life that left her feeling off-balance. Things were consistently calm among the four of them, even sometimes pleasant. Duncan would actually join them for dinner with a smile on his face, joking with Melanie and his parents, bits of food flying from his mouth as he laughed. It was almost a month since Calvin brought her home to that fight at the cottage, probably the longest lamb season that Melanie could even remember. It felt almost impossible to admit that maybe things really were changing for the better, that the Grand Plan of moving to Haverport was actually working.

But something deep down made her feel wary, the feeling like a heavy rock at the pit of her stomach. It all felt too good to be true. It was hard for her to even imagine this could be their new normal when a small sliver of her was waiting for the shoe to finally drop.

Melanie pulled on a clean Scoops shirt and her new khaki shorts. She had to get a few new pairs after growing out of the first set she bought. She didn't realize how thin she'd been, how the worry and stress just ate at the weight on her body like a disease. But slowly, over the past month, her body grew stronger. She had some weight again in her hips and thighs, enough that she needed to upgrade to a bigger size to fit her new body. She looked in the mirror and couldn't help but smile, her cheeks a rosy pink, the dark circles under her eyes all but faded away. The tan line from her halter bathing suit top peeped out from under her shirt, which made her chuckle. Rory was right, you really could get tan on a cloudy day.

She opened up her bedroom door and jumped backward in surprise. Duncan towered over her door frame, a grin on his face.

"Jesus, Dee, you scared me," she said. Ever since their taco night, when she howled with laughter as Duncan ate the six tacos she dared him to finish, she started calling him Dee again. Things between them felt really natural, and yet, completely different. Melanie had a hard time avoiding the distance that time had created between the two of them. But Duncan was acting like no time had passed at all. She decided to not bother psychoanalyzing the weirdness she felt between them, especially if Duncan showed no signs of feeling the same way. So she pushed them aside, as well as that sinking feeling in her stomach that kept coming back to her. Like this momentary happiness was just that —momentary.

"Mel Mel, what are you doing tonight?"

"Um, working, obviously," she said, pointing at her shirt. "Why?"

"Dumb," Duncan said, retreating to his room. Melanie followed him, noticing Leila was perched on his bed, scrolling on her phone.

"Can she come?" Leila asked.

"No, has to work," Duncan reported, plopping down on his bed. Leila sat up and rubbed his back, then twirled one of his curls loosely with her finger.

"Come where?" Melanie asked, curiosity getting the best of her.

"Party," Leila said. "My folks are out of town, so I'm having some peeps over for the Fourth."

"Should be super chill," Duncan said.

Party, Melanie thought. She should have known. Even if things at home felt really good, even if Duncan was actually participating as a member of the family again, Melanie knew he was still going out and drinking. He didn't hide it from her anymore. It's like having a single drink with him was the magical key to his secret life. He shared everything with her now, and he kept inviting her places. All the time.

Melanie quickly glanced around Duncan's new room. She had yet to step foot in it, but this particular moment felt like an invitation. She peered around the room, noticing a few open boxes half unpacked. His lacrosse sticks and all of his gear were tucked haphazardly into the closet next to a heaping pile of clothes. A couple mugs sat on his night-stand, next to a few old prescription bottles, likely from when he had strep throat earlier that year.

Melanie pointed to the bottles. "Why do you still have those?"

Duncan looked over at his nightstand, then shrugged. "Never know if I'll need them again."

"Planning on getting strep again?"

Duncan just chuckled, changing the subject. "So, think you can come? After work?"

Melanie looked at her brother, his gaze full of hope. She didn't want to squash it. Didn't want to ruin whatever was happening between the two of them, this sweet kinship that made them so close again. That had him talking to her, inviting her, *hoping* for her to be with him.

She sighed. "I'll try."

Duncan beamed, bolting from his bed and giving her a big hug, squeezing her so tight she could hardly breathe. She punched him playfully on his back so he would let her go.

"Just so you know, though, I have no idea when I'm getting out tonight," she said. "It's the Fourth, and according to Scoops, it's going to get bloody tonight. Whatever that means."

"Right, right, of course," he said excitedly. "You could even bring them, your co-workers. Maybe that dude that looks like he has a stick up his ass. He needs to loosen up a bit, he could use a party."

Melanie chuckled. "I—I don't know, we'll see."

"I'll text you the deets," Duncan said, flopping back down on his bed, hugging Leila fiercely. Melanie liked seeing him this happy, it was contagious. It frustrated her sometimes, knowing all it took was for her to say yes to him once. Maybe if she had done it sooner...

~

She arrived at Scoops with a smile on her face. She knew she looked dumb, but she didn't care. It was just nice to have Duncan back in her life.

But that smile quickly faded when she took a look at Calvin as he stood near the board, scowling at the schedule, his arms crossed.

"What's going on?" Melanie asked.

"Don't freak out."

"Well, that's always how I love a conversation to start," she bantered. "Tell me why I shouldn't be freaking out."

Calvin let out a long, frustrated sigh. "Tyler's sick."

"Oh," she said. "So?"

"And I really don't want to call someone on the Fourth of July and ask them to cancel plans and work."

"Oh."

Calvin finally looked in her direction, his glance partly an apology, the other part a challenge. "I think it's just you and me tonight."

Melanie slumped down into the desk chair. "That sounds..."

"Like a nightmare, I know," he said. "But we'll make great tips."

"We'll probably get out late," she mumbled, thinking of Duncan, the look of hope dazzling in his eyes. The thought of disappointing him left an acid taste in her mouth.

"We can keep closing to a bare minimum," he said, assessing the shop like he was planning an attack. "Make the people opening up do a majority of the work."

Melanie squeezed her eyes shut and let out a long breath, resting her head against the back of the chair. "Fine."

When she finally opened her eyes she saw that Calvin was staring at her, the bright blues of his eyes looking dim, like he had failed her. She smiled shyly. "Dude, it's all right."

"*Dude*," he chuckled. "Since when do you use the word *dude*?"

"Dude, do you have a brother?" Melanie quipped. "Dude is, like, the most important word ever, dude."

Calvin smiled gingerly. "No, no brother. No siblings."

Melanie paused for a moment, realizing she really knew nothing about Calvin. He clearly spent time with his grandmother, he was close with Ron, and he had a thing for pocket-sized paperback novels, but the rest was a complete mystery. She wondered if that was the point. If he meant to keep it a mystery on purpose. Strictly professional.

Melanie sat up, heading to the sink to wash her hands. "Well, we better get to it then."

"How about a challenge?"

Melanie wiped her hands dry and looked back at him. "Um, okay?"

Calvin leaned against the board, crossing his arms. "Instead of splitting the tips at the end of the night, what if we made it a competition?"

"What do you mean?"

"You keep what's in your jar, and I keep what's in mine," Calvin said. "We see who makes more."

Melanie thought about it for a moment, tightening her ponytail. "What if we up the stakes?"

Calvin smirked. "Oh yeah? Go on."

She hesitated, looking at the way his lips curled up into his cheek. She felt heat rush through her body at the way he looked at her, the challenge in his voice. She thought about Rory and their first conversation on the beach weeks before, about her getting kissed this summer. She wondered what it would feel like to kiss those lips that smirked at her, tucked underneath a dimple on his cheek.

She put her hands on her hips to try and steady herself, steady her thoughts, bringing them back to the present. "Whoever makes the most keeps it all."

Calvin lifted an eyebrow. "You do realize that I know practically everyone in this town."

"You do realize you don't know how to flirt, right?"

Calvin looked at her playfully. "Have you seen me with the grannies? They love me."

"Until they meet me, of course."

Calvin's smirk slowly turned into a grin, his teeth showing again. The last time she saw him smile like this was the day she met his Gram, the smile for his grandmother utterly adorable. Melanie stood firm, hoping the melting feeling in her knees wouldn't actually make them give out.

"Fine, headband," he said, turning to sign himself in for their shift. "You're on."

"I PUT a little extra dollop of whipped cream on there, *just* for you," Melanie said, blinking flirtatiously at her customer.

"This is probably the *biggest* kiddie cone I've ever scooped," Calvin said, handing a kid behind his counter a cone that looked...exactly how it was supposed to.

"Don't worry, I'll add extra rainbow jimmies to that," Melanie said with a wink.

"Oh, now, don't you ladies look nice," Calvin said, leaning against the counter to face a small crowd of giggling old ladies. "Off to see the fireworks?"

"Oh my god, I *love* your dress," Melanie said to a

woman with a bright red sundress. "Did you get it from Lacey's? I'm now obsessed with that place."

"I'll make it *extra* chocolaty for you."

"I made sure to give you the *big* waffle cone."

"I threw in an extra scoop of M&M's, I know you love them."

"Now I know you said one scoop, but I couldn't help but make it a little extra big. It's a holiday, after all!"

"Stop, ladies, you don't have to," Calvin said, his voice sweet and syrupy as he watched an old lady place a ten in his tip jar. He glanced over at Melanie and winked at her.

Melanie just smiled mischievously back at him as the man behind the counter placed a twenty in hers.

He balked at her, stepping over to her counter and looking in her tip jar. It was bulging.

"Wait, is that?"

Melanie nodded, confirming that yes, there was in fact a fifty in her tip jar. She shrugged. "Sugar makes people do crazy things."

Calvin shook his head in disbelief. "I better up my game."

"And you better fast," she said, glancing at the lines now dwindling behind their counters. "We only have an hour left, and by the looks of it, things are dying down."

"Oh, headband," he said, that smirk permanently etched on his face. "Don't you worry, we still have the after-fireworks rush."

Melanie groaned. Even if Scoops was supposed to close at ten, it was a known rule that you were never supposed to turn away a line. If the line was long and it was past closing time, you had to keep serving customers until the last one was served. The rule was extra brutal on a Friday or Saturday night when it felt like practically *everyone* in town ended their day with an ice cream cone. They were techni-cally supposed to be out of the shop by eleven, but last week they'd inched closer to midnight.

"We're never getting out of here, are we?" she grumbled.

"Why, got somewhere you need to be?"

Melanie frowned, serving the last customer in her line. They didn't tip, but she didn't care. She was now visibly frustrated. "No, just, a family thing."

"Are they doing the usual Fourth of July bonfire on the beach?"

Melanie's brows furrowed. "How do you know about that?"

"Sandy Cove, they always throw a rager on the beach," Calvin said. "Last year the fire department was called. Someone accidentally kicked Dan's drink into the fire and the beachgrass took it hard."

Melanie chuckled, imagining the sheer panic on Jan and Dan's faces, and the judgmental look of disapproval from Mrs. Pearson who was no doubt avoiding the party at all costs...while keeping a close eye from her window at cottage two.

The two of them silently cleaned the surfaces of the shop. Both of their lines were now completely empty, a lull in the shift that left Melanie feeling a little uneasy.

"This is weird," she admitted, leaning against the counter, not sure what else to do with herself. "I don't think I've ever seen this place dead at night."

"Wait till the fall when all the summer people are gone," Calvin said. "It's even more excruciating when it rains. I've gone through entire shifts and only made three bucks in tips."

Melanie exhaled audibly. "Brutal. When do the fire-works start?"

As if they could hear her, a lone spark shot up in the night and a burst of bright red sparkles covered the sky.

Melanie's breath caught as she watched another firework buzz next to it, a circle of blue bursting open and fizzling into white shimmers. She pressed her hands into the counter and stood up straight, watching one firework erupt after another, the show taking her breath away.

They were actually in the perfect spot to watch; Scoops was the closest shop on Main Street before turning into Hillside Park, where the fireworks were being lit. Melanie noticed how customers came through with blankets and chairs and picnic baskets, grabbing a quick cone before claiming their spot in the park to watch the sky explode with shapes and colors.

Melanie was so mesmerized by the show, she didn't realize Calvin had slid right next to her, his hands also pressed down on the counter, so close their pinkies could almost touch. Melanie could hear her heartbeat hammering in her ears, much louder than the crackling fireworks above them.

"What do you think?" he asked softly.

"They're amazing," Melanie admitted, not daring to take her eyes off the fizzling sky.

"Not bad for a small beach town, huh?"

Before she could respond, she felt his pinkie brush up against her own.

Her breath caught in her throat. She didn't move an inch, loving the way he playfully stroked her hand. Melanie felt like she couldn't breathe as he curled it around hers, their pinkies locked like a promise.

Her mind was racing. Despite his playful demeanor tonight in a ruse to get more tips, Calvin wasn't the kind of guy to flirt or mess around. This simple gesture clearly meant something. She felt her heart pounding faster when she realized that he actually might not just see her as boss and employee. Or just friends. He certainly saw her as something more, at least.

The two of them stood there in silence as they continued to gaze up at the sky, their pinkies threaded together. She noticed Calvin glance over at her, his eyes roaming her face. She wondered what he was thinking, but was too scared to look him in the eye yet. This little gesture he made toward her was so small, yet it was probably the most intimate she'd ever felt with someone. His gaze, his touch, made her feel vulnerable yet somehow certain. Like maybe she could trust him with the darker parts of herself. With the pieces of her that she kept pushing aside, creating a pile so massive that at some point she knew it would all come crashing down.

Dozens of fireworks shot in the sky all at once. Calvin looked up as the grand finale erupted before them, ending with a bright burst of sizzling light, leaving streaks of smoke in the sky, like a distant memory.

They kept standing there, pinkies locked, the silence dancing comfortably between them. Melanie didn't dare move, afraid she would break whatever spell was cast between the two of them.

She finally looked up at Calvin's gaze, his bright eyes back to searching her face, like she was some kind of puzzle he wanted to solve.

Then, the phone rang, and they both flinched.

"Um, I'll get it," Calvin said. He squeezed her pinkie with his own before letting go, taking long strides to the back before picking up the phone with a huff. "This is Scoops."

Melanie turned, leaning her back against the counter.

Her heart was hammering away, the sound thud-thud-thudding in her ears as the moment lingered between them, like the smoke that lazily moved through the starry night.

"No, Tyler, do not come here," Calvin barked. "You're sick, I don't want your germs. Do you even remember 2020?"

She waited as Calvin turned to face her, rolling his eyes. "We're going to be fine, Melanie and I can handle it."

He kept listening, shaking his head. *Sorry*, he mouthed.

Melanie smiled shyly. His demeanor softened as he looked at her, his eyes knowing. Like he was as much in disbelief as she was about what just happened between them. Like the exciting first spark of a firework.

"Okay, okay, fine, you owe us each a shift," Calvin said. "Now please, for the love of god, shut up so I can get off this phone."

Calving nodded a few times before finally hanging the phone up on the wall. "Tyler says he'll cover any shift you want, just say the word."

"Does Haverfest count?" Melanie teased.

Calvin chuckled. "Why? Trying to get away from me so quickly?"

She shrugged, making him outright laugh, the sound of it causing Melanie's toes to curl. If she thought the sound of his chuckle made her weak, she wasn't nearly ready for the way her body responded to the sound of his laugh.

"Excuse me, are you guys still open?"

Melanie turned and noticed a customer standing at Calvin's window. "Oh, of course! But you're actually at the wrong window. I'll serve you over here."

"Cheater!" he yelled, rushing toward his own window and swinging it open. He flashed a big smile at the line, teeth included. "I'll take whoever's next!"

~

Calvin slammed the window shut at his counter, flipping the sign to *Closed*.

"Don't bother filling," he said as she came up with a container of peanut butter cups. "Let's just get this place cleaned and get out of here. They can fill in the morning."

Melanie looked down at the candy canisters, all of them practically empty. "Are you sure?"

"Headband, if we fill, we are definitely getting out of here after midnight."

She looked up at the clock hanging above the door frame leading to The War Room. It was already 11:25.

"Crap," she said. "I didn't realize how late it was."

"That rush was anarchy," Calvin said. "I'll tackle up here, you get the dishes in the back."

She nodded, the two of them working quickly in silence.

"If only Jay were here to serenade us!" Melanie shouted, rinsing off the clean scoopers in her hands.

"Hard pass," he yelled back. "I'd give up all of my tips to never hear him sing again."

"*All* of them?" Melanie asked. "Because I'm pretty sure your tips are mine tonight, Ball."

Their banter was cut off by the loud sound of the whirring vacuum. She waited for his response after he turned it off, but instead found him barreling toward the desk with the two tip jars. "We'll see about that. I had a second wind."

Melanie shook her head. "Think that second wind will cover a fifty?"

"I'm feeling confident," he said, sitting down as he started counting through the tips.

Melanie's phone buzzed in her back pocket, distracting her from watching him count through the money. She reached for it and noticed Duncan's name on the screen.

Her throat tightened as she answered the call, turning from Calvin. "Hey, Dee."

"Mel Melllll! Where are youuuu?"

"Still at work," she grumbled. "We were slammed tonight."

"You're always slammed! That dumb job is stealing you from me. You should quit."

She chuckled. "I don't want to quit, I like this job."

She peeked over at Calvin as she said it, noticing a small smile on his face as he kept counting the bills in front of him.

"Lame. Are you coming?"

"I—I don't know." She was exhausted, and the last thing she wanted to do was go to her first party ever in her Scoops uniform, looking haggard.

"But Mel Mel, you prommmisssed."

"Okay, I didn't promise, I said I would *try*," she corrected him. "Big difference."

"Oh, whatever," he said, sounding irritated. "You're just blowing me off again."

"No, Duncan, that's not it," she stammered. She was ruining it. "I do promise to come to another one, just not tonight."

"All right, fine," he huffed. Then the line went dead.

Melanie stood there, stunned. She wanted a way to fix the mess she just made. Who cared what she looked like, who cared how tired she was, she should just go. Make him happy. Go back to whatever they were right now.

"You win," Calvin said softly.

Melanie twisted toward him, looking down at the piles

of money. Hers was clearly bigger than his, but the look on his face was telling. Something sorrowful, and she didn't like it.

"You didn't just put your money on my pile to make it look bigger, did you?"

His face went red. *Red.* "No."

She rolled her eyes, heading for the garbage. She started tying up the bag tightly, the rage blazing inside of her.

"Melanie—"

"Stop," she growled. "Stop trying to protect me. Stop pitying me."

"I'm not pitying you," he muttered.

"Do you see your face right now? It's written all over it, and I don't want it."

"That's not—"

"It's the same look you gave me when you dropped me home," she said, her head pounding. She wanted to scream.

"I was just—"

"And the other day, with the walk-in," she told him, the pitch of her voice much higher, on the verge of yelling at him. "You told them not to lock me in. You taught me how to get out just in case. I don't need your protection. You know nothing about me or my life or what I can handle. So stop trying to shield me from getting hurt, because the damage has already been done."

She was on the verge of tears as she lifted the garbage bag from the bin, bolting out the back door. She stormed to the dumpster and flung the bag in with fury.

He looked at her just like *they* did—everyone at Garrison Prep. After it all happened.

In Haverport, she was able to escape their rueful glances, full of sympathy and intrigue, as if she weren't actually a person but just collateral damage from a whirlwind storm. She couldn't imagine having to deal with that again, not here.

Melanie turned around to head for the back door, but watched as it swung open instead. Calvin was now hurtling for her, his face determined like he was ready to have another go.

Melanie took a deep breath, preparing for whatever nonsense he was about to send her way. But before she could say anything, Calvin was stepping right up to where she stood. He curled one arm around her waist, the other cradling the back of her head, and pressed his mouth to hers.

Chapter Eleven

Calvin's lips were soft and utterly mesmerizing. His touch was tender, yet she could sense a yearning from him, like he'd waited his entire life for this moment. Or maybe she was just projecting what she felt herself.

She leaned into him, arching her head back, letting the kiss go deeper. Her movement toward him was his confirmation as Calvin pressed into her further. He curled his arm even tighter around her waist, her shirt twisting up as his fingers brushed against the small of her back. Melanie wrapped her arms around his neck as he lifted her slightly, the feel of his calloused hands against her skin sending a shiver down her spine.

He placed her down gently, slowly releasing his lips and pressing his forehead against hers. "I wasn't trying to protect you because of what's going on at home." He moved his head back, twirling a piece of hair loosened from her ponytail behind her ear. "I did it because of *this*. Because I *like* you."

Melanie was stunned by his confession. By his kiss. By the feel of his hands still firmly on her, like letting go was the last thing he wanted to do. This time, she was the one to lean in, to make sure kissing him the second time was just as mind-blowing as the first.

And it was. She saw his lips curl into a smile as she leaned in, his hands moving up to cradle her face as he kissed her back fervently, like he couldn't get enough of her. He stroked a pinkie finger down her neck, causing her to melt into him, wrapping her arms around his waist and pressing her body against his. She worked her hands up his spine, feeling him shiver as well, her touch making him just as powerless as his was to her.

When they finally slowed, Calvin kept dropping soft kisses on her lips, her nose, her cheeks, the lids of her eyes. He pulled away and looked down at her, his eyes sparkling so brightly among the stars, even though they were shrouded in darkness behind Scoops. Next to the dumpster.

Melanie smiled shyly. "A pretty odd spot for a first kiss."

Calvin's eyes went wide with embarrassment. "Wait, like...first kiss, first kiss?"

At that moment, Melanie was feeling very thankful they were practically in pitch-black darkness, otherwise, he would notice how red her cheeks probably were. "Um, yeah."

Calvin stepped back, scratching his head.

Crap, Melanie thought. *He's going to think I'm nuts.*

"Well, this won't do," he finally said.

"What does that mean?"

"That means," he said, wrapping Melanie up into his arms again, pressing his nose against her. "This didn't count."

She tilted her head back, looking confused. "Excuse me?"

"This didn't count, no first kiss," he said, letting her go. "We'll try again."

"B-but—"

"Nope," he said, refusing to hear what she had to say, now heading for the door and pointing at her. "If I'm going to be your first kiss, Melanie Albertson, then I'm going to do it right."

She shook her head, following him back inside and closing up for the night. It was well past midnight, but at that point, she could care less. He may have thought it wasn't the best place for a first kiss, but to Melanie, her first kiss tasted sweeter than any Strawberry cone she'd ever had.

CALVIN OFFERED HER A RIDE HOME, and this time, Melanie didn't hesitate.

She pulled the elastic from her hair, releasing her ponytail as she rolled down the passenger window of his truck. The air was warm and balmy, the humidity of the day still stubbornly hanging on. She felt Calvin's pinkie brush against hers, interlocking it again. She looked up at him and noticed he was staring down at her, smiling softly.

"Eyes on the road, Ball."

He chuckled, turning his head back to the road in front of him, that smile persistent across his cheeks, his features relaxed and content. She liked him like this, different from the guy who was rigid with rules and guidelines. Tonight she saw an entirely new side of him, one that knew how to be goofy, who knew how to laugh and play and smile and kiss without abandon. She wondered if anyone else knew this side of him, or if maybe, for some odd reason, she was the only one he chose to show it to.

He turned the curve into Sandy Cove, driving slowly across the sand. She wished the truck would move even slower, not wanting this moment to end. She looked at him as he parked the car in front of cottage five, wanting desperately to lean in again for a kiss, to make sure it wasn't all just a dream.

The cottage was dark and silent. Melanie wondered if they were all sleeping, and if Duncan made it home safely. But her heart twisted when she didn't see his car in the gravel driveway.

"Hey," Calvin said softly. "Here."

She turned to him and saw he was holding out a fat stack of bills. "You did win, fair and square. I didn't even come close, not with that fifty."

Melanie smirked deviously as she unbuckled her seatbelt, sliding across the seat as she closed the space between them. She reached for the money but rested her hand on Calvin's slightly, her face dangerously close to his.

"I know what you're doing and it won't work," said Calvin, his leathery laugh making Melanie's toes curl again. "I am the textbook definition of patience."

"Didn't seem very patient tonight," Melanie taunted. "Just couldn't wait to get your hands on me."

"That was before I knew that your *first kiss* was on the line," he said. "Trust me, I'll make it worth it."

Melanie pouted. "How long do I have to wait?"

Calvin slipped his hand around her cheek and to the back of her neck, pulling her in close, his nose brushing against hers. Then he froze. "Not long, I promise."

Melanie pulled back. "Tease."

The two of them jumped as they heard a knocking on the passenger door. Melanie swirled her head around and noticed her father waving at them, holding up a cooler. He smiled mischievously, almost as if he waited his entire life to experience this embarrassing moment.

"Well hello, you two," Dad said. "I'm about to head back to the bonfire, care to join us?"

"Oh," Melanie said, looking toward the beach, noticing that a fire was indeed still blazing, a few shadowy figures sitting on chairs circled around it.

"Sure," Calvin said. Melanie watched in horror as he unbuckled his seatbelt and cut the ignition.

"Do you need to call your parents? It's pretty late," Dad asked.

"No, sir," he said, causing Dad to roll his eyes at Calvin's use of *sir* again. "Late night shifts are the norm."

Dad gave them a thumbs up, winking at Melanie slyly before heading toward the beach.

Melanie turned to Calvin. "You seriously do not have to."

Calvin was already opening up his door and stepping out of the truck. "And miss the infamous Sandy Cove bonfire? I don't think so."

She scrambled out of her own seat, slamming the door and scurrying around to his side of the truck. "Okay but, you know, in my head, when I had my first kiss, I didn't think meeting the parents would also happen *on the first night.*"

"What first kiss?" he asked, his eyes dancing playfully. "Besides, I've already met your parents."

Melanie rolled her eyes, walking right at his heels as Calvin stepped confidently toward the fire. "Calvin, wait—"

"Headband," he said, turning toward her, lifting her chin with his hand as he rubbed his thumb back and forth. "It's going to be fine. I also know all of these people."

Of course he does, Melanie thought to herself. "Small town."

He nodded. "Small town. Now stop freaking out, it's not like we kissed or anything."

Melanie slapped his arm playfully as he chuckled, turning his heels and walking toward the fire.

"Calvin!"

Jan jumped out of her seat and wrapped her arms around him, squeezing tight. Dan stood up as well, slapping his back. "Good to see you, son."

He smiled back genuinely, giving Jan a tight squeeze as well, before releasing her. "Haven't seen you guys at the shop yet, when are you coming to visit me?"

"The jams, you know how it is," Jan said. "We could use an extra hand, actually. Melanie has yet to come over and help us."

"Hey," she said, crossing her arms with a frown. "You haven't invited me over yet."

"Do you even need an invite, my dear?" she teased.

Melanie shook her head, smiling up at Calvin.

"That's probably my fault," he admitted. "Keeping her busy at Scoops."

"That's what I hear," Dad called out, walking over to them with two bottles in his hand. "Especially if you're making tips *like that*."

He stepped right up to them and held out the two bottles for each of them to take. She felt like her throat was closing up as she looked down. Was her father offering her beer? After everything they'd been through?

Before her mind started spiraling, Dad nudged Melanie with his elbow. "It's cream soda, honey."

"Oh." She exhaled, taking a bottle from him as Calvin did the same.

They made their way around the circle as Jan introduced Melanie to everyone—the Roberts in cottage eight, the Bentleys in cottage one. And Calvin, true to his word, knew them all. They asked about Scoops and Ron, and about his Gram. But never about his parents. Melanie wondered why no one ever mentioned his parents to him. She wondered if he even lived with them.

They finally made their way to where Mom and Dad were perched, the two of them laughing at whatever Tim Mackey, cottage six, was saying.

Mom gave them a nonchalant smile that Melanie already knew was practiced. She could tell by her mother's gaze that she was holding back hundreds of questions at that moment. She stood up and hugged Melanie. "Good to see you again, Calvin, come sit."

The two of them sat down in front of the fire as it popped and crackled, the unrelenting humidity finally starting to fade as a cool breeze rolled up from the sea. Melanie shivered as her Dad came over with a blanket, placing it over both of their shoulders.

Calvin chuckled, turning to Melanie and whispering in her ear. "Well, I think this is going well."

She hugged the blanket tightly as she curled her legs up, her thighs brushing against Calvin's. She leaned into him. "Wait till I tell them how bad of a kisser you are," she whispered back.

"How would you know that? You've never kissed me before."

Melanie rolled her eyes, taking a sip of her soda. She listened to the gentle melody of voices around her as the neighbors continued to talk and joke, their laughs rippling into the dark July night. She felt warm and content as she leaned further into Calvin, placing her head on his shoulder as he wrapped an arm around her, laughing along at whatever everyone was saying. She smiled, feeling the deep staccato of his chuckle rumbling out of him, the sound of his voice feeling like a safe place to land.

TWIRLING her wet hair into a towel, Melanie stepped into her room and slid right into her bed, not bothering to take off her bathrobe. It was well past two in the morning but she was buzzing, and it wasn't just from the sugary soda. She opened up the text that Jan sent her again and clicked on the picture.

Calvin was laughing, his smile wide, his teeth showing, his arm around Melanie as she leaned her head on his shoulder. She was giggling as well, the blanket wrapped tightly around them.

She couldn't stop staring at him, the way his cheeks were colored, the silver chain he always wore peeking out from behind his shirt. His feet were bare and tucked into the sand, and Melanie's thighs were tucked under his own.

She heard a muffled knock at her door and looked up, noticing her mom peering down at her with a grin. "So, still just friends, or...?"

She chuckled as her mom slipped onto the bed next to her, pulling the quilt over her legs. "Okay but seriously, is he your boyfriend? Are things 'official'?" she asked, holding her hands up and making air quotes.

"Wait, are we talking about Calvin?" Dad said at the top of the stairs, now shuffling his way into her room.

"Oh, God," she said, rolling her eyes. But she loved the way her father also curled up on her bed on the other side, his feet still slightly damp from rinsing off the sand.

"Nothing *official*," she admitted, dragging out the word purposely. "Let's just say we sort of established that we like each other."

"Did you kiss yet?" Mom asked.

"I don't need to hear that," Dad coughed.

Melanie thought about their kiss, the way Calvin's hands felt tracing the small of her back, the way his lips eagerly kissed her own. She couldn't help but smile sweetly, her left pinkie tingling under the quilt, recalling the way it felt twirled together with his.

"No, not yet," she said sheepishly. She would wait, at least give him the chance for whatever their *real* first kiss would be, then decide which story she wanted to tell them.

"Well, I like him," Dad blurted out.

"Harold, you barely know him," Mom said. "Besides, aren't you supposed to not like the boy that's taking your daughter out?"

"Am I?" Dad said, leaning into Melanie and winking at her. "Guess I'm terrible at this then."

She snickered, leaning her head against her father's shoulders, holding her mother's hand on the other side. The three of them sat there for a moment, sandwiched together on Melanie's bed. She felt it again, the satisfaction of having them all to herself. Maybe it wasn't normal to discuss relationships so openly with your parents, but she didn't care. She had the two of them here with her, holding her close, their demeanor at ease, their smiles infectious, the permanent worry from before washed away like a soft wave on the shore.

She should have known that the moment would be short-lived, that it was foolish to think such happiness could exist for them.

A door slammed outside and then they heard heavy footsteps trudging up the cottage steps.

For the briefest moment, Melanie had completely forgotten about him, and she felt guilty. Guilty for not worrying about him, guilty for letting him down tonight.

Mom moved abruptly from her spot, swinging her legs out of her quilt. She braced herself for it, the screaming, the lying. But before Mom could even say a word, she heard as Duncan paused suddenly at the top of the stairs.

Then puked all over the floor.

Chapter Twelve

Duncan barely talked to her after that New Year's night almost two and a half years ago.

Melanie had tried to win his trust back day after day, but he kept pulling away from her. She knew she'd failed him miserably by confessing to Mom what he'd asked her to do. Duncan was beyond grounded after that night, but that didn't stop him from drinking and sneaking out to be with his new friends.

She heard whispers at school, rumors that spread like wildfire about the crazy things Duncan Albertson would do. People at Garrison called him Ed because he was notoriously the fastest one to finish "Edward Fortyhands" competitions amongst the entire lacrosse team, chugging 40 ounce beers that were taped to his hands. He was also known as the reigning beer pong champ throughout the entire school. And, of course, there was the persistent rumor that Duncan somehow broke into Principal Eddy's office and sucked down a water bottle of vodka he snuck into the homecoming dance, while sitting in the principal's chair. Melanie wasn't even sure if she believed that one, but it seemed that everyone at Garrison Prep did. Duncan was a legend, and Melanie was no one. And her brother didn't seem to care that his twin was no longer a part of his new life.

So she took the polar opposite road, diving into her books like they were a lifeline. She was perfectly okay with being known as the quiet one, perfectly okay with being the ghost that no one seemed to pay any attention to, having a few class acquaintances but never any true friends. Her mind was too preoccupied with trying to get into Yale, to make her father beam with pride. Even if it killed her that, after almost three years, it still seemed that Duncan wanted nothing to do with her.

It wasn't until she stood over his hospital bed that horrible night, staring at his pale face, that Duncan really looked at her. His eyes were bloodshot as his lips parted, dried and cracked. "Am I fucked?"

She wanted to reach for him, to comfort him at that moment. But all she'd felt was anger. Anger that, after all this time and even after everything that just happened, he still was only concerned for himself.

"Yes," she'd answered coldly. She didn't reach for his hand, she didn't bother smiling. "You're fucked."

MELANIE WOKE up the following morning to an ominously calm household. The cottage was quiet, but as she lay there, rubbing her eyes, she heard a faint creaking from her open bay window, the sound of the porch swing on the patio rocking back and forth.

She slipped out of bed, still in her bathrobe, pulling her hair from her towel that she'd fallen asleep in. Her parents bolted from her bedroom the night before, shutting the door, cleaning up the mess Duncan made. There was no yelling or protesting, just the dull sounds of her parents helping Duncan into the bathroom, the occasional murmuring interrupted by his persistent retching.

She'd eventually plugged her headphones into her ears, hoping their noise canceling abilities would drown out the sound of Duncan getting sick, and dull the thudding pain she felt in her heart. She'd laid there wondering what tomorrow would bring, wondering if she could have done something different so none of this would have happened. If she hadn't been so distracted by Calvin that night, maybe she would have been able to help him, stop him from getting this bad again. She'd cried and cried, and at some point, fell into a fitful sleep.

She stepped over to the mirror in her room now and noticed how puffy and red her eyes were, her hair mangled and frizzy from sleeping with the towel on her head. She pulled it up into a messy bun, tied her robe tight around her waist, then slowly opened her door.

Duncan's door was open, and he wasn't in bed. Her heart lurched at the sight of his empty room, quickly shuffling down the stairs to figure out what was going on. But her parents' bedroom was still closed, the coffee still not made. She looked out the front window and noticed it was Duncan sitting on the swing.

Melanie stepped out cautiously, watching as he rocked back and forth, his gaze out on the ocean. He was holding an old iPod mini, his ears covered with a pair of headphones that were way too small for his head, the cord curling behind his ear.

She cocked an eyebrow at him as he released the headphones, placing them around his neck. "So," she said.

"So," he said back.

Melanie smiled shyly at him, not sure what to say. She wanted to know how he was feeling, wanted to know how the rest of the night went. But she didn't want to scare him away. She wasn't even sure if they were still acting like friends again. "Um, cool iPod?"

Duncan shrugged. "They took away all of my technology. Phone, laptop, earbuds, stereo. Even my car keys." He pointed down at the iPod in his lap. "Found this in an old box in my room."

"What are you listening to?"

"Nickelback, it's terrible," he said. "Why did you ever let me listen to them?"

"You were obsessed, there was no separating you from your first love."

He chuckled, moving slightly on the swing to make room for her to sit, his arm slung lazily on the bench behind her. "Remember when we got these for Christmas?"

"Mine was pink," Melanie said. "But I secretly wanted your blue one."

"You tried trading me," Duncan said, his voice full of nostalgia. "And your offer was awful."

"You hated chores, I would have happily done them for a month so I wouldn't carry around a pink iPod," Melanie said. "Really glad Mom and Dad figured out how much I hate pink after that."

"And yet, you love strawberry ice cream."

"How'd you remember that?" she whispered.

Duncan just smiled, his gaze contemplative as he stared down at the iPod on his lap.

She looked out toward the driveway and noticed his car wasn't anywhere in sight. "Um, how'd you get home last night?"

"Leila. She didn't think it was a good idea for me to... well...you know."

Her chest tightened. "Yeah...I know."

The two of them sat there as Duncan rocked the swing back and forth with his foot, watching as the sun continued to rise over the bay.

"Dee?"

He looked up at her, his curls bouncing as he did so.

"I'm sorry I couldn't come last night," she said.

"It's okay, Mel Mel," he responded. "Clearly not my best moment."

It was the first time he'd actually admitted it to her. Maybe not an apology, maybe not an outright confession that what he was doing was wrong. But a mere admission that maybe he didn't make the wisest choice.

Melanie sucked in a breath, wanting to ask him more. She wanted to know *why* he did it, why he kept partying and drinking, why it was so important to him to have this kind of lifestyle. Especially after what happened to him that spring. But the words sat in her mouth like dried-up sand.

"Next time?"

She just nodded, feeling like a failure. "Yeah, next time."

They swayed in silence, until the smell of coffee brewing inside alerted them that Mom and Dad were finally awake. Duncan escaped upstairs, locking himself in his room.

THE LAST PLACE she wanted to be was in the cottage. It felt like a prison, Duncan locked up in his tower, Mom and Dad sitting on the deck like watch dogs. She tried to spend her time wisely as she looked through the AP course list from the community college, then scrolled through Yale's admission guidelines for the umpteenth time. But after an hour of the stifling silence, she couldn't take it any longer.

Unfortunately, it was Sunday, and she didn't have a shift to get her out of the house. She thought about calling Calvin but decided against it, realizing that he kept Sundays free every single week probably for a particular reason. She wasn't even sure if calling him to hang out was even in the cards yet for...whatever their relationship was now. Plus, she didn't want to seem desperate; they did spend the entirety of the night before together...even if she couldn't stop thinking about the way his pinkie felt locked with hers.

Which is why Melanie found herself on the porch of cottage four, knocking on the door.

Jan swung it open, wearing a tie-dye shirt underneath a pair of old denim overalls, bleached by years in the sun. "Melanie! What a surprise."

"Do you need help with jam?"

"Do we need help with jam," Jan scoffed, pulling Melanie into the cottage. "Is that even a question?"

MELANIE PLACED a tie-dye sticker with *Fletcher Fam Jam* in bold white bubble letters onto a jar of Strawberry Rhubarb. "I think that's all of them."

"Read off the full list," Dan said.

She lifted the lined piece of paper with her hastily scribbled notes. "Okay, there's twenty-four jars of Strawberry Rhubarb, twenty-four jars of Raspberry, twelve of Grape, twelve of Peach, twelve of Blackberry, and thirty-six jars of Hot Raspberry Preserves."

"That's not the full name," Jan singsonged, pointing her purple-stained wooden spoon at Melanie with a wink before going back to stirring the bubbling pot of jam in front of her.

"*Mel's* Hot Raspberry Preserves." She sighed. "Seriously, do you need thirty-six jars?"

"We brought our first batch of twelve last week and it sold out in less than an hour," Dan said. "The Haverport Instagram account featured it for this week's market, so I'm honestly afraid we won't have enough."

"Well, if we don't, we just make more the following week, do a few IOU orders," Jan said, flicking the stove off and giving the jam one last good stir. "It seems everyone wants Mel's tasty preserves."

Melanie chuckled, shaking her head. There seemed to be no fighting them on this one, they were determined to name the jam after her.

Her phone buzzed next to her on the table. She flipped it over and noticed it was Calvin calling her. She stumbled out of her seat, her chest full of nervous energy as she stepped away from the table into the Fletcher's psychedelic living room. "Hello?"

"Headband, where are you?"

"At the Fletchers', making jam," she answered suspiciously. "Why, where are *you*?"

"At your house."

Melanie flung herself to the window in the kitchen to get a glimpse of the front porch at cottage five, not caring that both Jan and Dan were now staring at her.

Sure enough, he was indeed at her house, standing on

the front porch. He was wearing a plain black T-shirt, sneakers, and a pair of swim trunks.

"Do I see a bathing suit?"

Calvin chuckled as he walked up to the edge of the patio, leaning against the railing to get a closer look at Melanie through the Fletchers' kitchen window. "Maybe. It's sort of needed for what we're about to do."

"And what are we about to do?" she asked, her body humming with excitement.

"Depends, are you ready for your first kiss?" he answered, winking at her.

"Depends, will I be graded?"

Calvin grinned playfully. "This is more of a pass/fail kind of course."

"And how does one pass?"

"Just follow instructions," he said. "And grab your suit."

CALVIN VEERED the truck off Boston Ave, up a winding narrow road that Melanie had never seemed to notice before. The road curved and curled as they climbed up to the top of a hill, the sky hidden by a thick forest of oak and evergreen trees. She leaned her arms against the open passenger window, placing her head down as she took a deep breath, the scent of pine and salty ocean air easing her body.

She sat back up in the truck, not being able to contain the smile on her face. "Are we going to a private beach or something?"

"Not exactly." He shot her a mischievous smirk. "You'll see."

After a few more moments winding up the hill, he finally slowed the truck as the road abruptly ended, pulling into a dirt alcove and parking. He jumped out and reached into his trunk, swinging a backpack over his shoulder and grabbing two beach towels. He reached for Melanie's hand, but instead of grabbing the whole thing, he simply curled his pinkie with hers, her heart skipping a beat from his touch.

He pulled her down a steep hiking path, taking his time, turning toward her to make sure she wasn't going to fall. When the cliff got too steep, he threw the towels to the ground and lifted her down.

Soon, a clearing formed amongst the dense trees. Calvin walked up to a massive rock that overlooked a river that flowed into the bay. On the other side of the river was the entire town of Haverport, glistening in the late afternoon sun.

Melanie stood there stunned at the view as he placed his things down, kicking off his shoes. "This is incredible."

"Just you wait," he said, peeling off his shirt. Melanie glanced over at him, his arm muscles flexing as he pulled his shirt over his head, lean abs and pec muscles rippling. She flushed, turning from him.

He smirked. "Ready for it?"

To take off her shirt in front of him? Absolutely not. But then she realized he meant the river below them...and jumping off the rock.

"Wait," she said with panic. "We're going to jump?"

Calvin grinned, nodding his head. "We're going to jump."

The excitement and nervous energy drained out of her. She took a step back. "Oh my...I don't..."

Calvin reached for her, pulling her into his arms, his

skin warm against her now clammy hands. "I promise, I've got you every step of the way, and I won't let go."

She smiled shyly. His eyes were so deep and blue, they resembled the river below them. She wasn't sure what confidence had come over her, but she didn't question it as she kicked off her sneakers as well, tugging herself out of her jean shorts and pulling her shirt above her head.

He was staring at her, but his eyes didn't roam her body, almost like it was a rule he'd set for himself. Instead, his gaze was firmly on her face, looking at her like she was even more stunning than the view before them. He reached for her hand, holding on tightly with all five fingers this time. "Ready?"

Melanie nodded, avoiding the taste of bile in her mouth as Calvin counted down from three. When he hit one, they both took a running start and then jumped, hands still clamped tightly together as they plunged into the cool water thirty feet below.

She pushed above the surface, catching her breath as a laugh bubbled out of her chest. The sun was just starting to set over the bay, the reflection turning the water glittery and golden.

His hand was still holding on to hers as he tugged. Her body floated toward his as he wrapped his arms around her waist, planting his forehead against hers.

For a moment they stilled, holding each other, drops from his eyelashes sprinkling down onto her cheeks. Then he leaned in to kiss her, his lips surprisingly warm despite the chilly water. He pressed his fingertips into her back as he sealed her tightly to his chest. Melanie wrapped her arms around his shoulders, kissing him back as she melted into the golden, perfect moment.

When the kiss finally slowed, he brushed her wet hair

from her shoulder, pressing his lips against her neck before glancing up at her. "So, how was your first kiss?"

She looked out at the sun, how it set above the bay with streaks of orange, red, and purple. The glittering water and the boats bobbing in the distance. She looked back at Calvin, his eyes twinkling up at her, his look tender and sweet, not a hint of a smirk or a tease or a jaunt.

She grinned, brushing the back of his neck.

"It was magic."

"So, did I pass?"

The two of them sat on beach towels at the top of Sunset Rock, which Calvin explained was the name for... the exact reason he just showed her. Melanie sat in between his legs, leaning her back against his chest as he twirled his fingers through her drying hair.

Calvin smiled. "With flying colors."

"Who knew 'flying' would be taken so literally," Melanie mumbled, causing Calvin to burst out laughing, making her smile. He reached for his backpack and grabbed a white paper bag, retrieving a rather long sandwich.

"Picnic dinner?" Melanie asked.

"I don't think grinders need to be confined to meal times," Calvin answered, unwrapping the sandwich, the smell of salami, oil, and oregano wafting toward her. "They're perfect for any time of day."

"Any time of day?" she teased. "Also, what's a grinder?"

"Headband, didn't you grow up in Connecticut?"

"Yeah, but I've never heard the word 'grinder' before."

"Summer people."

Melanie slapped his leg playfully as he chuckled,

breaking apart the sandwich and handing her half. "It's the same thing as a sub, or a hero, or whatever you want to call it. But here in the Port, we call it a grinder."

"Why do you guys call it the Port?" Melanie asked, picking off a string of lettuce dangling from her sandwich.

"Easier to say, I guess. I don't know, I just say it because the locals have for years."

"Did you grow up here?"

"Oh, good, questions," Calvin said. "I also have many questions."

"Mmm," Melanie answered, her mouth full of the most delicious bite of sandwich—er, grinder—she'd ever had in her life.

"Cool, I'll go first," Calvin said. "Why did you move to Haverport?"

Melanie swallowed. "Really jumping into it, aren't we? I believe my question was first."

"Fine." He placed his half-eaten sandwich on the paper bag. "Most of my life. I moved here when I was five."

"From where?"

"That's another question, you have to answer mine first."

Melanie glowered, then took a deep, steadying breath. "Duncan did something really stupid back in Garrison that got him expelled. Haverport High said they would let him attend here, but he has to retake his junior year."

"And how do you feel about it?"

"My question first," she taunted. She also didn't know how to answer that one...or how to continue telling Calvin why they were here. She wasn't sure if she was ready for that yet.

He sighed heavily. "Boston. My mom brought me here

to stay with Gram for the summer and when she came to pick me up, I told her I didn't want to leave."

She wanted to dive in more, but he was also being massively cryptic, which she guessed was to be expected. It's not like she was giving him full answers as well.

"I honestly don't know how I feel about it," she admitted to him. "There really wasn't much for me in Garrison besides my education. I had acquaintances from my classes, but didn't really make any friends because..."

Because I didn't want them finding out, she thought to herself. She hesitated, not sure if she wanted to go that deep yet. Not sure if she wanted him to know the full truth about what faced her at home. Right now, with him, it all felt too good to be true. And she really didn't want to ruin whatever this was.

"Because they were all so competitive. It's been nice to escape all that pressure."

"And have a fresh start," Calvin said, combing her hair with his fingers again.

She sat up, turning to face him. "How did you—"

His face flushed. "Your application," he said quietly. "I read it when you handed it to me."

"Oh," she said, feeling a bit embarrassed as she slumped back down. "And I'm guessing you made sure it was at the top of the pile?"

Calvin leaned into her sheepishly. "Guilty. Also... Strawberry, really?"

"Okay but...Oreo, really?"

"It is a misunderstood flavor. People don't appreciate it enough."

Melanie shook her head, a bit relieved that they were no longer talking about Duncan. She decided not to ask him about his parents either, maybe as a way to leave those heavy subjects alone. For now.

She reached up and touched the silver chain around his neck, noticing a pair of metal dog tags dangling at the center. "Whose are these?"

"My grandfather's," he said, his voice full of pride. "He fought in Vietnam. He passed away ten years ago."

Melanie read one of the dog tags she held in her hand.

Frank Calvin Ball

"Is this why they keep calling you army boy at Scoops?"

He shook his head. "Not exactly. That nickname came way before Jay's time."

"I feel like there's a story here."

He let out a throaty breath, leaning his head back. "Please don't make me."

"Too late," Melanie said, sitting up and turning to face him, crisscrossing her legs.

Calvin's cheeks dimpled as he smiled at her, brushing a hand up and down her arm. "So, the same year Ron gave me the job at Scoops, he got in a bit of heat with the sanitation department."

"Uh oh."

"Yeah, wasn't good. Apparently, an inspector came through and reported that no one was wearing hats, which didn't comply with the cover your head laws, or whatever."

"Major uh oh."

He chuckled. "So the department told Ron that employees needed to either start wearing hats or buzz the hair off their heads."

Melanie held up her hands to her mouth, trying not to laugh.

"So that night, I went home, and I buzzed all of my hair off."

"Calvin."

"What? That job means everything to me. I literally would do anything to make sure Ron succeeds."

She melted at his words. "He really means that much to you, huh?"

He nodded, pulling her into him, letting the silence speak for itself. She still had so many questions, but the moment no longer felt right. He would tell her in his own time. And maybe at some point, she would have the strength to do the same.

He started stroking her hair again, the two of them watching as the sun began to set, the moon peeking out behind the ruby-colored sky.

"I like your hair like this," he said softly.

"A frizzy mess? Should I buzz it all off?"

"No, it suits you," he admitted, kissing the top of her head. "Although I do miss the headband."

Chapter Thirteen

MELANIE ARRIVED at Scoops fifteen minutes early, hoping to catch Calvin at the end of his shift before starting her own. But when she stepped through the back door, he wasn't there.

Tyler hunched over the sink as he washed dirty scoopers and spoon containers, humming to himself.

Melanie frowned. "Where's Calvin?"

"Called in his favor," Tyler replied, not taking his eyes off the sudsy dishes. "Asked me to cover for him last minute. Why, you need him?"

She realized at that moment that absolutely no one at Scoops knew about them. Even if *everything* had changed, the scoopers had no idea.

"Nah, just curious," she said lazily, making sure her tone of voice sounded like she didn't care, despite the fact that her mind was spiraling.

Where was he? Never in her almost two months at Scoops did she ever witness Calvin call out for a shift. Sure, everyone else traded around shifts like it was one massive game of hot potato. But never him. He kept to the schedule that he meticulously made every week. Until now.

She perched her Scoops hat on her head and went up to the front of the shop, scanning what needed filling before the night shift. Blake was serving the last few customers on his line, fumbling through the money in his hand as he counted out the change.

He sighed as he watched the customers walk away, closing the window. Melanie pointed down to the dip containers, the lid wide open.

Blake winced. "Right," he said, closing it shut. "God, why am I so bad at this? You caught on quickly, and I've had two more months than you. I should technically be better."

"I don't think it's supposed to be a competition," she reassured him. "Besides, you're doing great, look at that tip jar."

Blake smiled deviously. "It's the schoolboy look, gets people every time."

She chuckled, watching as his attention quickly snapped to a guy that came up to the counter. He was taller and unfairly suave, with dark bushy black waves and dimples for miles. He pushed a pair of sunglasses onto his head. "Hey."

Blake blushed. "Hello."

The guy leaned against the counter. "So, what's good?"

"Um, our best seller is the Strawberry Cheesecake."

"Hmm," the guy said, his eyes teasing as he glanced at Blake. "But I don't want what everyone else wants. What do *you* like?"

Melanie saw the color of Blake's cheeks go from pink to deep, deep red. "Uh, um."

The guy just kept smiling at him, like Blake was the most adorable creature in the whole world.

"Blake, weren't you just raving about Birthday Cake? Pretty sure you got in a fight with Jay about it," Melanie said casually, now filling up the chocolate jimmies.

"Oh, yeah," Blake said a little more confidently. "People usually don't love cake batter ice cream, but this one is actually really good."

The guy's smirk was so devilishly handsome, Melanie had to look away. Was this how Calvin looked when they talked to each other?

"Birthday Cake then, two scoops."

"Sugar, cake, or waffle?" Blake asked.

"Whichever you want to give me."

Blake exhaled, reaching for a sugar cone and heading for the freezer. He looked at Melanie and flicked a clean scooper in her direction. "Don't."

"Wasn't going to say anything," she said, the smirk on her face telling a completely different story.

Blake handed the guy his cone. "On me."

Handsome shook his head, dipping a five in the tip jar. "See you."

"Yeah, okay," Blake said wistfully, watching him walk away.

Melanie finished up her filling and walked over to where Blake stood, leaning her elbows against the counter, her eyebrows raised in his direction.

"That's Zach," Blake whispered to her.

"He seems nice," she said with a smile.

"My parents don't know."

"About Zach?"

"About...any of it."

"Oh," said Melanie, thinking through what to say next, but realizing it wasn't her silence to fill.

"I actually haven't told anyone yet," Blake admitted

quietly to her. "I noticed I liked guys almost eight years ago now, but never did anything about it. Until..."

"Until Zach."

He nodded, looking at Melanie, his face full of expectation for what would come next. Like standing on the edge of a rock with a thirty-foot drop, wondering if he was ready to take the plunge.

"Are you ready to tell them?" Melanie asked.

"I've always thought I wasn't, but now...I really want them to meet him."

"So then do it," she encouraged softly. "I mean, he's probably the most handsome human I have ever seen in my entire life."

"I know, it literally makes no sense to me." His freckled face flushed once again.

"Why? You're hilarious and fun to be around, but also a secret softie." She nudged him back.

Blake looked out the window, watching as Zach walked down the Main Street sidewalk. "I know this is cliché, but remember the day that you saved me from the walk-in? I keep having nightmares about it."

"Seriously? God, I'm going to hurt them."

"No, not because of them," he admitted. "Because I was locked in a closet that I couldn't get out of. I don't want to be locked in anymore."

"Then don't."

Blake looked at her with such tenderness, it made her heart break. "This is your life, Blake," Melanie reassured him. "You don't have to live it to anyone else's standards but your own. Why waste your time pleasing others when the life you want is right in front of you?"

The advice even surprised herself, realizing that maybe these were the words she also needed to hear.

Blake smiled shyly at her. "You're so good at your job *and* you're nice, it's infuriating."

"What are the little children gossiping about," Jay asked, joining them up front, his Scoops hat backward on his head. Apparently, they were "little children" until they graduated from being newbies.

Melanie stood up straight. "Birthday Cake ice cream."

"Seriously, that again? Blakey-boy, it's disgusting."

"Says the guy who likes *Pistachio*," Blake jested.

The entire shop went silent. Melanie heard Rory take a dramatic breath in The War Room, then cackled like an evil witch as she charged to the front. "PISTACHIO?!"

"He's lying," Jay said coldly.

"Oh, no, I don't think so," Rory said, pointing a finger at him. "You're acting like you got caught."

"What are we all laughing about?"

Melanie twisted toward the counter, noticing Duncan was there. He was leaning against it, Leila glued to his side, rubbing his arm lazily.

"Depends, how do you feel about the Pistachio ice cream?" Melanie asked.

"It's number 24 of 32," Duncan said. "Surprisingly decent for Pistachio, but still terrible."

"Wait, you've ranked all of them?" Blake asked.

"Five summers ago, I tried every flavor," he said. "I found my old notebook with all of my ratings in it when I was looking for something to do that wasn't just staring at a wall."

"Wait, so what was number one?" Blake asked.

"Birthday Cake, obviously."

"HA-HA!" Blake said, holding his hands up in triumph.

"You did that on purpose," Jay said flatly.

"Sure didn't," Duncan said, chuckling a bit at the banter

he was witnessing at Scoops. "Hey, Mel Mel, when do you get out?"

Her heart hammered in her chest. "Hopefully 10:30. It's a weekday, shouldn't be as busy."

"Sick, so, wanna come to a party after?"

Jay shoved Melanie aside, sliding into Duncan's view. "Did you just say party?"

Duncan nodded. "Wanna join us?"

"Are you kidding?!" Jay said, practically dancing with glee. "Dude, *yes!*"

"Calm down, tiger," Rory said.

"You can all come. Just make sure my sister gets there, she can't seem to escape ice cream boot camp these days."

"Oh, we'll make sure she's there," Jay said, throwing an arm around her shoulders like they were best friends.

"Ew, get your hands off her, who knows where they've been," Rory quipped, pulling her away from his grasp. She chuckled, high-fiving Rory in front of Jay's sulking face.

"I'll text you the deets, Mel Mel?"

She nodded, watching the two of them walk away, Duncan's hand curled around Leila's waist.

A party. It was finally happening. Her stomach was in knots. She felt like she couldn't breathe.

Jay looked at Melanie and Rory pointedly. "I want to be out of here at 10:15. *Sharp.*"

"That's impossible," Rory said. "Plus, dear lord, I have nothing to wear to this thing."

"I mean, me neither," Melanie said, looking down at her uniform, realizing she would be attending her first party in a Scoops shirt. Hopefully a clean one.

She saw Tyler come up behind Rory, touching her back softly. She turned and listened to whatever he had to say, nodding furiously.

"I'll pick you guys up," Tyler said, looking at Blake. "Want a ride as well?"

Blake nodded as he glanced down at his phone, texting someone, a shy smile on his face.

"10:15," Jay said toward Tyler. "We'll set a record for the shortest closing time. Even if we have to turn away a line."

"You know we can't do that," Melanie said.

"Who are you, Calvin?" teased Jay. "He's not here, so, uh, who cares?"

Melanie's heart twisted. She did care.

Where was he?

MELANIE FLIPPED the sign to *Closed* at 10:10, taking a look around her. The place was...spotless. And all the candy and sauces were already filled.

Rory rolled the vacuum up front, plugging it into the wall. "He's about to set a record for the shortest closing time."

Melanie glanced back, noticing Jay furiously washing the dishes in the back, his eyes determined and focused. No fooling around, no singing off-key.

"Maybe we should start calling *him* army boy." She chuckled. "What else is there to do?"

Rory shrugged, flicking on the vacuum. "Count the tips?"

She snatched both tip jars and went for the desk, counting out the bills and coins as Rory and Jay finished cleaning up Scoops. By the time she had three piles ready to hand out, the two of them were finished, and Jay was practically bouncing off the walls.

"It's 10:16, where's Tyler?" he asked impatiently.

"Did you check out back?" Rory asked.

Jay bolted for the door, opening it up and finding Tyler standing outside, his Jeep parked behind him. He wore a faded pair of jeans and a loose black T-shirt that still hugged his massive biceps tightly.

"You're one minute late," Jay taunted.

"I've been here since ten, wise ass."

Melanie flicked off the lights as they left, and Rory locked the knob behind them before sliding the extra key underneath the door.

Jay went straight for the front, opening the door to find Blake sitting there with his usual devious smile, his red bouncy hair spiked wildly in all different directions.

"Blakey-boy, out," Jay said.

Blake just smiled, flicking Jay off.

"Do you want to get to this party or not?" Tyler asked.

He rolled his eyes, climbing into the back next to Rory, who was now rifling through a duffel bag, Melanie on her other side. Tyler kicked the Jeep on and rolled it out of the Scoops parking lot, down Main Street.

"Okay, black, or florals?" Rory asked.

Melanie frowned. "Huh?"

"Right, why did I even ask," Rory shook her head. "Florals. You practically have flowers coming out your ass."

Jay belted out a laugh as Rory pulled a floral summer dress from her bag, handing it to Melanie. She grabbed a black dress for herself, then slipped off her Scoops shirt.

"Oh my god," Blake said, his face crimson.

"Yeahhhh, take it offf!" Jay whistled.

"Bras are basically bathing suit tops, stop freaking out," she said, slipping the silky black dress over her head and pulling it below her hips and thighs. She then shimmied out of her shorts, shoving them back in the bag and grabbing a pair of black leather sandals.

"Where did you get these?" Melanie asked.

"Tyler stopped by my place." She shoved the rest of her Scoops uniform into the bag. "We're neighbors. He has a key to my house, offered to grab us a few things."

She glanced up at the rearview mirror to get a look at Tyler. She noticed how he kept sneaking peeks at Rory as she got ready.

"Okay," Rory said, finally sitting still. "Your turn."

Melanie flushed. "I'm not taking off my shirt in front of everyone."

"Why not?" Jay teased, leaning over to look at her. "*It's just like a bathing suit.*"

Rory shoved him hard as Tyler pulled onto a dirt road that winded down to a sprawling beach house along the river. Cars were haphazardly parked, and she couldn't find Duncan's car in the sea of vehicles.

Once they were parked, Rory pulled Melanie behind the tree and helped her get ready, tying the bow of the floral dress as she twirled her hair into a braid.

"Crap, your shoes," Rory said, looking down at her pair of filthy Converse. Even after trying to clean them, they still had faint stains from various syrups and rainbow jimmies.

Melanie shrugged. "I doubt anyone at this party is going to notice."

"Says the girl who *still hasn't been kissed,*" Rory teased, holding up a pair of hoops to Melanie's ears, nodding, then gesturing for her to put them on.

Her stomach turned, realizing she hadn't told Rory the truth yet. "Uh, well—"

"Are you two done yet?!" Jay called out rather impatiently.

"Oh my god, chill OUT," Rory yelled, holding her back and assessing her work. "Decent, let's go."

She looped her arm through Melanie's as the five of them walked up to the house, music already booming from twenty feet away.

"I feel like I'm going to be sick," Blake admitted.

"And you haven't even started drinking yet," Jay jaunted, nudging his side.

Melanie exhaled. The thought of drinking really didn't excite her. As they walked through the entrance of the house, she heard a massive cheer as Duncan pummeled toward them, lifting Melanie up into a tight hug.

"Mel Mellll!"

He swirled her around, swaying slightly and almost dropping her to the floor. Tyler lifted up a hand to steady Duncan as he placed her back down.

"Shots!"

Duncan charged into the kitchen with Jay eagerly following behind, the rest of the Scoopers at his heels.

She stepped into the kitchen where Duncan was already handing out fluorescent green cups to each of them, a clear liquid swirling around at the bottom that smelled like gasoline.

"We're supposed to drink this?" Melanie whispered to Rory.

"Just pour it down your throat," Rory said softly back. "Helps if you plug your nose."

She nodded, watching as Duncan added a heavy pour to his cup before lifting it to all of them in a cheers. Everyone followed, then tipped their own cups back.

She hesitated, the smell of the drink already making her want to vomit. It didn't make any sense to her why people would drink this for fun. But with Duncan's eyes boring into her with such enthusiasm, Melanie knew she didn't really have another option. She pinched her nose and poured the drink down her throat, the burning causing her to cough viciously.

Duncan shrieked in delight, throwing an arm around her as he poured her another one. "Mel Mel, we finally did it! We're at a party together!"

Leila appeared in the kitchen, touching Duncan's arm. "They're here."

"Oh, shoot," he said, placing the big bottle of vodka down on the counter. He smirked at Melanie. "Boyfriend duties, be right back."

"B-boyfriend?" Melanie asked breathlessly.

Duncan smiled, teeth and all. "Officially off the market, Mel Mel!"

She smiled back at him as he left the kitchen, looking down at the very large shot that Duncan just poured her. She frowned. "This stuff is awful."

"Sure is," said Rory, reaching over with a bottle of fruit punch and pouring some in her cup. "Sugar makes it better."

"Sugar makes everything better."

Tyler tapped Rory on the shoulder as she poured. "Hey, you look nice."

"Oh my god, thank you, you're a lifesaver," Rory said, reaching around and hugging Tyler from the side. "We would look like the hot mess express without you."

Melanie looked up at his face, noticing the way it lit up when Rory hugged him. She discreetly lifted an eyebrow in his direction, noticing him bristle at her gesture. She smiled slyly back at him as she took a sip of her drink. Even with the fruit punch, it was still horrible.

"Jay's about to do a keg stand, wanna go watch?" Tyler asked.

"Oh, absolutely." Rory giggled, grabbing Melanie's hand and pulling her toward the back porch.

She held her drink in her hand for the majority of the night, pretending to take sips, but not actually letting any of it touch her lips. She realized that if she just carried around a cup with liquid in it, people were stupid enough to think she was drinking. Duncan included.

At some point in the night, he sloshed over to her, his eyes drooping and his gait sloppy as he plopped down on the couch next to Melanie, the cushions bouncing underneath him. He leaned into her, his breath a mixture of stale beer and a side of vodka. "Mell Mellllllllll."

She smiled tightly, patting his knee. "How you doing, Dee?"

"Ssss-so good. Sooo happy you're here."

It made her want to cry. She looked away, trying to fight back the tears in her eyes. She loved having him again like this, being a part of his life, talking to him regularly...even finding out that he has a girlfriend now. But she wondered if it was all worth it. Was it worth seeing him like this? Having to endure the drunkenness just to have access to her brother again?

Her eyes glossed over the room in front of her, noticing a lot of the other kids doing the same thing. Chugging drinks, cheering, drunkenly stumbling around the house. The whole scene made her anxious. Was everyone like Duncan when it came to alcohol? Was she the one who wasn't normal about it?

She looked at her brother who was now leaning his head against her shoulder, falling asleep. Her heart hammered in her chest as she started patting his cheek, panicking. "Dee, wake up."

He grumbled.

"Dee, don't fall asleep, wake up," she said, looking around the room. "Maybe it's time to take you home."

"I don't have the car," he mumbled, barely clear enough for her to understand. "No keys, remember?"

Shit. She noticed Leila slinking up to them, a wide smile on her face, clearly oblivious to the state her boyfriend was in. "Leila," Melanie said, her voice sounding as panicked as she felt. She didn't care. "Duncan, he's falling asleep, what if—"

"Chill out, sister friend," she said, reaching over to stroke Melanie's hair like a cat. "I'll take him upstairs, he can sleep it off."

"Um," she said, looking at Duncan, a tightness rising in her throat. "Will you keep an eye on him?"

"Of course," she said, her smile distant. "I got him, sweetheart."

Leila lifted him from the couch, patting his butt before disappearing.

Melanie sat there frozen for a moment, realizing she wanted out. *Now.*

She started searching the house, looking for Rory or any of the Scoopers. But after a few rounds around the party, she went from panicked to petrified. She couldn't find any of them.

She checked the back porch one last time and found Jay talking to some tall blonde, his arm curled low around her waist. "Jay, thank god, where are they?"

He bristled, his shoulders tightening as his face darkened. "No idea, those losers bailed."

"B-bailed?"

"Yeah, I don't know, whatever." A look flitted across his eyes that made it pretty clear he cared more than he was letting on. Before Melanie could ask, he turned back to the blonde next to him, focusing all his attention on her. She knew enough to know she was being dismissed.

Her hands were shaking as she left the house, heading for the tree where Tyler's car was parked.

But it wasn't there. It was gone.

"Oh god." She felt herself crumbling as tears flowed down her cheeks. Duncan was passed out, and she had no way of getting home. She walked toward the street and sat down on the curb, curled her legs into her arms, and sobbed.

Then, a rogue thought popped into her mind. *Calvin.*

She knew she shouldn't do it. He clearly canceled on his shift because something important came up. But as she sat there on the side of the road, she realized she didn't have many other options. Calling her parents would be a nightmare, and Duncan wasn't even supposed to be here in the first place. It pained her, knowing how pathetic she was for not having anyone else to call. And she had absolutely no idea how Calvin would feel after knowing the truth. About her, and her family, and Duncan.

But...she didn't think she had any other choice. So she took a deep, uneven breath, and dialed his number.

He answered on the second ring. She heard a screen door swinging shut in the distance on his end as he spoke. "Hello?"

"C-Calvin?" she said, her voice breaking, the tears streaming down her cheeks again.

He was silent for a beat. "Where are you?"

"We went to a party," she croaked. "And they left, and I don't have a ride."

"Where are you?" he asked again, his voice coming out

harsher this time. She could hear movement on his end, then the muffled sound of a car door slamming shut.

"I don't know, down a dirt road at this house on the river," she answered. "I-I have an address."

"I know where it is," he said, his truck roaring to life. "I'll be there in five minutes."

Melanie nodded to herself as the call ended. She wrapped her arms around her legs and pressed her face into her knees.

Soon enough, she heard the sounds of Calvin's truck pulling up next to her. He parked the car, not bothering to turn it off as he jumped out, kneeling down in front of her. She couldn't stop crying as he tucked her hair behind her ears, rubbing his thumbs against her cheek to catch her tears.

Before she could say anything, he was scooping her up into his arms, lifting her into the passenger seat of his truck, and gently closing the door. When he got to his side he pulled her close to him. She rested her head on his shoulder as he shifted gears.

Chapter Fourteen

CALVIN PULLED his truck behind Scoops and cut the ignition, the lights going dark. He slid Melanie into his lap and wrapped an arm tightly around her. He cupped her head as she continued to cry gloopy tears, his thumb brushing against her cheek.

"I...I'm so sorry," she whispered, her voice scratchy.

"You have nothing to apologize for," he murmured, squeezing her side.

"You were clearly busy."

"Trust me," he said, nuzzling her neck with his nose before looking up into her eyes. "It's really okay."

She exhaled, her breath uneven. He just sat there, stroking her gently, not pushing or prodding her about why she was so upset. She thought about the way she curled her body next to his by the bonfire just days before, how safe she felt. Even if he wasn't asking, the time felt right to finally tell him.

So she took a deep, sobering breath, and launched into her story.

WHEN THEY'D GOTTEN the call, Melanie's face was planted in her textbook, drooling right onto the page about Kinetic Molecular Theory. She knew she didn't need to cram like this—she could just take her AP Chem exam and probably be just fine. But with the end of her junior year at Garrison Prep coming to a close, Melanie knew these were the last grades Yale would see on her application. She couldn't chance at failing, not with Yale on the line.

She'd jumped as her door opened abruptly.

"Damn," she said, craning the side of her head to stretch out the kink in her neck. She looked over at her clock and saw that it was just past midnight.

Mom was at the door, looking frantic. "Get your shoes on."

She frowned, rising up out of her seat, feeling the air shift around her. "What's wrong?"

"Hospital," she said, not bothering to explain more as she stepped out of the room. "We need to go. Now."

Melanie felt dizzy for a moment as she listened to her mom's footsteps charging down the stairs, their car's ignition roaring to life outside. She snatched her sneakers and followed.

The hospital was only a thirteen minute drive, but to Melanie, it felt like a lifetime—even if Dad broke every traffic law possible to get there. She shoved her bare feet into her Converse, not bothering to tie them, her leg bouncing nervously as the three of them sat there in excruciating silence.

From pitch black darkness to blinding fluorescent lights, the three of them charged for the front desk.

"Duncan Chase Albertson," Mom asked the receptionist, her voice shrill. "Which room is he in?"

"I'm sorry, you can't see him yet. There are doctors with him running the necessary tests."

"Let me go in there with him then," Mom barked. "I'm his mother, he's still a minor."

"I will alert them that you are here," the receptionist said calmly, clearly used to people coming into the hospital completely panicked. "They will come find you, have a seat."

She leaned in looking like she was ready to scream, but Dad grabbed her, guiding her toward the waiting area.

"Thank you," Melanie mumbled to the receptionist. She sat down next to Mom who was keeled over, face in her hands.

Melanie turned to her father. "What's going on?"

"We got a call from the hospital, they said Duncan was brought in by an ambulance. Alcohol poisoning."

Melanie looked down at the cartoon turtles on her ratty, worn pajama pants. *Ambulance. Alcohol poisoning.*

"Wasn't he supposed to be at prom?"

Dad sighed. "I don't think he ever meant to go to prom."

Wow, she thought, letting his words sink in and realizing what fools they all were. It was a tale as old as time. Duncan thought of every lie in the book to get out of the house. No matter how grounded he was, no matter how much he let that lion roar and create a storm of fury at home, he always seemed to find a way. And her parents fell for it every single time.

This time, it was prom, obviously. Duncan had told them he was invited by one of the seniors on the girl's lacrosse team. He was even extra convincing this time; having her come over for dinner last week, the five of them sitting at the table like a normal, polite, civil family. Even though just days earlier, he'd thrown three dinner plates across that very same kitchen in a fit of rage about how unfair his life was.

Melanie never understood it. How could her parents just keep letting it happen, keep saying yes to him? She would sit through conversation after conversation with her parents as they explained to her the *newest* Grand Plan to get Duncan's life back on track. To help him focus on his schoolwork and find some kind of career that he could be passionate about. Something that would finally have him drop "this partying phase" for good.

The first few times, she really believed them with all of her heart. That their plans to take him on college visits and have him meet with Dad's colleagues would actually *work*. Would excite him enough to want to change. But after each brutal attempt, they always ended up at the same place—dinner plates or cell phones or Christmas ornaments smashing on a wall.

Yet her parents still had relentless blind faith in him—that maybe someday he really would turn a corner. Glancing at the colorless faces of both of her parents under the fluorescent lights of the hospital, she wondered if this was the moment where that faith would all come crashing down.

"Mr. and Mrs. Albertson?"

A man in a white coat was standing in front of them, his face emotionless. Like he'd experienced utter devastation many times before.

Mom jumped from her seat. "How is he? Can we see him?"

"Duncan is stable," the doctor confirmed. "We had to pump his stomach when he arrived, then ran tests to make sure none of his organs were at risk of failing. The scans thankfully show no signs of brain or liver damage. We have him hooked up with oxygen and an IV now. He's slowly recovering."

"Jesus Christ," Mom said, collapsing into the seat behind her. Dad wrapped his arm around her shoulders and rubbed fiercely.

"Is he awake?" Melanie asked.

"No, not yet," the doctor said, his eyes softening when they landed on her. "But he will be."

She thanked the doctor as she sat down next to Mom, who was now openly sobbing in the waiting room. She curled her legs up underneath her and leaned into her side, rubbing her arm, letting the tears fall down her own cheeks as well.

Melanie wasn't sure how long she was curled up in that seat before falling asleep, but when her father woke her up and handed her a steaming cup of hospital coffee, the sun was starting to rise over the parking lot.

"Any news?" she asked, her voice crackly from sleep.

"He woke up twenty minutes ago," he whispered. "Mom and I were just in there. She's still with him."

She sighed with relief, crisscrossing her legs as she took the coffee from him. "Thanks."

He took a seat next to her, reaching around the arm rest to pat her knee.

Melanie blew on the cup, steam rolling off of it. "Dad, what happened?"

He let out a breath. "I really should wait for your mother."

"Just tell me," she pleaded softly. "Please."

His sigh sounded almost frustrated, but that didn't stop him from angling his face so he could look directly at her. "Instead of going to prom, your brother decided to have his own party. But of course, he had nowhere to host it."

Melanie's eyebrows furrowed. "Then where was it?"

"He—" Dad hesitated, like he didn't even want to voice the horrible words. "He broke into the Holsteads' house."

Her eyes went wide as saucers.

"They're not due to come back from Florida for another two weeks, so Duncan decided that it would be a good idea to use their place for a party. But his plan didn't work out so well when a teammate found him on the floor with a blue face, covered in vomit."

Melanie pressed a hand to her face. "This is so bad."

"It gets worse."

Melanie looked at her father in disbelief. "How can it get worse?"

"Principal Eddy called this morning to let us know that Duncan has been expelled and should not come to school on Monday," Dad said, his face etched with so much pain. "Your mother and I will have to go in for a full meeting about it, but...yeah. There's that."

She wanted to scream. She felt like her own lion was building up in her chest, ready to attack everything in its wake. This couldn't be happening. Even though she'd come to have frequent nightmares about Duncan and his tantrums, they were never creative enough to be *this* horrible.

Mom approached the two of them, her face splotchy and red, her hair an absolute mess. "Melanie, come."

She'd followed dutifully behind her parents as they walked through the double doors and down a hall to Duncan's room. Mom gestured for Melanie to go in without them, and as much as she'd wanted to protest, she obliged.

Because she knew the last thing her parents needed was another teenager causing them heartache.

"MY PARENTS THOUGHT it would be a good idea to give him a change of scene," Melanie said, her voice scraggly and raw. "But I don't know, after tonight, seeing him like that...I just don't feel like anything is ever going to change."

Calvin was silent as he kissed her on the cheek, his lips lingering for a moment as her breathing slowed, squeezing his hand that was still tightly wrapped around her side.

"Thanks for trusting me with that," he whispered.

She nodded, leaning into him, realizing how heavy all of it pressed on her. And how relieved she felt to finally let it out.

"Come on," he said sweetly, opening up the door. He lifted her out of the car and set her down, reaching for her pinkie and leading her toward Scoops. She remained quiet as he unlocked the door with the set of keys clipped to his belt loop, pulling her through the back door. He lifted her once more as though she weighed nothing and placed her down on the desk, brushing his lips against hers. "Stay," he whispered.

She smiled wearily as he left her, flicking on the lights out front. She heard him placing cups down on the counter as he slid open the ice cream freezer, the tinkering sound of a scooper against metal, and the whirr of the milkshake machine as it roared to life.

Calvin finally came back to The War Room, flicking the lights back off, holding two large paper cups with straws. He handed her one.

"What is it?" she asked softly.

He smirked. "Strawberry Oreo milkshake."

She smiled. "That's...really cute."

Calvin leaned into her, curling an arm around her waist, and kissing her nose. "You're really cute."

She followed him as they left Scoops, her leg brushing against a large canvas bag on the floor when she slid into the passenger seat. She glanced down, noticing the bag was completely full of used, pocket-sized paperback novels.

"Did you just buy all of these?" Melanie asked curiously, picking up a copy of *Catcher In The Rye* as Calvin clicked his seatbelt into place.

He sighed heavily. "It's been a long day."

She felt overwhelmed with guilt, realizing her mess of an evening probably didn't help with whatever Calvin was going through at the moment. Because he *was* going through something, if her instincts were anything to go by.

"Hey," he said, sensing her shift in demeanor. He reached for her hand and squeezed it. "I won't let go, remember?"

Tears welled up in her eyes as he pulled the truck around Scoops and drove it past Hillside Park. They drove in silence, Calvin brushing his thumb across the top of Melanie's hand as he turned into a tiny beach community, parking in a dirt lot next to a worn-out wooden sign for Scallop Shell Beach.

Calvin reached underneath Melanie's seat, his hand brushing against her thighs as he grabbed a neatly folded blanket. She followed him out of the truck and down toward a set of docks to the left of the beach where a few sailboats were tied up and bobbing in the shallow water. When they finally reached the end of the docks, he spread the blanket down on the wood and motioned for her to sit next to him.

The two of them sat there silently for a beat, legs

dangling down over the water as they sipped on milkshakes and watched the lighthouse flashing in the distance.

"How'd you know where I was?" Melanie asked.

"That's Carl's place," he said. "He throws a party every Saturday."

"*Every* Saturday?"

He nodded. "Kind of a known thing in town."

She took a tentative sip. "Have you ever gone to one?"

"Nope," he said. "I don't drink."

Melanie exhaled, not realizing how relieved she would feel by that statement. "Why does it taste so bad?"

He shrugged. "I don't know. I've never had it."

"Oh," she said, her chest falling slightly. She wasn't sure why she felt like she failed in some way, but Calvin didn't seem to notice as he played with the straw on his cup.

He sighed. "My parents...they're addicts," he admitted, his voice quiet. "My dad's an alcoholic. I don't have a single memory of him sober. He left my mom when I was five."

His voice cracked slightly as he spoke. He placed his cup down and loosed a breath, submitting to whatever he was about to reveal to her. "When my Mom had me...her recovery was rough. They gave her these pills for the pain. And she..." He hesitated, looking up at the cloudy night sky. "She sort of didn't stop taking them. Found ways to get more."

She felt her throat go dry as he told his story, not sure what to even say to him. She wanted to be reassuring, but by the way he was sitting there, his body language militant and straightforward as he spoke, she could sense that he didn't need her reassurance. That he seemed resigned to his reality after so many years.

"That's what I was doing today," he continued. "She has this...habit of just showing up when it's convenient. Says it's to see me but it's really to try and squeeze money out of Gram."

Melanie felt her heart breaking at the mere thought of it, the horrors he must have experienced, having a mother show up and be so close, yet still so far away.

"The books?" she asked, curiosity getting the best of her.

His lips curled into a timid smile. "They help keep my mind off things. An escape when I need one."

He finally sat up straight, looking Melanie in the eyes. "Some people might turn to substances for an escape, but I don't even want to chance it. I'm afraid of what I'll become, that I'll be just like them. So, I read. A lot."

She just moved in closer to him, hugging his waist. "Thanks for trusting me with that," she repeated, not sure what else to say.

He stretched an arm around her shoulders, squeezing her tightly, like a lifeline. He kissed the top of her head. "I'm no stranger to addiction, Mel. I get what you're going through."

She pulled away from him slightly, looking up at his solemn face. "I—I don't think..."

But she did. Deep down in her gut, she knew.

Addict. Duncan was addicted to alcohol. If what happened to him that spring didn't scare him enough to put down the bottle, then there clearly was a bigger problem. And even if she didn't want to admit it to herself, Melanie knew it was true.

Her silence was telling as Calvin squeezed her tight, the two of them looking out across the bay, letting a comfortable lull settle between them. At some point, he shifted his body toward hers, cupping Melanie's face with his hands as he kissed her deeply. His hands and his touch were so tender, she didn't realize she was crying until he pulled away, kissing away the tears on her cheeks.

"I have a present for you," he whispered.

She chuckled, her voice gurgling from all of the emotion built up in her throat. Calvin reached into his pocket and revealed a light blue elastic headband.

She laughed out loud, the sound of her voice rolling off the waves. "Oh my god," she said as he stretched the head-band around her neck, then shimmied it into place at the top of her head. "You're ridiculous."

"The nickname doesn't exactly work if you're not wearing one anymore," he bantered. "And I couldn't help myself."

She shook her head, a big goofy grin on her face. Sure, things felt like an absolute mess, and the truth she finally admitted to herself about Duncan scared her down to her core. But looking up at Calvin grinning back at her, his expression just as sweet and gooey as her own, part of her really did feel safe with him by her side. And relieved that she wasn't so alone in it all.

Chapter Fifteen

MELANIE BROUGHT her yellow sunshine mug full of coffee back up to bed the following morning, peeling open a paperback that she swiped from Calvin's canvas bag—a copy of *The Sun Also Rises* that was missing the bottom corner of its cover. He said he got all of them from the 50-cent bin at the bookstore in town, full of paperbacks that had seen better days. It was how he was able to afford handfuls of them at a time.

She heard a soft knock on her door as it slowly creaked open. Duncan popped his head through the frame, his expression extra mischievous.

She placed the book into her lap, not even bothering with the small talk. "How in the *world* did you get home last night?" she whispered.

Duncan looked behind him before clicking her door shut, motioning for her to move over as he sat down next to her on the bed. He shot her a wicked grin. "I have my ways."

Melanie frowned at him.

"Mel Mel, chill out. I slept for a bit then Leila took me home," he said. "And somehow, I still beat *you* home."

She sighed. It was after 2 a.m. when Calvin finally got her back to the cottage, and another fifteen minutes before she even left his truck. That small moment of opening up to one another was like an electrical shock between the two of them. They couldn't stop touching each other, kissing each other, exploring each other. Melanie thought about the smooth skin along his abs as she slipped a hand underneath his shirt, the way Calvin's hand felt sweeping up her leg as he pressed her body against the window. Yet she also realized how his hand paused at her thigh, brushing his thumb against her skin, not daring to go further—like it was another strict rule he had set for himself. Melanie was surprised by how desperately she wanted him to let go of all those rules in his head as she pressed into him further—only to have her back accidentally push down on the lever of the passenger door, almost causing her to stumble backward onto the broken seashells along the driveway. But he'd caught her, holding her tight as the two of them tried to muffle their laughter.

She smiled to herself bashfully. "You caught me."

Duncan shoved her. "So where were *you* last night then?"

"Um—" She hesitated, realizing she really didn't want to deal with whatever Duncan was about to say about Calvin. He clearly didn't like him, and right now, Melanie just didn't want to hear it. "My friends sort of got in a tiff and had to bail."

"Shit, that sucks. They're cool though, I like them," he said. "You should bring them to the next one."

She felt her face darken. She had absolutely no desire to

go to another party with him, or maybe another one ever. "Duncan, I—"

He looked at her expectantly, his expression playful and familiar. Like they'd just finished building a castle in the sand. The sight of him sitting there on her bed had her thinking back to the summers they would share rooms, the two of them hiding under the covers as they played their Game Boys until the wee hours of the morning. She thought about mornings just like this, where he would jump up and down to tell her to get up so they could make a sand castle, the sand perfectly damp from the rain. They would rush past Dad flipping pancakes and Mom packing sandwiches and soda in coolers, gearing up for another sunny day at the beach.

Her words caught in her throat. *Duncan, I don't want to go to parties. I don't like them.*

But she just couldn't do it, couldn't risk breaking that look of happiness that was beaming down at her. Like he finally had a partner in crime to join him in all of his debauchery.

"I—I had fun," she said. "Thanks for inviting me."

He reached an arm around her and squeezed tightly, completely unaware of how bleak she must have looked. But he didn't seem to care as he jumped up from her bed, slamming her door open and demanding for Dad to make them pancakes.

APPARENTLY FOR DUNCAN, finally having a girlfriend was like obtaining the ultimate free hall pass from being grounded. Melanie silently watched the way Mom hummed to herself when he left to see Leila, the sickening look of hope in her eyes. She probably really did think Leila would change him. After what she saw at that party, though, Melanie wasn't so convinced.

But she didn't allow herself to think about it too much, especially when she had a constant distraction to keep her company. Since their night on the docks, she saw Calvin every day, the two of them stealing moments together whenever they could. They would linger after closing up Scoops for the night, waiting for everyone to leave before she curled her arms around his shoulders as he pressed her up against the brick wall. On days off, Calvin would take her back to Sunset Rock, the two of them plunging into the water below, drying off on beach towels as they split grinders and watched the sun lazily set before them. The days they worked separate shifts were especially excruciating because it meant Melanie would likely not see Calvin outside of work, and by the way he would sneak into the tiny bathroom and kiss her hungrily for a few breaths before returning back to his shift, Melanie knew it was equally as excruciating for him.

They still kept it a secret from the Scoopers. Melanie liked having him just to herself—like they were in this safe, beautiful, perfect bubble that no one could touch. She knew at some point the bubble would eventually pop and they would all find out. But for now, she enjoyed watching him gaze longingly at her from a distance as they shuffled around the Scoopers, brushing elbows as they scooped cones, catching glances across The War Room.

Yet even when the heat between them was hilariously obvious, it seemed the rest of the Scoopers were too caught up in their own lives to realize what was going on.

Blake was now openly dating Zach, the two of them holding hands any moment they were together, Zach twirling his fingers through his curls when he leaned down to kiss him before dropping him off for a shift.

Jess was drowning in a sea of cake orders as the town geared up for the weekend of Haverfest, her shift solely dedicated to making one cake after another.

Then there was the trio that wasn't speaking to each other—*at all*. Ever since the party, it was dead silence between Rory, Jay, and Tyler, the three of them grumbling at each other roughly as they passed one another during shifts. Melanie wanted to ask what was going on, but still felt too hurt after they up and left her at the party that night. Yet Rory seemed too lost in her thoughts to notice. Her constant jokes and banter had completely vanished, making everything at Scoops seem slightly dimmer.

"What do you think happened?" Melanie asked Calvin one day, the two of them curled up together at Scallop Shell Beach, sipping on Strawberry Oreo milkshakes after a shift as soft waves from the ocean curled at their toes.

"Jay probably did or said something stupid."

"Well, he was with some girl when I found him," Melanie recalled.

"Doesn't surprise me," Calvin said. "And Rory got upset?"

Melanie looked over at him, realizing Calvin was no stranger to the situation. "You know."

"I'm pretty sure everyone knows *but* Jay. He's an idiot."

"Yeah, no kidding." Melanie huffed. "Is that why you don't like him?"

Calvin bristled. "That...and it's like he doesn't have much respect for anyone in authority. Especially Ron. It drives me crazy."

She thought about the way Jay rushed through closing that night of the party, how he was quick to break the rules without Calvin there. She decided to leave that particular detail out of the story from that night, at least for the time being.

It wasn't until the day of Haverfest that Melanie would experience all of them talking to each other again. It was like the joy of that day brightened everyone's spirits, and for a brief moment, everything felt normal.

She showed up the morning of Haverfest ten minutes early for her shift. She found Jess furiously finishing up cake orders, a streak of bright purple frosting across her forehead as she trimmed a rectangular cake with a piping bag.

"You have some frosting on your forehead."

Jess reached up and touched the frosting. "Fuck, and it's purple."

"Is that bad?"

"Purple stains worse than any other color," said Jess. "I'll probably have a line on my forehead for days."

"Ooof, sorry," she said, tying her unruly hair into a ponytail. She stopped religiously straightening her hair and now left it to dry naturally, letting it go wavy and completely wild. It was like catnip for Calvin—he seemed to always be combing his hands through it.

"Shouldn't you be off today? Do you need me to do anything?"

Jess finished up the trim, pressing her hand into her back as she stretched up straight. "Only one more after this and I'm done. If anyone calls and asks for a cake order, tell them we're not taking them for the rest of the weekend. If I have to mix another bowl of frosting and dye I think my eyes are going to fall out of my head."

She looked at her sympathetically. "Do you ever want someone else to do the cakes? I don't mind helping out, I would just need to learn."

Jess paused for a moment, looking at Melanie earnestly through her smudged glasses. Jess looked bone-tired—her ponytail shifting out of place, small bags underneath her eyes.

"Um," Jess said, shifting in her spot uncomfortably before leaning back over her last cake. "I'll think about it."

Melanie nodded, knowing that was probably the most she would get out of Jess for the day.

Calvin came through the back door, Blake trudging behind him.

"Aw Blake, why the long face," Melanie teased.

"This is my first summer with a boyfriend and I have to spend the entire festival day here with you losers," he snipped, slinking into the bathroom.

Melanie chuckled as Calvin walked up to the sign-in sheet, stepping close to Melanie until their bodies brushed up against each other. Jess was too engrossed in the trimming of the cake to notice Calvin looking down at Melanie, winking at her as he signed in.

"CAKE!"

The two of them flinched as Jess flung by them with her last cake, Blake ducking to let her through. "I'm sorry, but this absolutely blows," Blake mumbled, signing in as well. "Scoops better be paying for lunch."

"Already ordered pizza from Penny's, they'll be here at one," Calvin said. "I know it blows, but I promise, the tips are worth it."

"Like, in the three digits worth it?" Melanie asked.

Calvin winked again before heading to the front of the shop, flipping the sign to *Open.*

"Wait, did Calvin Ball just *wink?*" Blake asked in shock.

She shrugged, watching as he pushed the windows open, his tricep muscles flexing with each movement.

She smirked. "The man is a mystery."

Working a night shift the first Saturday was one thing, and working the night of the Fourth of July was another. But Haverfest was an entirely different kind of chaos that had Melanie feeling like she was going to melt into a puddle by 2 p.m.

She stepped up to the front as Calvin handed a customer a double scoop of Black Cherry Chunk. "We have a problem."

He frowned. "What?"

"We are completely out of Strawberry Cheesecake, Cookie Dough, and Caramel Pecan."

"Like, *out* out?"

Melanie nodded solemnly. "Not one tub left."

"Shit," he said softly to himself.

"*Language!*" Blake chirped before whirring the milkshake machine to life.

Calvin pointed to the back. "Second drawer of the desk we have a few magnets we can stick on the board to let people know we're sold out."

Melanie nodded, heading for the desk to grab three bright pink magnets with *Sold Out* written in big, bold letters. She charged for the front, every muscle in her body aching already. There was no way she was going to get through the entire shift without collapsing.

Calvin kicked a step stool from underneath the counter in Melanie's direction, but even on her tip-toes, she could barely reach the board. She lost her balance slightly, stumbling backward.

Calvin dropped the cup he was holding and lunged

for her, steadying her from the small of her back, the feel of his hands on her causing her to break a sweat, despite the fact that it was always freezing inside the shop. He kept his hands on her as she finished pressing the magnets to the flavors, hearing customers moan with disappointment when they saw their favorite flavor was now sold out.

"Well, well, what's this?"

Melanie's heart skipped at the sound of Rory's voice right next to her. She looked down and noticed her grinning roguishly.

Calvin released his grip as Melanie stepped down, immediately putting all of his attention on his customer.

"We're sold out of three flavors," Melanie said assuringly, pretending like it wasn't weird the way Calvin was just holding her. "Had to put up some signs."

"Hmm, signs, huh?" she said, her eyes twinkling with mischief. She was wearing a pair of ripped jean shorts and a white tank, a red bathing suit top peeping out underneath.

The door at the back of the shop flung open with a dramatic smack as Jay sauntered in, wearing a pair of athletic shorts, sandals, and nothing else. He stepped up to the front. "How's it going, little children?"

"I hate you," Blake deadpanned.

"If you're going to be up here, put on a shirt," Calvin said, not even looking in Jay's direction, like he knew Jay would show up half-naked.

Jay rolled his eyes as he stepped in the back, pulling on a Scoops shirt before coming to the front. "All right, what do you guys need?"

Melanie frowned. "Huh?"

"Here to help," Rory said, jumping up to sit on the counter, licking a scoop of Rocky Road on a cone.

"But you're not even working today?" Melanie asked, looking rather confused.

"Part of the tradition," Rory said. "If you're going to work a double on the worst day of the year so we don't have to, we come in and help when we can."

"Blake could use a break," Calvin said.

"Ooo, looks like army boy is playing favorites," Jay razzed in Melanie's direction.

"Are we *sure* he's the favorite?" Rory whispered in her ear.

"Shove it," Melanie whispered back, causing Rory to chuckle.

"I don't need a break," Blake said through a clenched jaw, his eyebrows furrowed.

"Actually, I think you do." Calvin pointed to someone standing near the side window.

It was Zach, holding a fluffy cone of cotton candy in one hand, and two tickets for the Ferris wheel in another.

Everyone *ooh*ed and *aah*ed as Blake's face turned crimson, unable to hide his deliriously happy expression.

"Go," Calvin said. "Be back in an hour."

He didn't even hesitate. He left immediately, flinging his hat on the desk next to the empty pizza box as he bolted out of the shop. Rory and Jay shifted to the counter on the right, taking customer orders in Blake's stead.

"That took zero convincing," Melanie said to Calvin, leaning toward him. "How'd you know Zach would be here?"

"Because I called him and told him to come," Calvin said. "Don't worry, you get your break when Blake gets back."

Melanie frowned. "But what about you?"

"I don't need a break." He handed change to his

customer. They smiled, tossing the few bills and coins right into the jar. He smiled back before looking down at Melanie, his eyes sparkly and blue and perfect.

Her heart skipped a beat. She pulled at the keys dangling from his belt loop when no one was looking, teasing him as she tugged on it slightly. "Actually," she whispered. "I think you do."

~

JESS AND TYLER were next to show up, giving Calvin and Melanie a chance to bail. Blake was already back and in a very cheerful mood, floating around Scoops as he served customers.

Calvin turned Jess's way. "Okay, I think we're close to being out of Mint Chocolate Chip, and there's a—"

"Calvin, get out of here now before I punch you in the face," Jess said sternly. It was true—a faint purple stain from the frosting that morning left a streak across her forehead.

He chuckled. "Okay, *fine.*"

"It's not like I don't work here," Jess said. "Now leave before I change my mind about helping."

"All right, all right, I'm out." Lifting his hands in surrender, he followed Melanie out the back door. When the door clicked shut, he curled his arms around her stomach and lifted her from behind, making her squeal.

He kissed her neck before placing her down. "Okay, I have a plan."

"Do you now?" She turned toward him, noticing that he already had his phone pressed to his ear.

"Ed, hi," Calvin said on the phone. "Listen, I have a break and I was hoping—"

Calvin paused as the person interrupted him, chuckling

at whatever Ed had to say. "If I say yes does this mean you'll help?"

Calvin rolled his eyes, a big grin on his face. "Okay, we'll be there in five."

"Be where?" she asked as he ended the call, sliding the phone back into his pocket.

But he was too rushed to answer, grabbing her hand and pulling her as he started to jog, a big smile on his face. "Let's go!"

The two of them ran down the side of Scoops and onto Main Street into a sea of colors and people.

Haverfest truly was like a massive party for the town. Tents lined the streets with food vendors and local art, the smell of fried clams and buttery lobster rolls wafting through the air. Big bags of kettle corn swung from the tops of tents as people walked up and down the center of the street, holding massive mounds of cotton candy and dripping Scoops cones.

It was all a blur as Calvin kept his pace, weaving through the crowds until they finally reached a large patch of green outside of the Episcopal church, which magically turned into a summer carnival overnight. And right in the center was one of the most gorgeous Ferris wheels Melanie had ever seen.

"Wow," she said breathlessly.

He kept tugging her hand, pulling her toward it and skipping the entire line.

"There he is!"

An older gentleman with a thin gray beard wearing a flannel, faded jeans, and work boots pulled Calvin into a fierce hug.

"Is this her?" asked the man, turning Calvin back to face her.

Calvin nodded, that big, goofy smile on his face. Like he couldn't believe it himself.

The man slapped him on the back. "Well, damn, boy. She's even prettier than you described."

She felt her face flush.

Calvin turned toward the man. "Squeeze us in?"

"You bet."

He grabbed Melanie's hand again as the man motioned them into the next open pod, telling the people complaining in line to cool it as he clicked the door shut behind them. The pod jolted slightly, then started moving backward.

She turned to Calvin. "So, I'm guessing that's Ed?"

He nodded. "That's Ed, he's my neighbor. He's also the fire chief, but more famously known in town as Santa Claus during the Festival of Lights."

"There's another festival?" Melanie balked. "Haverport really knows how to party."

"More like we know how to squeeze money out of tourists," he quipped, wrapping an arm around her waist and tugging her closer as the pod slowly climbed higher and higher into the humid, sunny sky.

She rolled her eyes. "Summer people."

He chuckled, holding her tightly to him as he traced his other hand along her cheek before cupping her whole head and leaning in for a kiss. His lips were salty, sweet, and smooth like caramel as he tipped her head back, rolling his tongue against hers, making her shiver down to her toes. His hand around her waist teased playfully at the hem of her shirt as he brushed his thumb against her smooth skin. But he didn't push any further—just kept brushing the small of her back.

The pod jolted again as it paused at the top, causing their kiss to break apart, and making the two of them laugh.

"Tell me, was this just an excuse to get me alone so you could make out with me?"

"Always." He twirled an unruly wave sticking out from her ponytail. "But it's also the best view of town."

She turned her head to look outside of the pod, and sure enough, the view was breathtaking. Haverport was bursting with life as crowds of people weaved through the tents lining Main Street. Parents chased kids hyped up on sugar all throughout the carnival, with lots of laughter and cheers ringing from the green and the street below. From the top, you could even see the beaches at Hillside Park, completely packed to the brim with beachgoers. But it was the water that was truly showing off, the waves sparkling and dancing underneath the sun.

Melanie looked up at Calvin, his eyes like a portrait of Haverport coming to life, so intensely vibrant and blue. She realized at that moment that this town, this job, this *person* in front of her finally made her feel like she truly belonged —like the stormy gray clouds of her life had finally dispersed, making room for the bright, shimmering sun.

Chapter Sixteen

THE INSIDE of Scoops was an utter disaster. Chocolate and strawberry dip had slipped down the side of the canister and onto the counter, now hardened and impossible to try to scrub off. Smushed candy and crushed-up cones with paper sleeves lined the floors, trampled underneath feet that scurried from counter to ice cream freezer to sauce dispensers and back. They sold out of seven flavors by eight o'clock and yet somehow, they still had a tub and a half of Ron's specialty Blue Bombshell. It seemed the rest of the town agreed with the Scoopers' sentiment toward the new flavor. Calvin said not selling it out was a good thing; it meant Ron wouldn't order it again if they couldn't even get through the three initial tubs.

Melanie had to pause serving customers three times to fill up the spoon containers. She already had to dump the tip containers twice, the piles of money stacked on the desk making her head spin. She was coming out of the walk-in holding three new cans of whipped cream when she saw the rest of the Scoopers emerging through the back door. She watched in amazement as Rory, Tyler, Jay, and Jess all slipped their hats on and dispersed inside the shop. Jay flicked on the stereo and immediately started to sing, washing the dishes that were piled up in the sink. Jess and Tyler started grabbing stock for refills. Rory walked over to Melanie, the tip of her nose sunburnt from the sunny day, and reached her deeply tan arms up to Melanie's cheeks, smushing them together. "You did it, you survived."

"Barely," Melanie groaned. "I feel like I'm about to fall on my face."

"Well, don't worry," Rory teased. "Looks like you'll have someone to catch you when you fall."

She rolled her eyes and followed her to the front, placing the whipped cream cans inside the small fridge as Calvin flipped the sign to *Closed*.

"Don't we still have a line?" She eyed the line that still snaked down the Scoops parking lot and onto the street.

"There are some exceptions to the rule," Calvin said. "Today is an exception."

"Thank God," Blake said. "I think at this point, I'm going to be scooping ice cream in my nightmares."

All seven of the Scoopers bustled around the shop, going through the closing motions like exhausted drones. They chaffed and teased one another, and a few times Melanie even saw Calvin chuckling at someone's ridiculous joke. Rory and Jay were taunting each other again like two idiots, Jess even adding a quip or two to their banter. She felt like she was floating as she laughed with everyone else, handing out more cones and saucy sundaes pillowed with whipped cream and bright red cherries. Customers kept smiling at the happy little Scoopers inside the shop, tossing even more tips into the jar.

"Melanie!"

She turned quickly, spotting her mom calling at her

from Calvin's window, Dad by her side. She beamed at them.

"Here," Calvin said, reaching for the half-scooped waffle cone in her hand. "I'll finish this one, you take them."

Melanie half skipped over to them, a big smile on her face. "Hi, welcome to Scoops! How can I help you?"

Dad chuckled. "Well, don't you look happy after having to work all day."

Melanie blushed, sneaking a quick glance at Calvin scooping next to her, not able to contain the grin plastered on her face. "I am happy."

It was weird, seeing her parents like this—smiling, content, not a worry to be had. Mom reached her hand through the window and squeezed her wrist. "Well that makes us happy, sweetheart."

Melanie wasn't sure why, but the comment startled her for a moment. She wondered if she wasn't trying hard enough to be happy at home. Maybe her trying to focus so much on school and success wasn't exactly what her parents needed, but instead, they just wanted a kid that was happy and bubbly and smiling at them from inside an ice cream shop.

"Two scoops, Vanilla Bean and Death By Chocolate," Dad said. "Sugar cone."

"*Two* scoops? Harold, you don't need all of that."

"Oh, I certainly do, it's Haverfest," he dished right back, winking at Melanie as he did so.

Mom rolled her eyes. "Will you be coming home after, sweetie?"

"Actually," Calvin said from behind her, handing the other customer at the window their waffle cone. "We sort of have plans."

Melanie's eyebrows furrowed. "We do?"

"We *all* have plans," Rory rang out, scrubbing at the hardened strawberry dip on the counter like she was happy to be doing it.

"Oh. You guys really do love your traditions."

"Keeps us from killing each other," Rory joked, now turning toward the chocolate dip disaster.

"All right, well, not too late?" Mom said, looking between Calvin and Melanie in a very knowing manner. Like she *knew* getting home late had become a habit lately.

Rory glanced at her curiously, but Melanie ignored her gaze as her parents left and she called up the next customer in line.

With the seven of them working, it didn't take long to kill the line and have the shop closed up by 10:30. They all huddled together as Calvin counted the tips, making bets on how much it would actually be.

"I'm going to say one seventy five," Jay said.

"Dude, way too high," Tyler bantered. "Last year it was one ten."

"Last year it was raining," Rory said. "And we *still* made one ten. I say one sixty."

"You're all wrong," Calvin said, finishing up his counting. He exchanged piles of money from the bags in the drawer with some fifties, then divided up the bills he held into three and handed one stack each to Blake and Melanie.

Blake counted quickly, his eyes wide in shock. "One eighty seven."

They all cheered. Blake kept dusting off his shoulders playfully like it was all his doing as they ruffled his hair, hands patting Melanie on the back and squeezing her arms.

"A newbie record!" Jay cheered.

"Are you losers ready or not?" Jess asked.

They all went silent.

"Why do I feel like I *never* know what's going on around here?" Blake asked.

Melanie chuckled. "Seems to be a theme."

Jay bristled, crossing his arms like he was ready for battle. "I'm ready. Give us your worst."

They all remained silent as Jess reached into the cake freezer, pulling out a fluorescent blue cake that Melanie hadn't noticed all day, likely tucked into the back.

Everyone groaned.

"You did us dirty, Jess," Tyler said.

"Just you wait," replied Jess, placing the cake down on the counter. She turned toward Melanie and Blake. "Because you guys sacrificed your festival day for us, it is tradition here at Scoops for the rest of the staff to eat the most disgusting ice cream cake possible in your honor."

"Last year it was a combo of Mint Chocolate Chip and Black Cherry Chunk with gummy bears and grape jelly in the center," Rory explained. "The year before that was Pistachio and Caramel Pecan with every single nut we have in the shop at the center—and hot sauce."

"Pistachio, you must have loved that," Blake mumbled to Jay. Jay shoved his side.

"This year, it's quite obvious the flavor," Jess said. "Our favorite blue devil with a core center of maraschino cherries, marshmallow sauce whipped together with a sour green apple syrup, and crushed up toffee."

They groaned. Everyone knew toffee was the worst candy for ice cream—you would be picking it out of your teeth for days.

"Calvin, you first, as always," Jess said.

Melanie turned and saw that Calvin already had a container in his hand as he ladled a thick scoop of wet nuts onto the cake, spreading it on the top.

"Dude, every year," Jay said. "Can't you think of something original?"

"Not when you make that same comment *every year*," Calvin quipped, a sly smirk on his face as he returned the container to the front.

Jess turned to Blake. "Your turn, pick the worst possible topping you can think of."

Blake thought about it for a minute. "Anything in the shop?"

Jess nodded. "Anything."

Blake grinned sinisterly before he pivoted, heading for the frosting fridge in the back. He fumbled for a few moments before pulling out the rest of Jess's purple frosting piping bag from earlier.

"Now that's just mean," Rory said. "We'll all look like the purple people eaters for a week."

"I literally don't feel bad for you," Blake said as he started haphazardly piping around the edge of the cake, his dollops uneven and looking nothing like the beautiful lines Jess had come to perfect.

"Melanie, your turn."

She tapped her finger against her chin as they all watched her with anxious anticipation.

"The worst topping, huh?" she asked them.

They nodded as she picked up the cake and walked it toward the front, the Scoopers right on her heels. She placed the cake down on the front counter and peeled back a stainless steel lid.

"You wouldn't," Jay whispered in disbelief.

"Oh, she would," Rory said with pride.

"I'm going to throw up eating this," Tyler moaned.

Melanie lifted a ladle from the container of chocolate dip, then slowly poured it over the top as it hardened against the wet nuts and the frosting, dripping down the sides of the blue cake.

"This has got to be the worst one yet," Tyler said, truly looking like he was going to hurl just by the sight of it.

Jess beamed, like this was one of her proudest creations compared to the hundreds of beautiful cakes she decorated that summer already.

"Who's in my car?" Calvin asked, reaching for a switch as he flicked off the lights.

Everyone started fighting about who would ride with who, Jay declaring he'd take the front seat of Tyler's Jeep so he could pick the music, Rory chasing him out to try and claim the seat instead. Jess boxed up the cake and handed Melanie a stack of plates, spoons, and napkins as they left, Calvin pulling up the rear as he locked up Scoops for the night. When no one was looking, he dipped down to brush his lips against her, making her face tingle with delight as she followed him to the truck.

CALVIN TURNED onto the dirt lot that led to Scallop Shell Beach, Tyler's Jeep just a few paces behind. Out in the distance, Melanie could see a shadowy figure stoking at a flickering bonfire. As they drew closer and Calvin parked the car, Melanie noticed it was Ron who was poking at the fire with a long, scraggly branch.

Ron lifted his arms and cheered as they all hopped out of their cars, Jay wrestling Blake out of the back seat of the Jeep as Blake unleashed a few colorful expletives in his direction.

She followed the group to the fire, noticing that Ron had already set everything up for them. Beach towels were lined up around the outside of the fire as Scoopers started to claim their spots. Tyler opened up a big cooler that was already stuffed with sodas, and Rory grabbed one of the extra blankets stacked up on a bench.

"So, how much today?" Ron asked Calvin.

"One hundred and eighty seven buckaroonis," Blake interrupted with glee, like he still couldn't believe the number himself. He plopped down on a towel and cracked open a can of orange soda.

Ron's mouth fell open as he looked back over at Calvin, and Calvin shrugged. Ron shifted toward Melanie. "Well, hello, Melanie, how was your first festival shift?"

"Frightening," she answered honestly. "The lines would just never end."

Ron laughed. "Thank you for working today, I really appreciate it. And I'm glad you guys were able to take a break," he said, his eyebrows lifting slightly in Calvin's direction.

Melanie followed Calvin to the other side of the bonfire, walking close enough beside him so no one could hear. "So tell me, how many people know about us?"

Calvin chuckled softly. "Gram and Ed," he said. "And Ron."

"Are you *sure* that's it?" she whispered.

Calvin smirked. "Okay, and Kevin."

She rolled her eyes as she sat down on a beach towel, a distance enough from Calvin so things looked casual—even though the space between them pulled at her like a magnet.

She watched as Jess started slicing up their cake and handing fat slices to everyone.

"Well, here it goes," Rory said.

"I really don't think I can do this," Tyler said.

"Suck it up," Jay said. "You had to watch me eat these gross creations two years in a row."

"Yeah, but you probably *liked* the Pistachio cake," Blake quipped.

Jay gave him the finger as they all dipped into their slices, lifting their spoons in honor of the Scoopers who sacrificed their day, and took bites.

Tyler coughed. "Yep, bad."

"Honestly, is it weird to say that I think this green apple marshmallow concoction actually makes the ice cream taste better?" Rory asked.

Ron frowned. "You guys really hate our new flavor that much?"

All of the Scoopers chuckled uncomfortably. Calvin reached over to pat Ron on the back. "Not a winner, man, sorry."

Ron scowled, digging into his slice. "Well, I like it. And I don't think this cake is that bad."

"Of course you don't," Jay mumbled, causing Rory to cover her face and turn, stifling her laughter.

"Am I crazy for actually *wanting* to taste the cake?" Melanie asked.

Calvin smiled at her as he reached over for the cake box, slicing up three much smaller slivers and placing them on plates for her, Blake, and himself.

"Jay," Ron started. "Did my eyes deceive me or did I see you walking around town with a lady friend today?"

Blake raised his eyebrows at Jay as he took a plate from Calvin. "A *lady* friend?" Blake teased.

Jay grinned deviously. "You may have, perchance, seen me with, as you say it, a *lady* friend today."

"Ahhh," Ron said with a smile on his face, digging into

his cake, oblivious of the mood shift that swiftly traveled throughout the group like a cold front.

Rory took a big bite of her cake, wincing at the taste of it, keeping her eyes on the fire. Tyler's eyes were on his feet, silently kicking the sand.

"And are we going to meet this lady friend of yours someday?" Ron asked, still completely oblivious.

"Oh Ronny-boy," Jay said, his toothy grin shining brightly from the fire. "I can't just give up *that* easy, I've gotta keep my paws in the game."

"The game?" Ron asked, looking confused by every word that just came out of Jay's mouth.

"You know, can't settle down if I still got lots of game to play," Jay winked, digging back into his cake.

Calvin sighed audibly, shaking his head.

Jay sat up straight. "What, army boy? Got something to say to me?"

He spooned a cherry and a bit of ice cream, sliding it into his mouth. "Nope."

Jay scoffed. "That's right. What would you know about having game anyway? Never seen you with a *lady* friend before—you probably wouldn't know game if it struck you in the face."

Melanie glanced over at Calvin, noticing the big smirk on his face as he broke off another bite of his cake. "No game, huh?"

"Nope, none, zero, zilch," Jay listed off.

Calvin placed his plate down on his towel gently. Then, in one swift motion, leaned in toward Melanie, closing the space between them. He grazed a hand underneath her chin and pulled her face close to his, their noses just barely brushing against each other. "And what do you think, Mel? Do I have game?"

Melanie heard the sharp, dramatic inhales from the group, waiting with bated breath for Melanie's response. She smiled up at Calvin, his eyes playful and menacing. Like he knew *exactly* what he was doing.

Melanie nodded her head in confirmation. "Yeah, he's got game."

Calvin grinned down at her before planting a long, lingering kiss on her lips.

And the group went absolutely wild.

"WHAT?!" Blake said, bolting up from his blanket, pacing back and forth. "I was literally with them all day! How did I not know!"

"Called it!!" Rory cheered, lifting her spoon in the air like a trophy.

Jay was gaping at them, his mouth wide in utter shock, then started outright screaming.

Tyler kept nodding his head, a smile on his face. "That's dope, that's dope."

Melanie slowly pulled her lips apart from Calvin's, the two of them chuckling at the scene they just created.

"God, finally," Melanie quipped. She scooched over to him, taking a seat in between his legs as she leaned back against his chest. Making a show of it, she reached for his plate and took a bite of his cake with his spoon, then spooned another bite and handed it to him.

"I—I—I have no words," Jay said.

"God, you guys are all so stupid," Jess said. "It's been literally obvious from the beginning."

Blake frowned, dropping back down onto his spot with a thud. "How was it obvious?"

"If you guys paid even an ounce of attention, you would have noticed that Calvin can't take his eyes off her. Even during Mel's first shift he was trying hard to be his usual asshole self, but he kept sneaking glances at her when she wasn't looking."

Melanie's heart swelled as she tilted her head back to take a look at Calvin. *He* was now blushing like he just got caught. He smiled shyly and dipped his face down toward hers, planting a kiss on her cheek before pulling her in even closer to him.

"Well, I knew," Ron confessed.

"Of course you did, you're practically his Dad," Jay snipped, sounding irritated with every word.

Calvin shrugged in agreement.

"So how long has this little romance been going on?" Tyler asked, pointing his spoon at the two of them.

"Hmmm, three weeks?" Melanie asked, looking up at Calvin for confirmation.

"Nineteen days," he answered.

"You're pathetic," Jess mumbled. He reached over and shoved her shoulder, but Melanie noticed that Jess was actually *smiling*.

Tyler looked down at his phone, counting out nineteen days. "So that would mean the Fourth of July..."

The rest of his sentence lingered in the air as both Melanie and Calvin nodded. Melanie noticed Rory staring at her from across the fire, her face a mixture of confusion and hurt. That nineteen days had gone by and Melanie had yet to mention anything to her.

Tyler smiled again. "I guess I'm glad I called out sick."

"Melanie, Melanie, sweet Melanie," Jay said, folding his hands together like a prayer. "You do realize you don't have to do this, right? I get it, he's got that broody soldier vibe going on. But you are aware there are better *options* out there, right?"

"Sounds like someone is jealous," Calvin said, his voice full of sarcasm...and a hint of triumph.

"No, no, not jealous," Jay answered defensively. "Just, you know, looking out for a friend."

"Well you have nothing to worry about," Melanie said. "Especially if you have lots of game, right?"

The entire group roared with laughter as Jay scowled at her. Even Calvin couldn't contain it, his deep laugh rumbling out of him before giving her an extra squeeze and kissing the top of her head.

Chapter Seventeen

Duncan abruptly swung open the front door of the cottage after his run, his face steely and serious.

Melanie frowned, her mouth half full of the toasted ham and cheese sandwich she made for lunch—her attempt at trying to cook for herself while her parents were back in Garrison, meeting with their real estate agent who said they finally had an offer on the house.

"Why the face?" she asked.

He glowered as he reached into the fridge, twisting open the chocolate milk and drinking straight from the carton. She never touched the chocolate milk, always for that reason.

He wiped his mouth with the back of his hand, pointing out the window with the carton. "The sergeant is here to see you."

She twisted in her chair to look out the window, and sure enough, there was Calvin. He was standing outside of his truck, leaning against the door with one hand casually in his pocket, the other holding a small paperback open as he read.

She turned back toward her brother, noticing how the lines on his face went harsh and rigid. "Are you seeing that asshole?" he asked curtly.

She felt irritated at his tone of voice. "So what if I am? And don't call him an asshole. You don't know him."

Before he could respond, she left the cottage, heading toward Calvin's direction. He smiled brightly as she approached, sliding the book into his back pocket before curling Melanie into his arms. "Hey," he said sweetly.

"Hi," Melanie said softly. "Did Duncan talk to you?"

Calvin shook his head. "No," he murmured quietly to her. "But there was a lot of glaring involved, kind of like what he's doing right now on the porch."

She turned her head and sure enough, Duncan was now sitting on the porch swing, one arm slung over the top in an attempt to look casual, but the stern look on his face told another story.

She turned back to him and sighed. "While I do love an unexpected visit, want to tell me why you're here?"

"We're going out. I'm taking you to the beach."

"Like, what we do every day?"

"Nope. This beach is special, it's not even in town. We'll have to take the *highway*."

"God *forbid*," Melanie teased back, making him chuckle. "Is there a reason for this special occasion? Twenty-day anniversary?"

Calvin shook his head as he cracked a smile. "*Funny.* No, no special occasion. This is more like an apology."

Melanie pouted. "Why?"

"Because." Calvin sighed, glancing up at the sky for a moment before continuing. "Because I kind of feel bad that I told all of these people about us and didn't even ask you if that's okay."

"Oh."

He looked back down at her, his eyes full of anguish. "And then I got all caught up in trying to get at Jay and just kissed you in front of everyone and you just went along with it but I—" He hesitated, combing through a piece of her hair before tucking it behind her ear. "I'm not even sure if you wanted them to know and I kinda feel like shit now. I'm sorry."

Truthfully, Melanie hadn't thought much about it until this moment. She was so happy these days that sometimes, she felt light as a feather—like she couldn't get a grasp on reality because her head was just floating in hazy pink clouds. But as she briefly thought it through, she realized that maybe there was a deeper reason why Calvin couldn't help sharing his happiness with the world, and why she wasn't so quick to do the same.

"Please forgive me," he said, breaking up the silence sitting between them.

She reached up to touch his cheek, stroking it with her thumb. "I do, and I'm not mad. I guess I'm just—" She hesitated, looking over at her brother. Duncan quickly shifted his gaze out to the ocean, pretending like he wasn't watching this entire interaction intently from afar.

She turned back to Calvin. "I'm just scared that if I admit that something good is happening in my life, I'll just lose it."

"You won't lose me," he answered, his voice attentive and steady. "And I promise, I will do everything in my power to make sure of it."

Melanie gave him a gushy smile, reaching around his shoulders as Calvin pulled her in for a tight hug.

"Who knew the twenty-day mark meant getting so serious," she teased.

Calvin chuckled, his head bending in Duncan's direction. "I'm guessing kissing you would be a bad idea right now, correct?"

"Yeah probably," she whispered in his ear.

He let her go, pinching her side. "Go get your suit."

She bounded up the porch steps, Duncan's eyes on her intently.

She crossed her arms. "What?"

He swung back and forth for a few beats, making a point of it. "Why didn't you tell me?"

Melanie shrugged. "Didn't have much to say yet."

He looked at her with a hurt expression. "I told you about Leila right away. We're *twins*, we're supposed to tell each other stuff."

The irritation Melanie felt before roiled inside of her, boiling from annoyance to resentment and fury. "Twins, huh? Twins that barely talk to each other for over two and a half years?"

"That's different."

"No, it's not, Duncan." She flung open the front door. "You know it's not."

She beelined for the stairs, heading for her room to gather her things. She didn't care if she just woke up the lion and unleashed a whole new storm on their house. Because this time, she felt her own storm brewing inside of her, the one that slowly chipped away at her soul, day after day after day. And she was tired of trying to contain it.

SHE SAT in the passenger seat in silence, sipping on a Sandy Cove latte as Calvin veered the truck off an exit indicating Clipper's Island. She was deep in thought, pondering through every detail of her life over the past three years and trying to pinpoint where it all went wrong.

She felt Calvin's hand brush against hers, cupping it with a gentle squeeze. "Hey, talk to me."

She exhaled audibly, turning her head toward the oak trees that lined the road as they dispersed, revealing a rickety bridge that stretched out to a small island on the coast. "I just wish I had done something differently."

"With Duncan?

She nodded solemnly. "We used to be so close. And I just feel like it's all my fault that we're not anymore."

Calvin pulled the truck into an empty parking lot. He unbuckled his seatbelt and slid close to Melanie, their legs pressed together as he took her hand, threading his fingers through hers. "None of this is your fault."

"Then why does it feel that way?" she muttered faintly.

He sighed, looking out of the window toward the empty beach in front of him. "Because we love them. And when we watch them crumble before our eyes, we think we failed in trying to save them."

His use of *we* struck Melanie's heart. He was no stranger to this. He understood exactly how she felt, but on a much deeper level. She couldn't even fathom not having her parents by her side, how painful that must have been for him. How painful it still *was* for him, even though he never showed it. He kept it hidden deep within his fortress of rules and guidelines and structure.

He lifted her hand and kissed her knuckles as she looked out at the sea, the waves crashing into the sand at a much greater height than the calm, shallow waters in Haverport. "So...want to tell me why we're here?" she asked.

"Any time my grandfather wanted to go to the beach, he

meant here," Calvin started. "I think because no one really comes to this one, it's off the beaten path and there are no restaurants or anything. Pop said he enjoyed the purity of it compared to the packed beaches back home. Felt like an escape."

"So we're escaping?"

"Well, kind of," he replied. "I made this big deal about us to everyone yesterday, and I wanted to take you somewhere quiet."

Melanie hesitated for a moment. "Why *did* you tell everyone?"

He smiled sheepishly. "I just...rarely have good news to share."

Melanie felt like her heart cracked.

"I probably seem pathetic," he continued. "Sad boy gets an amazing girlfriend and now can't seem to control himself because he's way too excited about it."

"G-girlfriend?"

Calvin smirked. "Come on, headband. You don't kiss someone like *that* unless that's your girlfriend."

Melanie chuckled at the similar words her father had spoken. "I admit," she whispered. "I kind of like the sound of it."

Calvin rubbed his face, trying to contain the massive grin that he couldn't seem to control. "Me too."

She smirked. "Although...I never thought I would be dating someone who only allows himself one coffee a day. Seriously, who does that?"

He laughed, shaking his head as he reached for his herbal tea. "No one needs that much caffeine. Just one a day will do."

She rolled her eyes playfully as he stepped out of the truck, gathering their things.

They walked pinkie-in-pinkie down to the beach, plop-ping their stuff on the sand. Calvin immediately peeled off his shirt and ran for the water as she chuckled, her eyes fixed on the way his back muscles flexed when he lifted his arms before diving into the waves.

She now had a boyfriend. *A boyfriend.*

He popped out of the ocean, water dripping down his buzzed head and along his neck, gesturing for her to join him.

She peeled off her light blue sundress, the one she'd bought particularly at Lacey's to match the sky-blue elastic headband in her hair. She tugged that off as well, tossing it down on her towel as she jogged to the water, jumping in as Calvin quickly caught her waist, the two of them stumbling backward into a crashing wave.

~

"How do you take your tea, dear?"

"Um, I'm not sure," Melanie answered, looking over at Gram.

The two of them sat at the tiny round kitchen table, covered in a white lace tablecloth that looked like it came straight from a cozy English cottage. The entire house did, actually—full of knick knacks and big reading chairs with afghans slung over the top, piled with little embroidered pillows with seashells stitched in the center. Along the wall of the living room was a massive bookshelf heaping with paperback novels, the top of the shelf completely covered with books almost up to the ceiling and a few neatly stacked piles along the floor.

She glanced over at Calvin in the kitchen as he turned off the kettle, placing it down on a hot pad in the center of the table next to a basket of tea bags. He kneeled down in front of a tiny cupboard full of delicate, mismatched tea cups. "Which one do you want, Gram?"

"Hmm." Gram looked deep in thought about it. "I'll take the gold one with the flowers. Oh, but do give Melanie the yellow one."

"*Gram.*"

"Oh, stop that," she replied, patting Calvin's shoulder. "That's my favorite one, and I want her to use it."

He sighed. "Fine."

He stood up holding three cups, placing down a delicate cup with gold trimming and green tulips in front of Gram, and a clunky yellow mug in front of Melanie.

It was almost like her own yellow sunshine mug—but so much better. The mug had a sun painted on the front with a smiley face, the rays stretching across the side of the mug in bright orange and red colors. Clearly the work of a little kid.

"Did you make this?" she asked.

He flushed, pouring hot water carefully into Gram's cup.

"He sure did, when he was six years old," Gram explained, her eyes beaming with pride at the happy yellow mug. "He wanted me to have a special mug for my tea. But after a little while, he told me it didn't feel that special anymore and wanted to get me a *nicer* one. He's been buying me 'nicer' cups ever since." She gestured toward the little cupboard when she said it.

She looked at Calvin. "You bought her all of those? That's so sweet."

He smiled shyly as he nodded his head, now pouring water into Melanie's yellow mug.

Gram leaned in close to her. "I'm honestly afraid the boy has a hoarding problem," she said, gesturing toward the heaping bookshelf. "I can't even imagine what his home is going to look like when he's my age."

She laughed, mimicking the way Gram dipped her bag of Earl Grey into her mug as Calvin tore open a packet of Chamomile. "I don't even remember the last time I had a cup of tea," Melanie admitted. "Also, your home is lovely, thanks for letting me come for dinner."

Her eyes twinkled. "Oh I am just *thrilled* that I'm finally getting to know you. My Calvin has been very selfish and hasn't shared you with me yet."

"We've been...busy," he said, glancing over at Melanie, his eyes dancing at her flirtatiously.

A bolt of excited energy zipped through her as she thought about the two of them just hours earlier, cuddled up close on their beach towels at Clipper's Island, her leg curled over his. One of his arms wrapped tightly around her waist as the other reached over to play with her hair, their faces close enough to touch as they kept sneaking long glances at one another, feeling as lazy and content as the sun that set slowly behind them. They finally moved from their little cocoon when the sun got dangerously low along the horizon, Calvin inviting her to have dinner with him and Gram. They grabbed Chinese takeout on their way to Calvin's home, just two streets down from Scallop Shell Beach.

"Ah yes, how could I forget, the ice cream shop," Gram said, either oblivious to the way Calvin and Melanie were staring at each other, or at least pretending to be. "Calvin's first and forever love."

"No, *you* are my first and forever love," he said, making her giggle at the fierce way he leaned over to kiss her pale, wrinkly cheek.

"So, Melanie, tell me more about yourself," Gram said.

"Calvin has told me absolutely nothing. Will you be going to college in the fall?"

"Actually, I have one more year left of high school," she admitted. "But I'm hoping to go to Yale next year."

"*Yale*, wow," Gram said breathily. "So you *are* smart. Calvin told me you were, but that's on a whole other level."

Melanie smiled bashfully. "Thanks. We'll see if I get in."

"You'll get in," Calvin said. At this point, he was caught up about her dream of going to Yale. She told him about how hard she worked at Garrison Prep, how scared she was that it was all about to be for nothing. He reassured her, just like her father. Made her feel calm and secure as he stroked a hand through her hair.

Gram sighed in Calvin's direction. "I wish you were going to college, sweetheart. It's such a shame."

Melanie's gut dropped, realizing that in their extensive conversations about her own dream, she had yet to ask what Calvin was doing this fall. She was having a terrible start to this whole "girlfriend" thing.

"I am going to college, Gram," Calvin responded.

Gram rolled her eyes. "I don't mean a community college, I mean a *university*. I wish you would just let me help you pay for school."

Calvin shook his head defiantly. "We already discussed this. You've done enough for me, you are not paying for school."

Gram exhaled noisily, looking disgruntled. "You get that stubborn pride from your grandfather, and it drives me nuts."

He smiled at her comment, like he was proud to be compared to him.

"All right, now go get those cookies on the table that I

baked, secretly hoping you would bring her over today," she said, winking at Melanie now. "These were the only cookies Calvin ever actually liked as a boy, other than Oreos."

"Because Oreos are the best," he said, heading over to the kitchen to grab a plate of fresh-baked oatmeal chocolate chip cookies.

"They're stale and made in a factory, not with love," Gram teased. "But of course, that never stopped our Calvin here from ordering Oreo ice cream every day after school. I tried to get him to order anything else, but it was never an option. Too stubborn to change things up."

Melanie watched him closely as he sat down with the cookies, handing one each to her and Gram before grabbing two himself. A part of her could understand how that felt— to turn to something familiar when everything else felt chaotic and uncertain in life. For Melanie, it was textbooks. For Calvin, it was Oreo ice cream. Because sometimes, when everything felt unsteady and unsure, the familiarity of that one thing helped keep your feet planted on the shore.

Chapter Eighteen

MELANIE FELT her phone buzz in her pocket. She reached for it quickly, noticing it was a text from Calvin, then hid it behind her crossed legs as she opened the screen.

It was a picture of Gram, sitting at the kitchen table in her robe, holding her yellow sunshine mug with a fresh batch of oatmeal chocolate chip cookies in front of her.

CALVIN

She says she's ready for you to visit her again.

She chuckled, typing back.

MELANIE

She's almost as desperate as you are. It hasn't even been a day!

She watched the little gray bubbles dance with his immediate reply.

CALVIN

What can I say? The Balls are crazy about
you, headband.

"If you're going to join this meeting, phones must be away," said Mrs. Pearson curtly. "Otherwise, you may leave."

Melanie shoved her phone in her pocket, looking up at Mrs. Pearson's puckered lips, like she just ate something incredibly sour and was about to spit it out. "Sorry," Melanie mumbled.

Jan sniggered next to Melanie, singsonging quietly in her ear, "Someone got caught."

"Yeah, who ya texting?" Dan asked, leaning over her with a mischievous grin.

Melanie rolled her eyes as Mrs. Pearson stepped back toward the front, calling the official Sandy Cove Beach Association meeting into order. "It's that time of year yet again for us to talk details about the Sandy Cove block party," she said stoically, without an ounce of enthusiasm in her voice.

Regardless of her cold demeanor, the room burst out in cheers. Melanie was told she could join today's meeting as they talked about details for the party, especially since Mom had now coerced her into helping.

"As you know, each cottage will be bringing some kind of game or activity for everyone. Remember to *please* keep it kid-friendly," Mrs. Pearson stated, her eyes pointedly on Tim Mackey, who was snickering as she made her point. "Cottage one, you first."

Each cottage presented what activity they would be contributing to the block party, as well as any foods and drinks they planned on adding to the potluck lunch. The

Bentleys said they would be bringing corn hole—again—and the Lancasters (cottage three) would take on stocking the water balloons this year, which garnered a round of applause. Then it was their turn.

"We'll be doing a Jello treasure hunt," Mom announced with a grin.

Mrs. Pearson frowned. "And what is that?"

"We fill up two kiddie pools with Jello, then drop a toy soldier or something inside of it. The first person to find it with their feet wins."

"That's abhorrently vile," Mrs. Pearson said.

"That's *brilliant*," Jan said at the same time, turning toward Dan. "Oh, I'm *so* going to kick your ass."

The room's buzzing over the Jello-foot-treasure-hunt overpowered Mrs. Pearson's objections to the activity, and after many strenuous attempts to kill the idea, she finally resigned to it—writing "Jello atrocity" as cottage five's activity on the whiteboard behind her.

Jan turned toward Melanie, beaming with excitement. "Will you be making the Jello?"

Melanie nodded with a smile. "Yep. She's even recruited Calvin to help."

"Oh, ho, ho," Dan said, leaning back into his chair. "He's going *down*."

"Be nice," Dad said. "We don't want to scare him away."

"Oh, I think it would take more than that at this point," Jan said, nudging Melanie's arm and making her blush.

MELANIE PULLED into a practically empty parking lot at Hillside Park. Now that they were official residents of the town, her parents were able to buy a pass for the season at a discount—meaning Melanie could drive Mom's car over to the park when it was too cloudy or drizzly to ride her bike.

Rory was already there, arms crossed tightly across her chest as she sat along the ledge that divided the parking lot and the beach. She clutched a cup of coffee in one hand, another one by her side with *SC* written in big, bold letters. Shorthand for Sandy Cove latte.

She closed the door and sat down on the ledge, picking up the latte. "You didn't have to."

"Calvin said it's your favorite," she replied. "Although, he tried to convince me to buy you an herbal tea instead, not sure why."

She chuckled, making a mental note to give him crap about that later. "So, too cold to lay on the beach?"

"Too wet, actually," Rory replied, reaching down and grabbing a fistful of sand. "It's still damp from the rain last night."

She nodded, taking a sip of her latte. The break in conversation was agonizing as they sat there in silence. Talking to Rory had always felt natural to her. But now, with so much that needed to be said between the two of them, the words didn't come so easily.

Rory exhaled audibly like she was ready to get it over with. "Why didn't you tell me about Calvin?"

"Why did you ditch me at the party?"

Silence again.

"Okay, that's fair," Rory said. "That was a dick move and I'm sorry."

Melanie took a slow sip of her drink before she continued. "What happened that night?"

"Ugh, what didn't happen," Rory replied. "Blake bailed

early with Zach because Jay was being his usual dumb-ass self, and then Jay said something about my body that was really harsh."

Melanie rolled her eyes, shaking her head. "What a dick."

"Thank you, he is," Rory said. "Also, I don't think I've ever heard you use that word before, and now I feel like a proud mom."

"Only speaking the truth," Melanie replied.

Rory smirked. "True that. Anyway, I was upset, and then Tyler sort of went off on him, and it all just blew up. I should have gone through the house to find you, but I..." She sighed, taking a sip of her coffee before continuing. "I was so upset about it, that Tyler just wanted to get me out of there, get me home."

"I'm sorry," Melanie said softly. "That must have been hard."

"It was, but you shouldn't be sorry," Rory said. "I'm the one who screwed up and treated you like garbage. I do not deserve your friendship."

Melanie shrugged. "Too late."

Her shoulders relaxed as relief flooded her face. "Do you ever get tired of being nice? You're so goddamn good at it."

She smiled timidly. "Do you remember what you told me on my first day at Scoops?"

Rory grimaced. "Did I call Calvin an ass-hat? I'm sorry, I should have known you were into him."

"Well, no, but I am going to pocket that nickname for later," Melanie teased. "You told me that I was going to be fine as the new kid at Haverport High. Because I have you guys."

"Oh. Wow, maybe I am nice."

"Yes, *and*," Melanie continued. "You made me feel safe and welcome when I felt like my life had just turned upside down, and I don't think you realize how much that meant to me. How much that *means* to me."

Rory threw an arm around her shoulders. "Well, you are one of us now, even if you made the poor decision to become Mrs. Ass-Hat."

"I'll take it."

"Now," Rory said, letting go as she tucked a leg up underneath her so she could face Melanie full-on. "Tell me about your first kiss."

"Which one?"

"What do you mean which one?!" Rory balked. "You only get one!"

She laughed, then launched into her story, starting with the Fourth of July fireworks—and the curl of a pinkie that turned her summer right side up.

Melanie had a habit of arriving for her shift at Scoops at least fifteen minutes early. She liked having the time for herself for a brief few moments before clocking in, getting a sense of the front and what needed to be done before things would get crazy for the evening. At this point in the game, she no longer worried about stains on her shirt or milkshake explosions across the wall. She moved through the shop swiftly like the rest of them, sometimes scooping cones faster and even more efficiently than Calvin did.

She noticed the chocolate jimmies needed filling, so Melanie headed for The War Room to grab the box and found Jess standing awkwardly, waiting for her.

Melanie reached for the box, pulling it down.

"God, you're worse than Calvin," Jess said.

"I'll take that as a compliment," Melanie replied.

"Hey, do you um, have a minute?"

Melanie slowed, placing the box down on the desk. Jess had her arms crossed over her chest tightly, almost as if what she was about to do was physically painful. But she gritted her teeth and just went for it. "So, I'm, um, going to take a vacation with my boyfriend in a few weeks."

"Oh, wow, that's great!" Melanie replied, her enthusiasm making Jess wince.

She reeled in all of her bubbling curiosity. Since when did Jess have a boyfriend? How long had they been together? And...why was she still working here? Melanie couldn't help but take a peek at Jess's wallet when she left it open on the desk a few weeks earlier, realizing that Jess was almost 22—much older than the rest of them. And while the pay per hour was certainly generous, Melanie wondered if there was something more than the pay keeping Jess here.

"Yeah, whatever," Jess replied. "He wants to go to the Cape, which I think is so stupid because we already live by the beach."

She nodded, but decided to leave whatever was going on with Jess alone. Jess didn't seem like the kind of person that wanted pity or sympathy. Something she could completely understand.

"So I was thinking you could learn how to make the cakes," she continued. "Just for a week, if you're still up for it."

"Yes! I would love to help," Melanie said, resisting the urge to reach over and give Jess a hug. She just looked so tired—the bags under her eyes were even darker than the day of the festival. She really did look like she could use a vacation.

She smiled faintly. "Awesome. I'll make sure Calvin schedules us together for afternoon shifts next week so I can train you."

She nodded as Jess gathered her things and left, without saying another word. She carried the box of chocolate jimmies to the front and started filling when she felt a pair of warm arms coil around her waist.

Calvin dipped his head to kiss her neck, lingering there for a moment as she filled, a cat-like smile on her face as she relished the way his body felt curled around hers.

"I have a question for you," he murmured.

"No, I will not drink herbal tea instead of coffee."

She felt his chest rumble with amusement as he squeezed her tight, kissing her again. "The block party. Can I bring Gram?"

Melanie turned toward him, curling her hands around his neck. "Yes, of course, you don't even have to ask."

He grinned as he leaned into her, kissing her lips tenderly as he pressed her body up against the counter.

"Hey, this is a family establishment," Jay mocked, repeating Ron's words. "I don't want to be the cause of Billy-Bob's first porn-o."

Calvin didn't even look over at Jay as he flicked him off, causing Melanie to giggle with embarrassment, burying her face into his chest.

"Mel Mel."

Melanie twisted frantically, noticing Duncan was leaning against the counter on the other side of the window. His expression looked grim and full of shame.

Calvin released her, stroking her back gently for a beat

before stepping to the other side of the shop, checking that everything was set up for their shift.

"Dee," she whispered. "What's going on, why do you look upset?"

"I need your help."

She felt her chest tighten, anxiety pulsing through her veins. She had a feeling that whatever he was about to say wasn't going to be good.

"Okay," she replied, keeping her tone as calm and steady as she could. "What do you need?"

"I—I got myself into a little bit of trouble," he admitted, his eyes darting around, making sure no one else was listening to them. He eyed Calvin for a moment then leaned closer, not realizing that his words were still vibrating clearly through the front of the shop. "A bit of financial trouble. And, um, I'm strapped for cash."

Melanie froze. He was about to ask her for money. She did not feel nearly ready enough for this.

"Do...do you think you could help me?"

She coughed uncomfortably, her face and fingers now feeling particularly cold, nausea roiling through her stomach. "Um, h—h—how much do you need?"

"Three hundred," he said. "I'll pay you back every penny, I promise. Just need the cash up front now to fix the problem."

Melanie took a step back, her vision going slightly blurry. Three hundred dollars. What in the world did he do that he would need that kind of money?

"What is the problem?" she asked.

"It's nothing," he said, his voice short. "Something I can fix."

"Tell me, Duncan."

He squeezed his eyes shut. "I, um—I asked this guy to supply for a party, told him I would pay him back by today."

She knew he had to get his booze from somewhere, but until now, she never really thought through *how* he got the money to buy it. And it never occurred to her that he could actually be putting himself in danger.

She glanced over at Calvin briefly, noticing he was watching her from his periphery. For the briefest moment, he shook his head, enough to send a signal to Melanie without her brother noticing.

She turned back to Duncan, a placid look on her face. "I'm sorry, Dee, I can't."

"Oh, come on, Mel," Duncan pleaded. "You make that kind of money in a week in just tips alone. I'll pay you back as soon as I can, I promise."

She considered it for a moment, wondering if it really would be that big a deal to help him out, just this once. She *did* have the money to give him. Other than buying the occasional latte or dress at Lacey's, she'd been saving a majority of it for when it was time to leave for college.

But even though her heart wanted to give it to him freely and relieve him of whatever hardship and pain he was going through, Melanie's gut wasn't having it. She knew giving him money may not be a one-time ask, and if she were to do it now, what would stop him from coming to her in the future?

"No," she repeated, her voice catching when she said it. She cleared her throat. "I can't. I'm sorry."

He huffed, but to her surprise, he didn't yell. She expected the lion to explode on her like it always did when things didn't go its way, but something had shifted. Like he was almost embarrassed for even asking in the first place.

"Okay," he said, standing up straight. "Forget I asked."

He shoved his hands in his pockets and walked away from the shop, eyes cast down at his feet.

She felt a hand touch her arm, but brushed it off, not bothering to look in Calvin's direction. "I need a minute."

She stepped through The War Room and out the back door, taking in a big gulp of the stifling late-July heat. She sat down on the small patch of grass behind Scoops, tucking her head between her legs as she took big, unsteady breaths.

Melanie wondered if it was always going to feel this way. The constant back and forth of having good moments and bad moments, of feeling like life was either normal or anything but. She wondered if her parents were even aware that Duncan truly had a problem, or if they were just credulous in thinking that this was just a phase that would soon pass. Melanie even wondered if it was time to talk to them about it.

Nausea continued to churn in her stomach as she sat there, hoping her deep breaths would make it cease. But the thought of Duncan needing money and coming to her in such desperation seemed to be the breaking point as she turned her body away from the shop—and vomited.

"Do you want to talk about it?"

Melanie had ignored him throughout their entire shift. She let herself get lost in the work, not daring to look up and face the weird reality she was in—that she just denied helping her brother, that she shoved off her boyfriend, and that she puked her guts out behind Scoops. What she really wanted was to go home and sleep for an entire day. But instead, she was standing outside of Scoops, the night eerily quiet for a summer night in Haverport, with her arms crossed as she avoided looking Calvin directly in the eyes.

"Not really," she mumbled. "I'm tired of talking about this. I'm tired of this being my life."

Calvin nodded, rubbing the back of his neck as he looked away, hurt etched on his face. He took a moment to control himself before looking back at Melanie, stuffing away whatever he felt and putting all of his attention on her. "I know. It's not fair. None of it is."

Melanie nodded, not sure what else to say.

"Do you want me to just take you home?" he asked quietly.

To her surprise, she found herself shaking her head. She was tired, but she wasn't exactly sure what she would meet when she got to the cottage. And she wasn't in the right mind to face it quite yet.

Calvin popped open the tailgate and hopped up, taking a seat. He patted the spot next to him, motioning for Melanie to join. She did reluctantly, leaving some space between the two of them as she stared out at the lights that led down Main Street.

"Gram wasn't kidding when she said she used to take me here every day," Calvin started, his gaze down the street as well. "We used to come just once a week, but after Pop died, Gram got in this habit of spoiling me. So we came often."

Melanie crisscrossed her legs, pulling them close as she listened, feeling thankful that he'd changed the subject.

"That spring after he died, my class was having this career day where all the students were asked to bring their fathers to school so they could all share about their jobs," he continued. "It felt especially brutal because Pop was now gone, and I didn't want to be that pathetic kid with the only grandmother in the room.

"That day after my teacher announced it, Gram brought me here, like she always did. Ron was working at the counter, and at that point, he knew me by name. He always scooped my Oreo cone without me even having to ask, always with a big smile on his face."

Calvin smiled at the memory fondly as he spoke, playing with his hands. "When he handed my cone to me that day, I asked him if he would be my dad."

Melanie finally glanced over at him, her heart twisting in her chest. It didn't make any sense to her, why he kept choosing to open up. He was so set in his ways with everyone else around him, all about following the rules and doing everything by the book. And yet, when he was with her, all of his hard edges softened. He trusted her with all of the difficult things, and in that moment, as Calvin continued to share his story, Melanie wished she had the courage to do the same.

"He didn't even hesitate. He came to my career day and I was suddenly the coolest kid in the class because my dad ran the ice cream shop," Calvin said. "And he just kept showing up after that. He came to everything—school concerts, graduations, sports games."

"Sports?"

"It was...a very, *very* brief time in my life," he explained with a shy smile.

Melanie smiled back at him, his features relaxing as she did so, his eyes examining her face like he wanted to memorize it. "My classmates soon figured out that Ron wasn't my real dad, but I didn't care. Ron doesn't have any kids of his own, never really met someone he wanted to settle down with, so he was just as excited about stepping into the role as I was."

Calvin sighed, gazing back down at his hands. "Working at Scoops was kind of an unspoken agreement, and over the past year, it sort of dawned on me that he has no one to pass this place down to. So...I'm going to do it."

"To...take over the shop?"

He nodded. "That's what I'm going to community college for. Getting my associate in business so I can run this place someday."

Melanie glanced back at Scoops, marveling at the finality of his decision. "Wow, that's—"

"Not as cool as Yale, I know."

She frowned. "That seems harsh."

"Sorry, I just meant—"

"No, Calvin, I mean harsh to *yourself*. What you're doing is such a beautiful and honorable thing. I think it's amazing that Ron and this place mean so much to you."

Calvin nodded at her. "I don't think a lot of other people see it that way. Ron himself thinks I'm crazy, that I should be doing something more for myself." He sighed, looking up at the stars. "But...I honestly can't imagine myself doing anything else. The only family legacy I have is this town and Gram's cottage and this ice cream shop. I already don't have much, so what I do have...I can't imagine letting it slip away."

She shifted over to him, running a hand along his cheek, cupping the back of his neck before leaning in to kiss him softly. "I don't think it's crazy," she whispered.

He exhaled with ease, wrapping his arms around her waist, like the distance between them before caused him great pain. She relaxed in his arms, resting her head against his shoulder as they sat there in comfortable silence. She thought about how Calvin had his whole life figured out, that he knew exactly what he wanted to do and was just going for it.

Melanie knew she always wanted Yale; she had been working toward it fervently for the last decade of her life, ever since that day her father placed his hat on her head. Yet why, after spending so much of her time focused on it, was Melanie only just realizing that she had no idea what she wanted to do with her life if she got in?

Chapter Nineteen

MELANIE WAS in the middle of sealing up a bucket full of orange Jello with plastic wrap when Mom let Calvin and Gram into the cottage. Duncan begrudgingly watched as he shuffled down the stairs, his gaze toward Calvin stiff and uninviting as he sat down at the bottom step to lace up his sneakers. Duncan had yet to speak to her since asking for the money. The distance between them felt even more excruciating than it did before. She felt like she failed him all over again.

Calvin sauntered over, taking a seat on a stool next to the counter. The way he was looking at her had her thinking back to the night before, his hands running through her hair as he kissed her eagerly. He smiled at her now, almost like he too was thinking about it, causing Melanie to blush as she poured another batch of blue Jello into a separate bucket.

"I know you said not to bring anything, Alice, but your daughter likes these," Gram said, placing a large plate of oatmeal chocolate chip cookies down on their counter.

Melanie smiled at Gram as a thank you, slyly trying to reach for a cookie before Calvin playfully slapped her hand.

Dad turned toward Duncan as he stood up. "Hey, before you go, do you think you could help me—"

But Duncan didn't stay to hear the rest of Dad's request as he exited the cottage, taking off for his jog.

"Never mind," Dad puffed. "Calvin, maybe you could help me? I need to get the kiddie pools out of the shed and down the front yard."

"Yes, sir."

"Son, I am not a *sir*! You don't have to keep saying that."

"Whatever you say, sir," he responded as the side of his mouth curled into a half-smile.

He shook his head, pointing to Calvin with eyes dead set on Melanie. "Where'd you find this guy?"

Melanie smiled to herself. "At an ice cream shop, with a paperback novel in his hand."

His eyebrows raised as the two of them pushed through the kitchen back door. "Novel, huh? What are you reading right now?"

Calvin launched into talking about a Stephen King novel he was currently working through, their voices becoming distant as they maneuvered toward the shed.

"Coffee, Mrs. Ball?" Mom asked.

"Well sure," Gram replied. "But only if you promise to stop calling me that. I prefer to go by 'sir' moving forward."

Mom laughed brightly. Melanie mixed together more orange Jello in a bowl as she listened to Mom pour a hot cup of coffee into a mug for Gram, handing it to her.

"Why, this is just like my mug!"

She looked up, realizing Mom handed Gram her sunshine mug, the same one Melanie drank out of every morning.

"Oh, yes, that one is mine," Melanie said. "Although the painting was made in a factory, not with love."

Mom's face furrowed with confusion as Gram giggled. "Well isn't that just special that both of you have a little yellow mug with a sun," Gram said. "It's almost like it was meant to be."

She blushed as she looked out the front window, watching Calvin and Dad still chatting as they carried the kiddie pools out front. The entire moment felt pleasant, the small group of them hanging out in the cottage, getting ready for a rowdy block party in a few hours.

Yet it wasn't easy avoiding the obvious. To Melanie, it felt like a very large piece of the puzzle was missing.

"So, Gram," Mom started. "I hope you don't mind me asking, but are you raising Calvin?"

"Calvin didn't need raising," Gram said. "That boy is just as stubborn and determined as his grandfather. But yes, he's been with me since he was five."

Melanie remained silent as she stirred, listening intently. Even during dinner with Gram and Calvin that night, they'd evaded talking about his parents. She wondered if she was about to bring it up, now that he wasn't in the room.

Curiosity also seemed to get the best of her mother as she continued to pry. "And his parents?"

"Father is a deadbeat, who knows where he is," Gram said clinically. "His mother lives in Boston, stops by anytime her need to come home and see her son overpowers her need for pills."

Melanie froze. Gram just outright *said it*. She glanced over, watching the way her mother calculated this response in her head, waiting to see how she would react.

"That's...horrible, I'm so sorry," Mom said softly. "Your daughter?"

Gram nodded, taking a sip of her coffee.

"Does that—" She hesitated like she wasn't sure how to ask what she was about to ask. "Does that bother you? How do you deal with it?"

Melanie white-knuckled the wooden spoon in her hand as she listened very, very carefully.

"I remind myself that God has given me a good life," Gram said, a genuine smile on her face. She turned to look at Melanie before she went on. "And a grandson that is truly my saving grace."

Melanie smiled at Gram, her heart fluttering as she heard Calvin laughing outside at something Dad just said to him.

He really was a saving grace. For all of them, it seemed.

THE JELLO ATROCITY was an absolute hit. Everyone signed up for a chance to stick their feet in the gooey pool and find the little action figure hidden below. Melanie and Calvin were in charge of manning the station, filling up the pools with fresh Jello if too much spilled over the edges as they helped neighbors step in and out of the sticky mess. Gram had set up shop in the shade nearby, sipping on an iced tea and waiting for people she knew to come to her and gossip about the latest town news.

Jan and Dan finally showed up, half-soaked from the water balloon toss, both with their serious game faces on. "Get the Jello ready, Mel, it's time."

A group of neighbors crowded around the kiddie pools as they peeled off their sandals, calling out their predictions of who they thought would win. Tim Mackey was confident Dan would be able to find it first, but Melanie and Mom knew better.

"They don't know that Dan basically doesn't have any nerve endings in his feet," Jan whispered to them as she slowly stepped into her pool. "He doesn't even flinch when I touch them."

Melanie chuckled, taking a step back, deciding to make the most of the information she just learned. "Want to make a bet?" she asked Calvin.

Calvin smirked. "What do you have in mind?"

"Winner has to obtain two slices of Grampy's blueberry coffee cake in the morning," she replied.

"Good luck with that," Dan mumbled. "Impossible."

Which, of course, made Calvin grin. "Not if you know how."

Melanie scowled. She thought her tip from Rory was a secret, but apparently not. He really did know everything about this town.

"What if we up the stakes?" he replied, lifting an eyebrow at her.

She smiled back at him wickedly, remembering the last bet they made like this. "Oh yeah? Go on."

Calvin crossed his arms. "Winner gets to throw three water balloons at the loser."

Everyone around them *ooh*ed at that one like it was practically a death threat. She turned to Jan, who just nodded confidently.

"Fine," Melanie said, turning back to shake Calvin's hand. He tugged on it, drawing her just a few inches closer, making her heart skip a beat. "You're on."

Everyone was rumbling with nervous energy and excitement as Mom counted down *three, two, one*...and then they were digging.

Jan's face was full of concentration as she felt around for her toy figure, sweeping her feet around the bottom first like she had a planned strategy. Dan stomped around the entire surface area, hoping to just step on it, turning to Dad and asking if the action figure really was in there.

In just twenty seconds, Jan grinned, curling her toes around the action figure and lifting it with her foot. Half the group cheered, including Melanie, who turned to Calvin with a grin, pointing at the water balloons as he rolled his eyes.

"I'm sorry, man," Dan said, sounding defeated. "I really don't think it's in there."

Calvin frowned, pointing down at a little action figure that was floating toward the top of a mound of Jello. Dan frowned back.

Jan grinned menacingly at them as she handed three water balloons to Melanie. "Pay up, Ball."

Calvin groaned. "Fine."

He stepped away from everyone and peeled off his shirt. Melanie felt her face flush at the way Calvin tightened his muscles as he pulled his body into a straight line, holding his fists firmly in front of him. "All right, headband, do your worst."

She grinned, throwing a water balloon right at his chest, the neighbors cheering as the balloon splashed all over his face and down his arms. She walked around him and threw one at his back, his shoulder muscles tensing from the cold water.

"You know, we really should have specified the rules," Melanie said, rolling the third water balloon in her hand.

"Less fun that way," Calvin mumbled.

"I was hoping you'd say that," she said, untying the balloon carefully and pouring the contents of it over his head.

Calvin grinned. "Oh, you are *so* dead."

Before she could defend herself, Dan tossed Calvin a water balloon and he chucked it at her, right at her shoulder. It was like the first shot in a war as all hell broke loose; everyone was grabbing for water balloons and throwing them at each other, causing complete anarchy across the block party. Gram was cheering from her corner, the cubes inside her iced tea glass clinking in her hand. Jan attempted to throw one at Mrs. Pearson but was abruptly stopped with one warning finger, so she turned instead to Tim Mackey and chucked it at his butt.

Calvin and Melanie were viciously throwing water balloons at one another, laughing hysterically as they got soaked. She couldn't help but grin the entire time, even though the water was freezing with every balloon Calvin pelted at her.

When they'd completely run out of their supply, Calvin seized her in a fierce hug, kissing her half-wet, half-frizzy hair as they walked over to the coolers. He twisted open a cap for a cream soda, handing her the bottle.

"Hey, guys, stay *right* there."

They froze as Duncan peeled open the cooler behind them, rifling through the bottles of beer.

"Just grabbing a few of these," Duncan explained, bottles clinking as he handed them over to Leila while she discreetly stuffed them in her bag.

Melanie's breathing quickened, practically feeling like Jello herself as she involuntarily stood guard, allowing Duncan to just take the beer freely. Calvin reached his free hand over to Melanie, wrapping it around her wrist and squeezing it tightly.

"Okay, awesome, thanks broskis," he said, slamming the cooler lid down.

She turned her head toward Duncan, but Calvin didn't bother—just kept his gaze on the party. "Where are you guys going?" Melanie asked, her voice scratchy.

"A few of us are gathering at Rocky Point beach," Leila said sweetly, her expression light and devoid of any concern. "You guys should come."

"*Yeahhhh*, you guys should come!" he parroted. "Gonna be fun, everyone is bringing drinks and we'll have some good tunes."

"Um, I don't...I don't know—"

"Seriously, it's going to be great." To Melanie's surprise, he reached over, slapping his hand on Calvin's back like they were buddies. "And we can finally get to know one another, ya?"

She glanced over at Calvin. She couldn't read his expression. He was just calm; like this wasn't his decision, but one that she would need to make.

Wasn't this what she'd just been wishing for? A chance for Calvin and Duncan to connect and get to know one another, for Duncan to be a part of her life in this way?

But Melanie sobered. If it meant drinking, she didn't want it. Especially when that kind of environment was something her new boyfriend avoided at all costs. She couldn't do that to him. She didn't *want* to do that to him.

"We promised Mom we would help her today. Sorry, Dee."

"Eh, I tried," Duncan said, releasing his hand from Calvin's back and shrugging in Leila's direction as they left.

Melanie watched the two of them walk away, her breathing becoming steadier.

"Hey," Calvin whispered.

She looked up at him, his eyes sparkling beneath the August sun. "Thank you," he whispered.

"For what?"

His smile was shy, his expression vulnerable. "You know what."

MELANIE CARRIED A STEAMING cup of herbal tea over to Calvin as he stretched out on the couch, reading his book.

She was feeling particularly thankful that he'd stuck around; the perfect distraction from the uncomfortable pit that still sat in her stomach. Duncan had yet to show his face after sneaking off with Leila, and her worried expression must have been obvious enough to Calvin. He didn't leave her side for the rest of the day, razzing her with all kinds of goofy attempts to try and make her laugh. He even came back after taking Gram home, helping to clean up the remains of the party and rinse out the kiddie pools that were now stained with fluorescent shades of orange, green, and blue.

The entire neighborhood seemed to have a blast at the block party, including Mrs. Pearson. While she refused to stick her perfectly pedicured toes into the Jello, Melanie was surprised to find her laughing and agreeing to a match of corn hole with Tim Mackey. She even willingly invited the association members back to her cottage for a nightcap to commemorate the day.

Which left Melanie and Calvin in cottage five—alone.

He placed the book down with a smile, reaching for the

yellow mug. "This must be the sunshine mug Gram wouldn't shut up about."

"Apparently it means we're soul mates," Melanie teased, sitting down next to him carefully as she softly blew on her own tea.

Calvin smirked. "Is that herbal tea in your cup?"

She rolled her eyes. "Maybe. Turns out, herbal tea is kind of comforting to have at the end of the day."

"Imagine having it *during* the day."

"Nope. Coffee is for sunlight hours. You will not win this one," she quipped.

He laughed, and Melanie couldn't help but revel in the way it vibrated off the walls of the cottage. Her gaze lingered at the way he casually perched one leg up, his body leaning against the arm of the couch. She watched his right arm flex when he tipped the mug back, his jaw tightening as he took a sip.

Calvin smirked at her. "What's going through that mind of yours?"

She flushed. "Oh, um—I, well, was just thinking about Scoops and how they survived a Saturday without us."

"The place is probably up in flames. Jay probably gave out all of his ice cream for free."

"Well, if Jay's working, they may actually get out of there early."

Calvin frowned. "Care to explain?"

"The night we went to the party, Jay had us all cleaned and closed up by 10:15," she told him.

"Huh," he said, placing his tea down on the coffee table in front of them. "I feel like this is useful information I should take advantage of someday."

"It was impressive, I don't think I've seen him work that

hard at anything ever. Besides trying to flirt with someone, of course."

Calvin shook his head with a smug look on his face. "Now," he started, reaching for Melanie's legs and pulling her closer to him, making her yelp. "Want to tell me what you were *really* thinking about?"

She pressed her lips together playfully like she just got caught. The sound of his deep chuckle sent an excited tremor down to her toes as Calvin pulled her in for a kiss. His lips were warm from the tea, the taste on his tongue a mix of citrus and chamomile.

He shifted backward on the couch as he pulled Melanie down. She stretched out her legs, tucking herself in between the couch cushions and Calvin as he twisted his arms around her body, his hand cupping the back of her head.

She pulled back slightly, her eyes still sealed shut, as if opening them would break the spell. "They could come in here any moment," she whispered.

"I'm willing to take that chance," he murmured as he pressed back in, his desire to actually *break* the rules surprising her. He rolled his lips against hers with that same longing that Melanie felt every time he kissed her. It was a feeling that she thought about every night when her mind always seemed to drift back to him—a feeling that was more than just a need for a taste or a moment, but a longing for something much, much bigger.

She balled up his soft crew-neck sweatshirt into her fists and pulled him closer, letting her own need and longing take over. She savored the way his hands felt as they playfully brushed the small of her back, silently wishing he would keep exploring. Wishing he would keep breaking the rules.

The sound of distant yelling caused Calvin to slow, his

lips parting from hers. She whimpered, but he held up a finger to her lips, cocking his head up to listen to whatever commotion was happening outside of the cottage.

Calvin shifted, sliding off the couch and fixing his sweatshirt as he glanced out the window.

Melanie sat up. "What's going on?"

But before he could respond, his eyes went wide and he bolted out of the cottage.

She ran after him and found Duncan and Leila on the front lawn in the middle of a full on screaming match.

Duncan's hand was tightly grasping Leila's wrist, his face red with fury. "I will be the judge of what I can and cannot handle! You are NOT the boss of me!"

Leila was crying. "Duncan, look at yourself! You've clearly had enough!"

"Who are you, my *mom*?!" he screamed, tightening his grip on her wrist, her body withering underneath his strength. "I thought you were cool and fun, but you're just as bad as the rest of them!"

"Let her go, man," Calvin said, his voice calm and collected.

Duncan whipped his head around, his eyes bloodshot as he noticed Calvin and Melanie standing there, witnesses to what was going on.

"This has nothing to do with you," Duncan snarled. "Stay out of it."

"Dee," she said, tears streaming down her face. "Don't do this, let her go."

Duncan threw down his arm, releasing his grasp on Leila. But in less than a millisecond he was coming after Calvin, his arm winding up ready for a punch.

Calvin easily ducked out of the way, causing Duncan to stumble forward. Then, in one graceful movement,

Calvin stepped behind him and wrapped his arm around his neck.

"Ss—stop!" Leila screamed. "Please, don't hurt him!"

But he wasn't hurting him. He held his position tightly as Duncan's head lolled, and he fell asleep.

Calvin placed him down gently on the lawn, gripping his hands under his armpits. "Grab his feet."

Melanie and Leila dutifully followed, speechless, as they helped Calvin lift Duncan up the porch steps and through the front door. They placed him down on the couch, making sure he was lying on his side.

He turned to Leila next. "Do you need a ride home?"

She nodded, her face red and splotchy from crying, her shoulders trembling.

He wrapped an arm around Melanie's neck, kissing the top of her head. "I'll be right back."

She just nodded as she watched him lead Leila outside, listening to the rumbling of his truck as it pulled down the street. She sat down in the armchair across the couch, wrapping her arms around her legs as she pressed her face into her knees, crying silently. Embarrassment consumed her. Calvin and Leila both had to experience the storm of the lion at full rage, and part of her wanted to tell them to both run and never come back.

She looked up at Duncan, watching as his head rolled forward, his breathing staggered. She felt the urge to wake him up and scream in his face. She wanted him to understand how hard this was for her, wanted him to feel guilty for being so selfish. She wanted to plead and tell him to just stop and see reason, to realize his habit was ruining everything and everyone around him. To realize what his choices were doing to her heart and soul.

Melanie stood up before letting that urge consume her.

She left the room, taking the steps two at a time up to her bedroom, not bothering to change her clothes as she climbed under the covers.

She soon heard the crackling of the gravel driveway from Calvin's truck. She heard the faint jostling sound of keys and footsteps on the stairs. Then he was there. Without saying a word, he kneeled down by her bed, brushing a strand of hair behind her ear, stroking her cheek with his thumb as she openly wept in front of him.

"You don't deserve this," she whispered, her voice haggard and torn. "I won't be mad if you want to leave, if this is too much or too triggering—"

"Melanie, stop."

She looked into his eyes, so steady and blue. It reminded her of how calm the sea would look the night after a brutal storm, the sun rising and signaling a new day.

"I already told you I won't let go," he said, causing even more tears to flow.

He slipped off his shoes and climbed onto the bed next to her, cradling her in his arms as she continued to cry and cry. She could still smell the lemon and chamomile on his breath from his tea. She cried at the thought of how, in an instant, a perfect evening could easily switch into a horrible nightmare.

At some point, her crying slowed and her breathing steadied. Her eyelids began to droop, and before she knew it, she was fast asleep, wrapped up tightly in Calvin's arms.

Chapter Twenty

THE SUN WAS JUST STARTING to rise above the bay when Melanie blinked her eyes open. She was in her bed alone, still fully clothed from the day before. She glanced around the room, wondering what time Calvin had left, then noticed his sweatshirt was tossed to the floor.

She maneuvered out of bed, changing into a comfortable pair of sleep shorts, and pulled on his sweatshirt that smelled like old books and oatmeal cookies. She curled back up under the covers, letting herself fall back asleep without any plans of moving, not after the events of last night. She had no idea what awaited her downstairs.

She was floating in a golden sea in her dream when she felt someone kiss her, right between her cheek and the crook of her nose. The smell of coffee had Melanie blinking her eyes open and finding Calvin by her side again, holding a tray of drinks and a brown paper bag.

She smiled, sitting up slowly, leaning her head against his shoulder as he handed her a latte. She took a sip as she watched him retrieve two containers with slices of steaming hot blueberry coffee cake, handing her one with a fork.

"I think this is how I would like to always wake up," Melanie said. "Coffee, sugar, cute boy."

He chuckled, opening up his own container. She realized he was still wearing the same clothes from the day before.

She frowned. "Did you stay the night?"

He grimaced. "Yeah, I fell asleep."

"Do you think they noticed?"

"Well...my truck was here all night. And I may have just run into your dad downstairs when I tried sneaking back in."

Melanie sighed. "Looks like I'm about to be grounded for the first time."

"Well, he did just wink at me, so I have a feeling you might be okay."

She shook her head, bemused. "Was...um...Duncan still down there?"

"No. Must have made it up to his room at some point."

The two of them ate their slices of cake in silence for a moment, listening to the seagulls caw as they soared above the water.

"How'd you know how to do that?" Melanie asked shyly. "With Duncan...last night."

He took a sip of his coffee. "I went through this phase a few years ago where I kept thinking my father would come after me. It's not like he's shown up or anything since he left us, but for some reason, I kept thinking I needed to prepare myself in case he came back. So I learned, just in case."

She blew out a long breath. "Well...I—um, thanks."

Silence settled over them again, and this time, Melanie just wanted to fill it and change the subject. But he didn't seem quite done with the conversation yet.

"How often is he like that?" he asked.

Melanie didn't answer right away as she leaned her head on the bed frame behind them. He was patient, leaving space for her to answer him.

"Often," she whispered. "He hasn't tried attacking someone in a while, but back in Garrison it was constant."

"Has he ever come after you?"

She shook her head. "I tried to stay away from it, never said or did anything that would provoke him. Kept my focus on school."

He leaned his head against hers, reaching for her hand and threading their fingers together.

"I just feel so hopeless sometimes," she admitted. "I wish there were something I could just do to make him stop."

"I know," Calvin said, kissing the top of her head. "I know."

"I'm wondering if I should talk to them about it..." she whispered. "My...parents."

"What would you say?"

"That—I don't know. That it feels like a bigger problem than just moving towns and hoping for the best? That I think he needs help? I don't understand why they haven't tried getting any help yet."

He squeezed her hand. "And if they don't agree?"

She sighed, thinking about Mom's expression the day before as she listened to Gram. "Part of me thinks that deep down, they know. They sneak around all the time trying to hide it, and they don't mention it at all around him. I guess I'm just kind of hoping they'll talk to *me* about it."

Calvin nodded, letting a comfortable silence linger between them as they fell deep into their own thoughts—up until Calvin's phone alarm went off.

"I have to go," he whispered.

She frowned, realizing it was Sunday—the day Calvin always took off at Scoops. He kissed her head again before shifting away from her and reaching for his shoes.

"Don't leave. Please stay."

Calvin turned toward her, wrapping his arm around her waist. "I can't. I'm sorry."

She pouted, feeling selfish. But when in her life had she ever allowed herself to be selfish?

He exhaled, stroking her hair. "Do you want to come with me?"

Her eyebrows furrowed. "Where?"

He just smiled, bending down to kiss her nose. "Put on something nice, I'll be back in a half hour."

"Okay," she whispered, watching him grab his coffee cup and shuffle out the door. She lay there still, listening to the rumbling sounds of his truck as it distanced from the cottage, waiting for the gentle cawing sound of the seagulls to fill her room again before sliding out of bed. She changed, pulling on a white summer dress and a new pair of sneakers she decided would never see the light of day over at Scoops. Her face was puffy from crying, but she didn't care. After last night, she had nothing to hide anymore. Calvin had officially seen her at her worst as she sobbed in her bed, her tears seeping into his sweatshirt as he held her tightly. Yet after everything...he had stayed, holding her close, fulfilling his promise to never let her go.

She combed through her hair with her fingers trying to control the waves that didn't seem to want to be anything but wild. She gave up, sliding her elastic blue headband on her head before gathering the trash from their breakfast and creeping down the stairs.

Mom was standing over the coffee machine, her robe wrapped tightly around her. She smiled as Melanie tossed out the trash, grabbing her sunshine mug and sliding up next to her mother.

"You look nice," Mom said. "Is he coming back?"

Melanie nodded. "Says he wants to take me somewhere this morning. Are...are you mad at me?"

Mom sighed. "No. Not mad. Just worried."

"About what?"

Mom gave her the side-eye before pouring coffee into her mug, reaching over to fill Melanie's as well. "A boy just stayed the night in my daughter's room, what do you think?"

"Oh." Melanie was so caught up in her hurt about Duncan and the horror from the night before that it didn't even occur to her that her parents might have thought... well...that.

"Promise me you're being safe," Mom whispered.

"I promise," she said, hugging her Mom's side. "You have nothing to worry about."

But...did she? She took a sip of her coffee, glancing back toward the couch as she thought of Calvin's hands on her back, the need she felt as she pulled him closer to her. Were her mother's worries valid? Melanie always assumed that she would wait to fall in love before taking that next step. But as she glanced over at Calvin's tea from last night, still sitting on the coffee table, she wondered if that feeling wasn't totally off base.

HE PULLED into the parking lot of a tiny white chapel. It was hidden deep within the beach communities, on a street somewhere between Rocky Point and Misty Bay. Gram was sandwiched between her and Calvin, wearing a pair of light pink slacks and her white cardigan. She had one hand perched on the black handbag on her lap, the other patting Melanie's knee.

Calvin parked, quickly sliding out so he could help Gram out of the truck. Melanie got out on the other side, closing the door.

Calvin walked over to her, wearing that same outfit she saw him in weeks ago—black slacks, white button-down, leather shoes. His two top buttons were undone, and Melanie had a particularly hard time *not* glimpsing at his tan skin underneath.

"Church?"

Calvin nodded, rubbing his hands up and down Melanie's arms. "I know it's a bit strange and not everyone's thing. If it's too weird, you don't have to go in."

Melanie sighed, glancing over at Gram, whose eyes were intently focused on the chapel and not on her grandson and his girlfriend behind her. Melanie's heart melted a little, thinking about how Calvin took off every Sunday, just so he could take his grandmother to church.

She looked up into his eyes, wondering how she got him so wrong when they first met. Melanie thought he was the one with all of the assumptions about her, but clearly, she was guilty of the same thing. She thought Calvin was rude and abrasive, that he was out to make her training at Scoops miserable because he didn't want her around. But it was just a wall—a layer of protection to keep what mattered to him close. And now, standing in front of her, he was letting that wall come crashing down. She wondered why he just kept choosing to invite her in, but she knew not to take that invitation lightly. And if stepping into a church with her boyfriend was a way to show him how much it meant to her that he broke down those walls, she could do it.

"I'll go," she said.

He grinned, wrapping an arm around her waist as they walked up toward the front of the chapel. Gram was already ahead of them, hugging the other churchgoers and heading for the pews.

The church was small but utterly magnificent. Big sprawling windows lined the side of the chapel as streaks of sunlight poured through. At the front was a simple pulpit surrounded by flowers and greenery. The pews weren't packed, giving everyone room to spread out and get comfortable before the organ started to chime.

Calvin kept his hand firmly twined with hers as they listened to a small choir sing hymns and patrons murmuring prayers up front. A reverend delivered a brief message about hope in the midst of fear, which Melanie had a particularly hard time listening to. But Calvin kept squeezing her hand through the entire thing, almost like he somehow already knew this was difficult for her. She looked down at their hands threaded together, thinking that maybe this is what hope felt like. Clinging to something good when life seemed impossible. Allowing yourself to open up to another when it felt scary. Looking for moments of light amidst murky darkness.

Less than an hour later, they stood up for a benediction, watching the reverend ceremoniously walk down the aisle, ending the service. Gram said she would be right back, scurrying off to another group of poofy white-haired old ladies that were already gabbing in a circle.

Melanie joined Calvin sitting back down in the pew. He smiled at her, placing a hand on her thigh, brushing his thumb back and forth.

"When I told my mom I didn't want to leave Haverport, my grandfather said he had one rule if I were to stay: I had to go to church every Sunday," Calvin explained. "At first I thought it was stupid and the most boring waste of time, but he was persistent—I had to get up, put on my nice clothes, and go."

"I wonder where you get it from," Melanie teased.

Calvin pinched her leg playfully. "Right before he passed, he asked me to keep taking Gram to church. It wasn't like I really could do that as an eight-year-old. She still had to drive his truck. But I made sure it would happen—I got up early, put on my clothes, and made sure Gram sat in her pew."

"How did he pass?" Melanie asked quietly.

"Lung cancer."

"That's horrible, I'm sorry."

He sighed, looking up at the pulpit. "I don't know how I feel about all of it still, but I guess after all this time, it just feels peaceful to be here. And I like the idea that there's some kind of greater meaning to all of this, that maybe I wasn't dealt a bad hand and there's a lot more to my life that I don't even realize."

He squeezed her thigh. "Part of me thinks that all of the good things happening in my life are because of Pop. Like he's up there negotiating with that same stubborn attitude, making sure that I get to experience little miracles."

He looked at her when he said "miracles," making Melanie's heart flutter in her chest.

"I think it's sweet," she said. "And I am touched you let me come."

The way he was gazing back into her eyes was so intense that, for a moment, Melanie felt like she couldn't breathe.

"All right, you two," Gram proclaimed as she walked back over to their pew. "Lunch? Ice cream?"

"Ice cream," they both answered at the same time.

Her eyes twinkled. "Good, that's what I was hoping you'd say."

~

Melanie and Calvin were welcomed by the sound of screaming when they entered the back door of Scoops.

"You're SO SELFISH, you know that?!" Rory screamed.

"Selfish?! You're the one freaking out for no reason!" Jay yelled back.

"It is a reason! You can't just make everyone do what you want them to all the time!" Her face was bright red as she clenched her fists.

Calvin and Melanie stepped around them in The War Room. Tyler stood closely by, his arms crossed and tense, listening intently to the conversation unfolding very poorly in front of him.

"What's going on?" Calvin asked.

Jay glanced at Calvin with a serene expression. "Oh, nothing. Rory is freaking out here because I asked her to do me a favor."

"What kind of favor?" Melanie asked, her voice monotone.

"He asked me to go up front and flirt with him while he scooped ice cream," Rory explained, her eyes still glaring at Jay. "He wanted to make that blonde bimbo outside jealous."

She cocked her head to get a glimpse through the window out front, noticing a skinny blonde girl standing outside of the shop, scrolling on her phone and completely oblivious to what was going on.

"Don't call her a bimbo, you're being rude," Jay said

tightly. "I *really* didn't think this was a big deal, it's not like it means anything."

"Classic Jay, thinking his actions have *zero* consequences, all in an effort to get into someone's pants," Rory said viciously.

"Hate to break it to you, hun, but this is just how you have to play the game," Jay responded, crossing his arms. "Every guy knows that."

"Not every guy," Rory replied darkly.

"Oh, yes, every guy," he said, turning toward Calvin as he pointed a finger between him and Melanie. "Am I right?"

"Do not put me in the middle of this," Calvin said pointedly.

"Calvin doesn't need to play the game because he actually *knows* how to do it right," Rory jested, causing him to look over at Melanie with his eyebrows raised. "And Tyler would never try pulling off something like this either."

"Oh, Tyler?" Jay asked, more as a statement than a question. "If only you *knew* the games he plays."

"Jay," Tyler pleaded.

"Do you want to know the reason why he's always soooo nice to you? Why he'll pick up an outfit for a party or drive you home when you're upset, or hug you when you cry?" Jay spewed.

Rory's face went from bright strawberry red to dark cherry maroon.

Tyler turned toward Jay, his back facing Rory now. "Jay, please, stop."

"Because he *likes* you, moron!" he yelled, cocking his head around Tyler's huge frame. "Isn't it obvious? Out of everyone in this shop, he's the one who's been playing the game the longest! And he's clearly bad at it, because you never noticed."

Everyone was silent. Tyler squeezed his eyes shut, not daring to move or turn around to look at Rory. She stepped back slightly, her eyes on the floor.

"You're lying," Rory whispered.

"Oh, I most certainly am not," Jay continued, not caring about the disaster he was causing in the slightest. "Everyone here knows it, too."

"Jay," Calvin said firmly. "Get out."

Jay's eyes went wide. "You can't kick me out in the middle of a shift, army boy. What will Ron think when he gets back from lunch?"

"He'll think I made the right call in breaking this up," Calvin answered coolly. "Now leave right now before that mouth of yours causes any more damage."

Jay rolled his eyes. "Whatever, fine." He pushed past everyone and left, the aggressive slam of the back door causing everyone to flinch.

Calvin sighed, reaching into his pocket and handing Melanie his keys. "Get Gram a scoop of Caramel Pecan and take her home, please."

"Wait, you're staying?" she asked, feeling bewildered. She followed him to the tiny bathroom as Calvin unbuttoned his shirt, reaching for the extra clean Scoops tee and khaki pants he left in his cubby.

"Yes, someone needs to cover his shift," he said. "It's fine, I didn't work yesterday."

She exhaled, looking over at Rory. She was still standing there, staring at her feet. Tyler had escaped out to the front, likely hiding from embarrassment.

Melanie walked up to Rory, rubbing her hands up and down her arms. "Hey," she said softly. "Do you want me to take your shift when I get back? I don't mind."

Rory nodded, looking too shocked to actually speak.

"Go," Calvin said toward Rory as he signed in. "Tyler and I can handle this for a bit, no need to stay."

She nodded again and left, not bothering to look back at Tyler who was now standing in the door frame of The War Room, watching her go.

Calvin looked over at Tyler, placing a hand on his shoulder. "It's going to be all right."

"You're wrong," Tyler mumbled. "I don't think it can get any worse than this."

Calvin nodded. "Then it's only uphill from here, right?"

Chapter Twenty-One

MELANIE WAS LAYING on her bed reading, a steaming cup of coffee beside her on the end table when the email notification came in. The ding was soft enough that she almost didn't notice it, her phone tucked somewhere under her covers. She reached around for it, not bothering to take her eyes off the page as she swiped it open. When she glanced at the email, she dropped her book.

Yale University Applications Open In Two Weeks!

Two weeks. Her heart started racing when she realized how much of her summer had flown by and how completely unprepared she was. She turned to her calendar and, sure enough, they were exactly two weeks away from September first—the day Yale opened up the application for all new students. She should have her essay ready and answers for the questionnaire thoroughly fleshed out. And even if she already secured her teacher recommendations at Garrison Prep, she still had to collect all the other information and documents needed for her application.

And yet...a part of her was hesitating as she scrolled through the email. She thought back to the night sitting in the back of Calvin's truck, listening to how sure he was about his next step in life, how excited he was to carry on a legacy for the people he cared about most. Besides going to Yale, Melanie wasn't even sure what kind of legacy she wanted to leave. She had no desire to go into finance like her father, and she didn't have a home with deep roots like Calvin did—especially now that her family had left their life in Garrison behind. If Yale asked about what she wanted to study...what would she say? Did she even know what she wanted?

She heard a muffled knock at her door.

Melanie tossed her phone down on her bed and sat up. "Come in."

Dad opened the door slowly, poking his head into the frame. "Did you get the email?" he whispered, being careful not to wake up Duncan who was still sleeping across the hall.

Melanie nodded solemnly.

"Do you want to talk about it?" he asked.

"Um—" She hesitated, wondering if she should burden her father with all of this. It was probably fine; she could handle this brief little hiccup in her plan and figure out her next steps. She had done that for years already, and she's gotten particularly good at finding ways to *not* bother her parents with her problems. But her father was just standing there, his expression almost hopeful, like this was a conversation he *wanted* to have. Melanie softened. "Yeah, okay."

He nodded, sliding into her bedroom as he closed the door. He sat down on the edge of her bed. "So, talk to me."

Melanie exhaled. "I don't feel prepared."

"You're more than prepared," Dad said confidently. "You've been outlining your essay for years now, and you have recommendations from the top two professors at Garrison Prep."

"I know," she answered apprehensively. "I just...don't feel prepared about what comes next."

"What do you mean?"

"Like, say if I get in...what comes next? What do I do with my life?"

He nodded. "I see."

"Did you always know you wanted finance, that you would become an advisor?"

Dad shook his head. "Yes and no. I knew I wanted to work in finance just like my father, but only because I didn't really know anything else, and it was easier to just follow in his footsteps. The advisor part came with time, and it gives me the flexibility to work from home."

"What if I don't want that?"

"The flexibility to work from home?" he asked, looking confused.

"No, no, I mean finance. What if I don't actually—" She hesitated again, looking into her father's eyes, afraid to admit how she was really starting to feel about it all. "What if I don't actually want to do it as you did?"

His eyebrows furrowed. "You're scaring me, kid."

She felt a shot of nervous energy course through her body. Like she said too much. "Don't be scared, it's nothing. I just have no idea what I want to study but I'll figure it out soon."

He shook his head. "No, Mel. I'm scared because you think you need to do as *I* did. Is that why you want Yale?"

And make you happy, she thought to herself. *To feel proud of one of your children.*

"It's more than that," she admitted. It was a half-truth, at least, and not a lie.

He reached for her hands, cupping them in his own and squeezing them tightly. "Melanie, the last thing I want you to do is to make this decision because of me. I need you to be happy, and to find a life that brings you joy."

She'd always thought that a life full of joy meant walking around Yale's campus, coffee in hand as she scurried to her next class, glancing up at the stunning brick buildings rich with so much history and meaning. But at that moment, when her father said *joy,* Melanie thought of Calvin's hand intertwined with hers as they sat together in the pew of that chapel. She thought about how safe she felt next to him underneath a blanket by a bonfire. She thought about his laugh as she chucked water balloons at him, the way it felt with his arms wrapped tightly around her waist on the couch, the way he smiled to himself at Scoops when he thought she wasn't looking.

For so much of her life, Melanie thought that joy meant achieving something great. But maybe joy was a whole lot simpler than that—a small bead of hope in your chest after feeling like nothing was going the way you thought.

Melanie walked down the stairs in her Scoops uniform, clicking on her helmet when she found Duncan sitting at the kitchen table with a glass of water in front of him. He didn't look well—his face a pale, ghostly white, like all of the life had been drained out of him.

"Hey," she said softly. "Everything okay?"

"No," he replied. "Leila...she broke up with me."

Good. She felt bad that it was her immediate thought, but she was proud of Leila. Melanie loved her brother, but she knew he wasn't ready for a relationship. Especially with someone who seemed to instigate his problems even further.

The paleness of his face scared her, causing Melanie to wonder whether he ever figured out his money problems. She decided at that moment that she really needed to talk to her parents about Duncan. Tonight. Even if it didn't go well, she hated seeing him like this. She really did want her twin brother to experience a good relationship, something that felt as real and intimate as things felt between her and Calvin. But she knew that in order for him to get there, things would need to change in his life.

And if that meant Melanie would have to make things uncomfortable between her parents, she would do it. For Dee's sake.

"I'm sorry," she replied.

He pressed his lips into a thin line. "No, I'm sorry,"

Melanie's eyes went wide. She felt her fingers shaking slightly, crossing her arms tightly around her chest so Duncan wouldn't notice how much an apology from him was affecting her. "F-f-for what?"

"For how I acted that night," he said, gazing out the window toward the sea. "For coming after your boyfriend. For being an ass to you for two and a half years."

She felt tears well up in her eyes as she stood there. She was going to be late for her shift, the first one she had with Jess to learn how to make cakes. But she didn't care. This moment felt monumental. Like a first step toward the healing that they all desperately needed.

"Duncan," she whispered.

"Don't," he said, glancing at her, his eyes almost bloodshot. She wondered if he'd been sleeping much with all this weighing on him. "I don't want to hear it. I was terrible, and that's it."

"Okay," she replied. "You're right."

He nodded, looking back toward the ocean.

"Um, I have to go to work," she said gingerly. "But...Dee?"

He looked at her again.

"Th-thank you," she stuttered, barely able to get out the words through her tears.

"Of course, Mel Mel."

She smiled timidly, then left out the back door, wiping her eyes with the shoulder of her Scoops tee before rolling her bike toward the street.

"So once you scoop the ice cream into the cake mold, you have to pack it in," Jess explained, snatching a rubber scraper from a drawer. "You just press it down until it's a smooth service"—she started, pressing down the ice cream with the side of the scraper—"then we add the chocolate crispies and the fudge."

"Seems easy enough," Melanie said. She'd needed a few minutes after getting to Scoops to let the sobs out of her system, crying in disbelief at what had just happened between her and her twin. Still bewildered and in complete disbelief, she stepped into the shop, gearing up for Jess to be pissed at her for being almost twenty minutes late. But Jess had said nothing—just nodded her head and gave Melanie space to collect herself before diving into training.

"Seems easy until you have to pack in ice cream," Jess

mumbled. "You'll find yourself sore in places you didn't even realize after a cake shift."

"I'm gathering that's the theme of working here," Melanie quipped.

Jess smirked, which made her smile. She liked how easygoing and quiet she was as they worked together, the two of them side-by-side as Melanie handed over frosting bags, watching as she meticulously piped beautiful swirls onto cake edges.

"Pack in the next layer, and I'll show you how to level it." She reached for a stainless steel scraper in the drawer.

Following Jess's careful instructions for the rest of the shift, she scraped the tops of the ice cream into perfectly leveled lines, lifting the cake rings before scraping the sides. Her first attempts for frosting the edges weren't as even, but Jess didn't even hesitate as she scraped them off and had Melanie try again and again, not caring that she would have to mix more frosting now that so much was being wasted. But toward the end of the shift, she was able to produce a beautiful cake—with bright red trimming and cursive letters with *Happy 24th Anniversary* swirled together evenly at the center.

Jess beamed down at her, looking just as proud as she had of the disgusting cake that they'd produced the night of Haverfest. "Decent, you'll be fine."

She smiled. "Thanks. And thanks for trusting me with it."

"Don't trust anyone else right now. Jay clearly wasn't an option."

Melanie chuckled, glancing out front as she watched Jay and Blake serving customers. "Jess, did you just make a joke?"

"Rare, I know," she said, a smirk on her face again as she

placed the half-empty frosting bags into a container to go back in the fridge.

She glanced up at the clock, noticing that Calvin was officially fifteen minutes late for his shift. "I wonder what's holding him up," Melanie huffed.

"His mom is here," she answered, her tone of voice sounding straightforward and clinical.

Melanie's heart dropped slightly. He'd told Jess…but not her? "Oh."

"He texted me." She didn't bother looking up as she washed the dishes, as though she didn't want to deal with Melanie after hearing what was sure to have sounded like hurt in her voice.

"Gotcha," said Melanie, wondering if Calvin would be coming in at all. "I'm going to, um, fill up the spoons."

"Sounds good," she replied, vigorously washing the cake rings covered in milky, melty ice cream.

She took the steps to the upstairs storage two at a time, taking her time as she read the labels on the boxes, looking for the spoons.

Why didn't he tell her? She knew his situation with his mom was incredibly complicated. But after everything they had been through together…didn't she at least deserve a text? Was he trying to hide this from her on purpose?

She listened to the back door of Scoops open and a few mumbled exchanges before Melanie heard footsteps climbing the stairs. She turned around and noticed Calvin advancing toward her, his face anchored on hers.

"Hey," Melanie said.

He looped his arms around her waist, lifting her slightly and placing her down on the pile of boxes behind her. He pinned himself tightly to her, his nose brushing against hers, his eyes fixed on her lips. "Hi."

And then he was kissing her. But this kiss felt...different. Usually when Calvin kissed Melanie, it was playful and sweet, and he never crossed a line. He kept those militant boundaries, always being careful to never reach too far or make her uncomfortable.

But this kiss was intense and full of urgency. He pushed himself closer and closer to her, like he was in a hurry and wanted to get lost in it. Like there was an escape he desperately needed.

She pulled away. "Calvin," she whispered.

Almost like the sound of his name on her tongue was the invitation he needed to unleash, he moaned deeply. He slid a hand inside her shirt, tracing it up her spine farther than he ever had before, tucking it under the back of her bra right near where it hooked together. He rubbed the soft skin underneath with his thumb as he pressed her body closer to his, his mouth and his cheeks were warm.

But right now...it wasn't an invitation.

"Calvin."

He pulled his mouth off hers, his eyes closed tight, his rapid breathing in and out sounding jagged.

"I'm sorry."

He released his hand and pulled away, rubbing his head as he stepped back. "I'm—I'm so sorry."

And then he was crying.

Melanie straightened her bra before standing up and reaching over to him. He was gripping his face as his shoulders shook, keeping his sobs quiet enough so no one downstairs could hear him.

She grabbed his other hand, pulling him toward the boxes, and gesturing for him to sit down next to her. He did, tucking his legs up to rest them on a box below, wiping at his red face as he tried to control himself. But one look at Melanie had him crying quietly again.

"Calvin," she whispered. "What's wrong, talk to me."

He took a deep breath, shifting over toward Melanie. He reached for her hands, keeping his eyes intently on them as he spoke. "My mom showed up today," he started.

Melanie nodded, wondering why in the world she made such a fuss about this just moments ago. She didn't even give him time to come to her about it like he was right now. She squeezed his hands, waiting for him to continue.

"She...wanted money, of course," he said. "It's always the same—she tries to make it seem like a normal visit as if she actually cares about us, but it always ends with her asking for money. But this time, instead of trying to make the visit as brief as possible, Gram told her about you."

She felt her throat tighten.

"Told her about how beautiful and smart you are, that you work at Scoops with me, how kind you are to everyone around you," he continued. "And it...suddenly it all changed. Like the usual haze she was in had lifted. She started asking me a million questions. It was like she actually cared for once.

"I found myself feeling *excited* to tell her things. She laughed when I told her you didn't know what a grinder was. I told her your nickname and how we met. I told her about the Sandy Cove bonfire and Clipper's Island and the Jello atrocity."

She smiled shyly, feeling a large pit in her stomach. Waiting for the shoe to drop...a feeling she was far too familiar with.

"When it was time to leave for work, she followed me out of the house with more questions, like she couldn't get enough of it. It was absolutely wild," he said. "But right before I got in the truck, she—"

He started to cry again, his hands squeezing Melanie's so tightly, his knuckles turned white. "She said that she really would love to come here more and wanted to meet you, but she'd need money," he said, sounding more defeated than she'd ever thought possible. "That if she could just have the money she needed, everything would be fixed. She could come here more and see us. She could watch me graduate."

He shook his head. "I graduated over two months ago. We told her about it, but she forgot."

"Are you upset at her for not coming?" Melanie asked softly.

"I'm always mad at her," he said. "But no. I'm upset because this is the first time that she has explicitly asked *me* for money, not Gram."

Oh. She watched tears continue to stream down his face. She felt completely incapable of having this conversation. Calvin always knew exactly what to say to her when she needed it, and the moment he needed *her*, words eluded her.

She heard feet bounding up the stairs. He twisted his head so whoever was coming up couldn't see his face. Melanie glanced over, noticing Blake at the top of the steps, eyes wide. She shooed him off and he nodded, tip-toeing back down the stairs, murmuring something to Jay about not going up.

"I feel pathetic," Calvin muttered. "You handled your brother asking for money so well, and I'm just falling apart."

"If puking your guts out counts as doing well, then sure," Melanie responded. "Calvin, it's not even the same.

She's your *mom*. She should be taking care of you, not the other way around."

He shook his head. "No. Addiction is addiction. The situations may look different, but the pain is all the same."

Melanie didn't respond because she had no idea what to say. So she just nodded her head, letting go of his hands and wrapping her arms around his shoulders. He pulled her onto his lap, tucking her in close as he leaned his head against her chest.

"What are you doing tonight?" he asked softly.

"Nothing," she whispered. "Mom's making dinner I think."

"Can I pick you up after?"

"After your shift?"

He nodded.

"Okay," she answered. She kissed his forehead as he snuggled his head into the crook of her neck. They remained there for a moment, not daring to move from the comfortable shelter they made for themselves on top of the boxes, safely hidden away from the rest of the world.

Chapter Twenty-Two

Mom placed a plate of Caprese chicken and a billowing green salad in front of her, setting down a basket of toasted garlic bread on the table as well.

"Wow," she breathed. "This is fancy. What's the occasion?"

"Can't I just cook something nice for my daughter?" she asked, taking her seat. Dad was already slicing into his chicken, a grim expression on his face.

"Just not the usual hot dogs or burgers," Melanie teased. "It looks amazing, thank you."

Mom smiled, slicing into her own chicken, the three of them silent except for the clinking of silverware against plates.

"So...is Duncan not joining us?" she asked, gesturing toward his usual spot at the table.

"No, he's taking Leila out tonight."

Her brows furrowed. It was clearly a lie, given what he'd told Melanie just that morning. Her stomach dropped when she thought about where he really was instead...and what he might be doing.

She took a deep breath, placing her fork down on her plate. "Um...Mom, Dad?"

The two of them looked up at her, their faces full of concern.

"I feel like there's something, um, that we need to talk about," she started.

Dad nodded his head. "Yes, I think so."

Melanie exhaled a sigh of relief.

"I told your mother about our conversation earlier," Dad continued. "About Yale and how you're feeling about school."

She felt like the wind was just knocked out of her. "Oh, well, actually—"

"I didn't realize how you were feeling, Mel," Mom said. "How come you didn't come talk to us?"

She sighed, resigning to the conversation. "I guess I always just thought I would figure out what I wanted to study when I got in."

"I'm not so worried about that, sweetheart," she replied. "I'm worried about you feeling like you needed to go to Yale because your father did."

Melanie's eyes went wide as she glanced back and forth between her parents, feeling panicked. "But I—I never said that."

"No, not outright," Dad said, a softness lingering in his gaze. "But I put the pieces together enough."

"Because I don't know what I want to study," Melanie said defensively. Her parents were looking at her with that same look of worry, the exact expression she always saw when they faced Duncan. But now, it was all focused on her, and she hated it. She needed to fix it—immediately. "Isn't that normal? For a freshman not to know what they want to study?"

"Well, yes," Dad said. "But we just wanted to make sure there isn't more to it."

"You have nothing to worry about." She rushed through the words, hoping to eradicate their worries. "I was just feeling panicked because applications are opening and I wasn't feeling prepared."

"Is that maybe because—" she started, glancing quickly over at Dad.

Melanie frowned. "Because of what?"

"Maybe, um, a certain someone that is distracting you?"

She crossed her arms. "You mean Calvin?"

"He's a nice boy," Dad said. "And he says 'sir' way too often."

"But maybe..." she continued, steering Dad back to her point, "maybe you feel panicked because you haven't had time to prepare?"

She glared at them, not believing what she was hearing. "He's not the problem."

"Are you sure? Again, he's a nice boy, but—"

"Calvin is not the problem." Her voice was curt and firm. She picked up her fork and forced her lips into a tight smile. "Don't worry, I'll be fine."

As they fell back into silence and ate their chicken, Melanie couldn't help but wonder if her parents really did have a reason to worry. Was Calvin the problem? She had spent so much of her time that summer focused on him and working at Scoops, that she hadn't even given her Yale application much thought. So much so, that a simple email reminder had her feeling startled and unprepared.

Dad reached over, resting his hand on Melanie's. "If you need us, sweetheart, we are always here to talk. We just want you to be happy."

Melanie nodded at her father, digging back into her

chicken. If being "happy" meant seeing her parents like this, full of worry and concern, she didn't want it. She would focus on Yale and make her parents proud. It had worked well for her in the past, so there was no reason why it couldn't continue working for her now.

They finished their dinners and cleaned the dishes in silence. Melanie was so hyper-focused on what she needed to be doing next—which classes she should take at Haverport High, her checklist of things she needed to do for her application, the process of choosing a major—that she didn't realize until after her parents went to bed that she'd completely forgotten to bring Duncan back up.

Melanie was crouched over her laptop, scrolling through the list of majors on Yale's website, when the front door creaked open.

"Hey," Calvin whispered. "Still good?"

"Oh," she said, tilting her laptop away from his line of sight. She forgot that Calvin had asked her to hang out after his shift, her mind completely lost in her application process.

His eyebrows knitted together with concern. "Is everything okay?"

She huffed. "Yes, just...stressed."

"Do you want me to go?"

Yes, she thought selfishly to herself. Her mother's words floated back into her head, about how Calvin might be the distraction holding her back from focusing on Yale. She knew she should stay on track with plans for her future, and everything else that needed to get done before the school year started.

But she couldn't help thinking back to the way Calvin broke down in the storage room at Scoops. He needed her tonight, just like she'd needed him only a few nights earlier. And it wasn't like she was going to figure out her entire future at that exact moment.

"No," she finally replied, closing her laptop. "Let's go."

"Grab a sweatshirt."

She shuffled up the stairs, grabbing her sweatshirt and sneakers before sneaking out of the house and shutting off the lights behind her.

Calvin drove his truck out of town, winding through a series of backroads that she'd never seen before. She sat right next to him as she inched her blue elastic headband onto her head, brushing through her hair before resting her head on Calvin's shoulder, their hands intertwined.

"Where are you taking me this time?"

She could feel his jaw move as he pressed his lips into a smile. "You'll see."

Melanie rolled her eyes. "It's always a surprise with you, huh?"

He chuckled, squeezing her hand. Soon they finally pulled into a parking lot next to an open soccer field. Calvin cut the ignition as the headlights flicked off, enveloping the field before them in complete darkness. He snatched his blanket underneath the seat and reached over Melanie to grab the thermos perched inside the cup holder.

"Let me guess," she teased, pointing to the thermos.

"Make fun of me all you want," Calvin bantered. "But when we're lying down on the blanket and you're freezing cold, you're going to thank me."

She smirked as she followed him from the truck down a grassy field that was still wet from the rain earlier that day. Calvin spread the blanket out as Melanie tugged her sweatshirt on, curling up next to him as he lay down, tucking one arm around her shoulder and the other behind his head.

The sky was covered in stars sparkling brightly in the pitch-black darkness. Melanie's eyes gazed over the vast number of them, drawing invisible lines from one to the next, trying to find the constellations she read about in her textbooks.

"This is incredible," she muttered. "How do you know about so many cool places?"

"Small town," he said.

"Ah, right, how could I forget?"

He chuckled. "So, what were you working on tonight?"

"Hmm?" she asked him, completely infatuated with the stars.

"On your laptop," he continued. "You seemed sort of stressed."

She let out a frustrated breath. "I got an email this week that made me realize I have focused none of my time on Yale stuff. I feel so behind."

"What do you mean? Haven't you been working on this forever?"

"Yes, I guess the part where I get in...but it's more about what happens next," she sighed. "I just don't know what I should do with my life."

"Well, I think it's pretty obvious what you should do."

Melanie frowned, pressing up slightly to face him. "You do? Care to enlighten me?"

Calvin pressed up as well, making his face level with hers. "You're meant to do something with people. Helping them in some way."

She balked. "That's—crazy, no."

He shook his head. "I don't think it's crazy at all, I think it makes perfect sense."

Calvin traced a finger up and down the side of her waist. "Did you know that the day you spoke to Blake about his boyfriend, he went home and came out to his parents that night?"

"Um, no, I didn't," she said, feeling an ember of pride radiating through her.

"And Jess, when you offered to help her with the cakes," he continued. "She came up to me later that day and told me that you were one of the good ones, and that she would beat me up if I did anything stupid."

"Jess is truly a riddle I can't solve."

"Agreed," Calvin chuckled. "And then...there's me. I've never really had a girlfriend because I've been so afraid of anyone actually knowing the truth about my life. I thought it would be too much for someone to handle, so I just never really bothered. I did my work, I finished school, I took care of Gram. But then it's like I met you and all of that changed, and I feel safe enough to share these things."

"Why me?" She couldn't help it, she had to know.

Calvin just looked into her eyes with a telling expression. "Headband, you know why."

Melanie could feel her heart hammering in her chest. Calvin reached a hand up toward her face, stroking the elastic headband slightly with the tips of his fingers before combing them through her hair.

"I knew since the moment you ordered that Strawberry cone," he confessed. "I am completely in love with you, Mel. When I told you that I wouldn't let go, I meant it. Because I can't bear the thought of losing you. I've lost more than enough in my life to know that when you're blessed with something so good, you hold on to it with everything that you have."

She gazed into his eyes that gleamed underneath the

stars, her heart pounding in her chest. *I am completely in love with you. I can't bear the thought of losing you.* His confession was so beautiful and raw, yet she was left tongue-tied. Nerves coursed through her body at every passing second, those three words practically on her lips. But she couldn't seem to let them free.

But Calvin didn't seem to notice her hesitation as he cupped his hand behind her head and kissed her, tipping open her mouth with his. The smoothness of his lips and the feel of his hand as he methodically massaged her neck had Melanie melting into his touch. They leaned back down onto the blanket as she wrapped her arms around his shoulders. He traced slowly down her back as he reached under her sweatshirt, his hands warm on her cool skin.

But he didn't go any farther. He continued to brush his hands on the small of her back and kiss her, but he didn't explore her. She thought about the way his hands had felt underneath the back of her bra just hours earlier and how much she wanted that feeling again, wanted his hands on her. She wondered if maybe he was waiting for her permission to break all those rules in his head.

She released her lips from his. "Calvin," she whispered.

"Mmhmm," he said, tracing his nose against her cheek.

"You don't have to hold back anymore."

He shifted back slightly, looking into her eyes. "Are you sure?"

She couldn't help it as her lips curled into a smile. "Yes. I'm sure."

He nodded, brushing his lips against hers, grinning. "Okay...me too."

As Calvin dipped down to kiss her, letting his hands finally explore her as he pinned her body beneath his, she hoped she would soon have the courage to say those three words back...even though she felt them deeply in her heart.

SHE BLINKED HER EYES OPEN, the sky still dark, realizing the two of them had fallen asleep. Calvin's body was wrapped around hers, his arms and his legs and his neck covering her, like he was her own personal armor. She reached for her phone and tapped on it, realizing it was 2:30 in the morning. She panicked. Her phone was almost dead, and she didn't have any service.

"Hey," she whispered, rubbing Calvin's shoulder in an attempt to wake him. "We should probably go."

He huffed, curling his arms around her even tighter. "Five more minutes."

"Tempting," she teased. "But I really should be getting home."

Even though her parents didn't keep close tabs on her, after their conversation tonight, she really didn't want to chance it.

Calvin blinked his eyes open, reaching over to kiss Melanie's cheek before peeling himself slowly off her. They collected the blanket and half-empty thermos of tea before heading back toward the car. His arm was wrapped tightly around her shoulders, hers around his waist.

"I'm pretty sure this is the best night of my life," he admitted, pulling her in for another kiss.

She smiled as she felt her face flush. "Yeah, me too."

They climbed into his truck and took off, winding down the roads back toward civilization. Melanie felt her phone buzz in her pocket, meaning she finally had service again.

It buzzed again.

Then again.

And again.

She furrowed her eyebrows as she reached for it in her sweatshirt pocket, watching as a stream of notifications came through on her screen.

Nine texts from Mom.

Three from Dad.

Five missed phone calls.

One voicemail.

She hastily tapped on the message, pressing the phone to her ear.

It was from Mom, a mixture of screaming and sobbing.

Melanie, where are you!! We're on our way to the hospital, your brother...

Calvin glanced over at her, looking concerned. "What's going on?"

Tears pooled in her eyes, spilling down her cheeks. "Baybrook Hospital," she whispered.

Calvin quickly switched gears and pressed hard on the gas.

Chapter Twenty-Three

Melanie rushed into the hospital, her vision a complete blur—a mixture of tears and utter disbelief that this was happening all over again. Calvin found out which room they were in, and she didn't wait for him as she bolted down the hall. She pushed open the door and found Mom and Dad kneeling on the floor, curled up together as sobs ripped through them.

"N—no," she croaked. "No, please."

But it was too late.

Duncan Chase Albertson left the world on August 19 at 2:19 a.m.

He drove back to Garrison that night to see old friends for a back-to-school party to celebrate the start of classes that he wouldn't be attending. His blood alcohol levels weren't as high as the night of prom, but close enough.

Then he got behind the wheel.

His head injuries from the crash were irreversible, and as the alcohol had taken over his system, his body gave up in defeat.

The doctor came in and mumbled something to

Melanie, but she couldn't hear him over the sound of her own screaming as she charged for the hospital bed.

Calvin tried reaching for her but she pushed him off, his touch feeling like burns against her skin. She climbed onto the bed next to Duncan, begging for him to come back to her, wishing this was just a cruel nightmare.

But her life, it seemed, was a mixture of dreams and nightmares. Light...and darkness. And that night, as Melanie curled up against Duncan's body despite the doctor's pleas, pressing her face in his dirty blonde curls, the darkness had won.

MELANIE DIDN'T REMEMBER MUCH of the moments and days that followed. She remembered being lifted from the hospital bed and into Dad's car, then eventually brought up to her room. She remembered her mother's attempt at trying to get her to eat something as she held out a paper plate with a slice of peanut butter toast, which Melanie refused. She remembered briefly hearing Calvin's deep voice mumbling with Dad downstairs days later, discussing arrangements.

But she didn't remember how the black dress hanging on her door had gotten into her room—somehow appearing unnoticed as the crashing waves of grief consumed her. She had gone through phases of denial lying on that hospital bed, refusing to believe that any of this could actually be real. But as she waded through moments of sleep and wakefulness, the nightmare had yet to cease. And it was unrelenting.

At some point, Melanie heard the creak of her door as it slowly opened.

"Mel, get dressed," Mom said quietly. She didn't wait for her to respond before closing it.

Even though she moved off the bed, following the usual rhythm of getting dressed, her entire body felt numb. She zipped up the side of the dress that she'd never seen before. She decided that after today, she would also never see it again. She slipped on her pair of black flats, the one's she hadn't worn since her last day at Garrison Prep, and decided that those would have to go as well.

Melanie didn't even bother looking in the mirror before leaving her room, shuffling down the stairs. She knew Dad put his arm around her shoulders, but felt nothing, the words he spoke sounding muffled like she was underwater. Her vision was already blurry from tears as he guided her to the car.

The three of them drove silently to the little white chapel, the same one Melanie went to with Gram and Calvin. She had no idea if Calvin had tried to contact her. She wasn't even sure where her phone was at the moment, probably dead in the small pile of untouched clothes that she stripped off after that horrid night.

Melanie felt her dad's hand gently reach for her arm, pulling her out of the car. He steadied her as they walked toward the chapel, Mom clenching his other hand tightly. When they stepped inside all murmuring ceased, but Melanie didn't bother to look into their sorrowful eyes as they made their way down the aisle, taking a seat at the front pew on the left.

At some point, she felt the warmth of a body sitting next to her. He was wearing his usual black slacks, but this time with a black T-shirt underneath a blazer. Calvin didn't reach for her or touch her. But he sat close enough to let her know he was there if she needed him.

The reverend started with prayers about peace. Melanie glanced up at the closed coffin before them. A bouquet of white roses had been placed at the top of the casket, and more roses lined a large framed picture of Duncan displayed on the side. It was a picture taken at some point that summer, his bouncy curls flying in the wind, his cheeks pink with life as he laughed, the most glorious grin covering his face.

"Duncan was a light to us all," the reverend started. "He knew how to make us laugh and how to bring joy. His infectious love for his family and friends reminds us that life is a precious gift."

Melanie heard a sob cut through the reverend's words. She glanced up and saw Leila in the front pew on the right side, her face crumbling with sloppy tears as an older woman held her close, rubbing her back. She quickly skimmed the pews, noticing the Fletchers sat behind them, along with some of the other Sandy Cove neighbors. Rory was there as well, sitting next to Blake, followed by Tyler, Jay, Jess, Ron, and Gram. Their eyes locked briefly. Rory didn't smile, but lifted her hands slightly and shaped them into a heart. Melanie just stared back at her blankly before turning back toward the front.

"Yet there is a darkness in this world that tries hard to consume us, and Duncan...he struggled with that darkness," the reverend continued. "He was no stranger to pain and the tendrils of evil that lurk among us. And for our poor brother, it overwhelmed him."

She felt it in her chest—that same storm that thundered inside her so many times before. In the past she'd always found ways to contain it, to control the anger that burned through her like a mighty flame. But all of that strong willpower that she relied on for years had completely depleted the day she lost her twin.

Without even comprehending what she was doing, Melanie let her lion roar. She stood up abruptly and walked around the pew, making the entire congregation gasp. The reverend paused his homily as Melanie launched down the aisle and flung open the door, leaving the chapel.

The door swung closed, and soon after, she heard a faint click as the door opened. She didn't glance back, crossing her arms tightly around her chest as Calvin came up to her side.

"Is that it?" Melanie croaked. "Is that really all he gets? He—he didn't even have a *chance*."

"I know," he whispered, his voice sounding ragged and torn. She turned to face him, noticing tears had formed in the corners of his eyes.

He didn't reach for her—he knew not to. After that night, Calvin didn't touch her again. Melanie thought about the way his hands had felt on her skin at the hospital, how the places he touched felt like scorch marks, leaving scars that reminded her of how deep her shame was. Of completely missing the moment her family needed her most.

She looked away from him as she felt that same shame to flood through her entire body. "I can't go back in there," she admitted. "That man has no idea who Duncan is or how to honor him. Nobody here does."

"Then how do you want to honor him?"

She shifted her gaze, but not to his face—just down at his shoes.

"What is the way that *you* want to honor Duncan, Mel?" Calvin asked again.

The idea came to her gently, like a whisper in the wind.

She lifted her head and started for Calvin's truck.

MELANIE PRIED OPEN the doors of the shed behind cottage five, squinting at the dim shadows within. She eyed what she was looking for and crouched down, wiping off the layer of dust before pulling out stacks of colorful plastic buckets. She handed the stacks to Calvin, his blazer already off and folded neatly on the banister leading to the house.

She grabbed a net bag of plastic shovels and rakes before standing back up. As soon as she left the shed, she kicked off her shoes near the trash can, then started for the beach.

Calvin followed with the stacks of buckets and placed them next to Melanie as she knelt down in the sand. She used her arm to level out a large flat surface in front of her.

"What would you like me to do?" Calvin asked.

She peeled off a bucket from one of the stacks, shoving it in his direction. "Go find crabs."

Calvin did what he was told without a word, rolling up the ends of his slacks before wading in the water, lifting up rocks and dutifully catching crabs, placing them gently in his bucket.

Melanie got to work too. She did exactly as Duncan had always taught her, filling the bucket with some water before packing in dry sand, making each tower sturdy. She pressed the sand in tightly with her fist before turning it over on the flat surface.

The first tower completely fell apart, but she just swept the sand off and tried again. The next tower was able to stand despite parts of the top slowly crumbling away. But she didn't care as she kept building tower after tower, using buckets of different shapes and sizes as she stacked the towers overtop of one another. Her shapes looked like blobs but she kept moving, hoping that somehow at the end, the castle would turn into something magical. Like Duncan had reached down and fixed it himself.

"Here," Calvin said softly behind her.

She turned around and took the bucket from him, then delicately tipped the crabs into the center of the castle, into their new home. The bucket she held bumped one of her towers, causing a large part of the right side of the castle to come tumbling down.

She threw the bucket and let out a cry, dropping to her knees. Her dress was now wet and covered with sand, but she couldn't care less. She hugged her legs tightly toward her chest, pressed her forehead to her knees, and bawled. She didn't bother wiping her face as the tears fell and snot dribbled from her nose.

She felt a hand on her shoulder but she shoved it off, pulling her legs even tighter together.

Calvin stepped back. "I'll, um...I'll be on the porch."

He left her alone as she continued to cry at the pathetic sand castle next to her.

"You were so much better at this, Dee," she said, her voice gurgling with each word. "You were better at every-thing. I wish the world could have seen it. How deeply you loved and how much joy you brought to the world."

She sobbed for a few moments, then took a deep, steadying breath before continuing. "I can't do this without you. I don't even know how."

Melanie wasn't sure how long she sat there, rocking back and forth, letting herself openly weep on Sandy Cove beach. All she knew was at some point, her father's arms wrapped around her as he lifted her up, the sky already deep shades of purple, and the sun already gone.

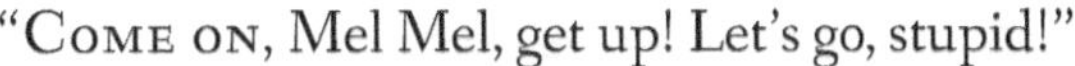

"Come on, Mel Mel, get up! Let's go, stupid!"

Duncan was jumping up and down on their bed. It was early—or at least it felt that way after spending the majority of the night before playing their Game Boys under the covers.

"No, so tired," Melanie moaned, throwing the quilt over her head.

He reached for the blanket and pulled it off of her, throwing it on the floor. "Mel Mel, the sand on the beach is still damp. It's *prime* castle-making conditions, get your stupid butt out of bed."

She flung herself at her brother to try and punch him, but he wrestled her, shoving her face in his armpit, and yelling at her to smell it. She pinched his belly, causing him to yelp and jump back.

"Okay, fine, let me get my suit on," she moaned.

"No time," he said, grabbing her hand and tugging her down the steps of the cottage. "If we wait, the sand will be too dry."

"Where do you two think you're going?" Mom asked, already at work putting together their picnic lunch for the beach.

"No time to chat, we have work to do," he said, dragging Melanie toward the front screen door.

"Well, do you want breakfast?"

"Pancakes," Duncan ordered. "But when we get back."

Mom rolled her eyes as they stepped outside. They picked up the sandy buckets and shovels that lined the front of the house, then she chased him down to the beach. The sand was perfectly damp, the ends of her bright blue pajama pants getting coated with wet sand and strings of dry black seaweed.

Duncan was already on the ground, making a level surface for them to start building. "Start packing the buckets with sand, Mel Mel. As tight as you can."

She did as he said, packing sand tightly into buckets and handing them over to her brother. He assessed her work, fixing her packing job to make sure the tower wouldn't topple over, before gracefully turning the bucket over and sliding it off, making a perfectly shaped tower every single time. He stacked the towers on top of each other, stepping back to evaluate his work with each new tower like an architect. She loved to watch her brother's creativity come to life, the shapes of his castles always getting bigger and more intricate with each summer they spent in Haverport. She always thought about how naturally smart he was compared to her, and secretly wished she could be just like him.

"Okay, I'm thinking we'll need to stack a few more towers on the side here to make a little lookout, kind of like a fort. To make sure no one steals our crabs."

"And will we assign a crab to be our little watchman?" Melanie teased.

"Mel Mel, have an imagination," he pestered, knocking at her head playfully.

They finished up making the small towers, then the two of them rolled up their sandy pajama pants and headed for the water, turning over rocks to find little crabs to place in their new home.

"How many flavors do you have left to try at Scoops?" she asked.

"Thirteen," Duncan answered. "I've decided to skip Rum Raisin. It's not worth massacring my taste buds for something so *vile*."

She laughed, making a joke about him smelling vile, causing him to reach over to tackle her, but her swift karate chop movement kept him away.

"Do you have a favorite yet?" she asked.

"Birthday cake was FIRRRE," he belted. "But honestly? Oreo was also pretty deese."

"Deese?"

"Short for decent, keep up Mel Mel," Duncan teased. "How are your crabs looking?"

His bucket had over double the amount as Melanie, but he decided their collection looked good enough. They walked back up to their beautiful castle, with windows and doors intricately drawn along the sides of the towers, traced by Duncan with a small twig he'd found in the sand. He crouched down when they approached the castle, tipping the bucket toward a small open window at the front, watching closely as the little crabs crawled and jumped in.

She stepped back to give him room, almost stepping right on top of the most stunning little scallop shell she'd ever seen. She picked it up, admiring how perfectly symmetrical it was. The shell had a magical mixture of light pinks and grays that made it so astonishingly beautiful, she couldn't help but press it in the center of the front of the castle, like a little shrine.

The two of them stepped back, admiring their work. Duncan had a massive grin on his face. He reached for Melanie's hand and squeezed it. "Probably our best one yet."

She sulked. "It was mostly you, I just followed instructions."

"Oh, shut up," he said. "I could have never done this without you, Mel Mel."

Chapter Twenty-Four

Melanie wasn't sure how long she lay there in bed, letting the memories come at her in waves. The idea of trying to get up and function without Duncan in her life seemed utterly impossible. So instead, she let the days and the nights melt together, refusing to leave for meals or even walk outside as the summer season of Haverport drew to a close. Sometimes she would have the energy to sit by her bay window, staring out at the sunshine and the ocean, nibbling on a piece of toast or some crackers her mother forced her to eat.

That's where she was when she saw Calvin's truck pull up to the cottage. She shuffled away from the window so he wouldn't see her, but stood close by and listened as he knocked on the screen door.

"Hey, Calvin," Dad said.

"Sir," Calvin said, his voice sounding heavy and exhausted. "How is she?"

He sighed. "Still hasn't left her room."

Awkward silence lingered between the two of them for a moment.

"Has she eaten anything?" he asked.

"Barely."

More silence.

"Reading anything good lately?" Dad asked, obviously trying to make light of the heavy situation they were in.

"I honestly haven't been able to since, well—" He trailed off. "Plus, I started school last week."

"Ah, so it looks like summer is over for you then."

"Unfortunately. But it's okay. I'm actually liking my classes."

"Good, that's what I like to hear," Dad said. "Listen, Calvin...we appreciate you a lot for helping us out with the funeral, which was above and beyond the call of duty, and Alice and I are incredibly grateful. But right now—" He hesitated for a moment as if he didn't want to say whatever it was that he needed to say. "We're still trying to figure out what to do next, and with your classes starting, I would hate for us to be more of a burden. You should go and enjoy the start of college."

"You are never a burden," he declared pointedly.

"You're a good kid," Dad replied. Melanie heard the muffled sound of a hand patting a shoulder. "But I think right now she's going to need space to heal. Let her come to you when she's ready."

Another soul-sucking silence.

"All right," Calvin said softly. "I can do that, sir."

"Please stop calling me that, it gives me the creeps," Dad joked.

"Never," he replied. She heard him walk down the front porch steps, the broken shells and rocks crunching underneath his sneakers as he headed toward his truck. Melanie peeked out her window and saw him sitting in the driver's seat, scratching his head that looked freshly buzzed. She saw him let out a long breath as he glanced up toward her window, causing her to shuffle back behind the curtain. Shame washed over her again as she thought about that night, about what she'd done with him while her twin brother was dying at the hospital. Melanie didn't have the energy to face him, didn't even want to look him in the eye. It was all too overwhelming.

She watched him discreetly as he crossed his arms against the steering wheel, pressing his head against his forearms. His shoulders moved slightly as he sat there and cried.

MELANIE WAITED for the sounds of the house to still. It was late at night, and her parents were already in bed and likely fast asleep. She slid out of her covers and tip-toed out of the room, heading across the hall. She creaked open the door.

Duncan's room looked like no one had touched it in the week and a half since his accident. His bed was unmade and his computer was tucked into the covers from watching his shows late at night. A few coffee cups lined his night-stand, still stained from the coffee he never finished, too lazy to bring his mugs downstairs. His old prescription bottles were also still there, scattered next to his mugs, some even on the floor.

Melanie's heart twisted thinking of him. She hoped that coming in here would help her feel his presence in some way, make him feel tangible and alive. But this room and the moments leading up to his death didn't remind her of the brother that she lost, but of the lion that tormented her nightmares. She felt horrible for thinking it, for feeling some kind of relief that she wouldn't have to experience it again. But then the yearning hit her at full force, and she wished he could somehow come back and be the same boy that woke her up those early summer mornings, forcing her to make sand castles in her pajamas.

She was about to turn and leave when she noticed a small box open next to his bed. She stepped forward and peeked in, noticing it was full of Duncan's treasures from his past. His blue iPod was stacked on top of a raggedy old DVD organizer. His notebook was open, with the meticulous list of all of the Scoops ice cream flavors. He highlighted Birthday Cake, drawing a crown next to it as the clear winner of the summer. But she also noticed a blue star next to Strawberry, with a very small almost illegible scribble next to it.

Mel Mel's favorite, don't forget!

The tears came, something she couldn't seem to control these days. She lifted the box and carried it over to her room, setting it down on her bed. She started removing all of the items, admiring each slowly. His first-ever lacrosse jersey from third grade was rolled up tightly in a ball. She found an old photo from Halloween, the two of them dressed up as Luke and Leia in their Star Wars garb. She chuckled, remembering how desperate he was for her to dress up with him that year. "They're the most badass twins out there Mel Mel," he said, in an attempt to get her to say yes. "Besides the whole kissing thing, of course."

She smiled, opening up the frame and placing it on her nightstand. When she looked back down, she found a small jewelry box that must have been tucked underneath the picture. She lifted it up, the contents making her sob so hard, she didn't care if she was making noise.

It was the scallop shell. The same one Melanie had found for their castle years ago.

She lifted it delicately, the shell so dainty and small. The light pink had faded over the years, but it was still completely perfect. He must have secretly run out there at some point that summer and found it, preserving it well in the little box. She wondered what he could have been saving it for.

Maybe Duncan didn't even know himself at the time, but right now, as she twisted it underneath the moonlight that softly streamed through her window, it felt like a small gift from her twin. A little nudge of hope letting her know that even though he was gone, she would always be his Mel Mel. And he would always be her Dee.

MELANIE WOKE up the next morning to the sound of raised voices downstairs. She rubbed her eyes as she sat up slowly, brushing off Duncan's items that she must have fallen asleep with. She listened intently as she left her room, standing at the top of the stairs. "What's going on?"

They abruptly stopped, looking up at her.

She noticed a stack of broken-down packing boxes neatly piled at the front door, like they'd just been delivered. Mom had one shaped and open at her feet as she emptied bowls from the kitchen cupboard.

Dad was standing on the other side of the counter, arms crossed firmly against his chest, not looking pleased.

"Sweetheart, you're up," she said, placing down the

stack of bowls in her hand. "Do you want something to eat? Maybe some eggs?"

Melanie made her way down the stairs. "No...I want to know what's going on."

She glanced over at Dad briefly, who just shrugged back at her. He seemed aggravated.

"Honey," Mom started, looking back at Melanie. "We were thinking—"

"You were thinking," Dad interjected.

"*We* were thinking that, well, we did move here for Duncan..."

Melanie froze, realizing what her mother was about to say.

"And we took you away from all the opportunities you had in Garrison," Mom continued. "That wasn't fair, and we're sorry."

Dad looked over at Melanie, his face full of remorse, like he too was sorry. But she could tell he was annoyed at what was happening.

"You want to move back," Melanie whispered.

"The buyers haven't signed yet so the house hasn't officially sold. We can go back on our deal."

"You want to leave Haverport." The weight of what was going on sat deep in her stomach, like a heavy rock at the bottom of the sea.

"Sweetheart, we're so worried about how you've been feeling about school, and we thought maybe going back could help you make those decisions," she said. "Be back in a place that has been so good to you for so many years."

Good wasn't the word Melanie would use to describe Garrison Prep. Words like exhausting, stressful, and lonely came to mind. But never good.

She looked over at her father. "Is that what you think, too?"

He released his arms, running his hands through his hair in frustration. "I told her to ask you first," he admitted.

Melanie felt it, the rage fuming inside of her. "But you didn't," she said, turning to her mom. "You just assumed, like you always do."

Mom crossed her arms. "What's that supposed to mean?"

"You think you know what's best for everyone, so you just barrel through with another Grand Plan, thinking it will fix everything," Melanie spewed.

She stared at her, mouth agape.

"He wasn't okay," Melanie whispered at first, her voice gradually getting louder. "He was *struggling*, but you just pretended like everything was fine. But he wasn't fine."

"Melanie—" Dad started.

"*No!*" Melanie yelled. "It wasn't just a teenage phase! Duncan had a serious problem, but neither of you did anything about it."

Dad slumped down into a chair. "We did. We tried to get help."

She stared back at her father, stunned. Mom turned away from her, her knuckles going white as she clutched the edge of the sink.

"What are you talking about?" Melanie asked, bewildered.

"We took him to different doctors and counseling, back in Garrison," Dad explained. "We knew he had an addiction, but we also found out he had bipolar disorder."

Mom twisted her head sharply at Dad, like he'd said too much.

"He had medication, which sometimes he took. But sometimes," Dad said, with a sigh. "He didn't."

Melanie's throat went dry, her mind immediately flashing to the prescription bottles on Duncan's nightstand. How he'd brushed it off and changed the subject weeks ago, pretending like it was from his bout with strep throat. He'd lied to her.

Melanie's eyes roamed slowly from her mother back to her father. "How long have you known?"

"Almost a year," Dad said.

Melanie clenched her hands into fists. "And you didn't tell me?" she asked through gritted teeth.

"We didn't want to bother you with it, sweetheart. You were so focused on Yale and your studies that we didn't want to put more on your plate. It wasn't your problem to worry about."

Melanie squeezed her eyes shut, not believing what she was hearing. It was exactly what she would have done to them—try to shield them from any more hurt or pain.

But this was her *brother*. All of those seasons of the lion and the lamb, those stretches of having good days and bad days. It sat heavy in her chest, the fact that they didn't think it was wise for her to know. It had her seeing red.

"We thought about it, telling you," he admitted. "But then we moved here, and for a while, things were working out. He was taking his medication, he wasn't drinking at first—"

Melanie took a deep, aggravated breath. "And you thought your plan was working, so you kept me in the dark."

Mom finally turned toward her. "We did what we had to, to protect you."

"Protect me from *what*?!" she yelled. "From not knowing what was going on with my own brother?! I live here, I *saw* what was happening, I listened to the screaming!"

"Melanie, please honey, calm down, we know we screwed up by not telling you," Dad admitted.

She was silent from his confession, and for the first time, she really saw them. Not just as her parents, the people that gave her advice and provided for her and told her what to do. She saw them as broken, flawed, imperfect humans. People who screw up. People who didn't have it all together. She realized in that moment that none of them did; no one truly had it all figured out. And even if they thought they were doing the right thing by hiding all of this from her, Melanie understood that even her parents could get it all wrong.

"Okay," she whispered. She didn't *feel* okay about any of it, that her parents kept this massive secret from her. But at least they could admit it was a mistake.

Dad's shoulders relaxed slightly.

Mom leaned against the sink, her arms tightly wound across her stomach, her mouth pressed into that firm line. "Principal Eddy said you're more than welcome to come back. You would have to make up the first two weeks of classes, but they're all confident that you can do it."

Melanie could feel the panic rising in her chest. The thought of going back, of being in that house without Duncan, of walking the halls of Garrison Prep, of going back to her life as a nobody...it had her mind spinning.

"No."

They both froze, staring at her with eyes so wide, their eyeballs looked like they were going to fall out of their heads.

"Melanie," Mom started. "Honey, but—"

"No," she said, firmly this time. "No, I won't go back."

"But what about school?" she asked. "What about your dreams?"

Her mind was too preoccupied to answer at first. She realized right then and there that her dreams were no longer what she thought them to be. When she thought about her dreams, she imagined being here. Her hair flowing behind her as she rode her bike down the streets of Haverport. Laughing with Rory on the beach on a cloudy day. Pressing scoops of ice cream into cones. Counting jam jars with the Fletchers while listening to the Grateful Dead. Eating an abhorrently disgusting ice cream cake around a bonfire. Sitting on Sunset rock, wrapped tightly in a pair of arms that belonged to a guy who promised to never let her go.

She hoped he still hadn't let go. She hoped he hadn't given up.

She hoped she could still say those three words to him.

"I have new dreams," she said confidently.

With that, she slipped on her ratty pair of flip-flops and charged for the back door.

Chapter Twenty-Five

SHE DIDN'T HESITATE, didn't even bother going up to her room to grab her helmet or change out of her old tank top and sleep shorts, didn't turn back as her parents yelled for her. She hopped on her bike and sped down the streets of Sandy Cove, racing toward downtown.

Scoops was packed. Melanie had no idea what day it was, but she hoped it wasn't a Sunday. She turned her bike into the parking lot and around the lines of people, then hopped off, dropping it down carelessly on the grass as she walked toward the shop. She was ready to barge into the back and demand to see him, fully planning on biking the entire town of Haverport until she found him.

But she didn't have to look far. Calvin was at the window, nodding at a customer who was placing an order.

Rory was the first to notice her as she approached Scoops. She tapped him on the shoulder, then pointed outside. Calvin's head quickly turned and he froze, staring at her like she was the only thing that truly mattered. Without taking his eyes off her, Calvin handed Rory the teal cup he was holding, then bolted for the back door. He appeared from behind the shop and was charging for her. He looked haggard—like the past two weeks had torn him up from the inside out too.

Melanie inhaled, then stopped moving. What was she going to say to him? The last time they spoke was at the funeral, and she had pushed him off. Just like she did at the hospital. She had no idea how he felt, if he was angry at her for pushing him away, or if he'd decided to move on like her father had insinuated.

Before she was able to string together her words, Calvin folded his arms tightly around Mclanie's waist. Tears welled up in her eyes as she returned the embrace. He picked her up, holding her tightly, burying his face in her hair as she wrapped her legs around him.

She was now openly sobbing in front of everyone, but she didn't care. Calvin held her close, kissing her neck, his own tears brushing her cheeks.

"I'm—I'm so sorry," she muttered, wiping a hand across her face now covered in tears. "I pushed you away, I let go."

"You have nothing to apologize for," Calvin said, tears still streaming down his face. But he didn't wipe them away, didn't care that everyone was watching them—including Rory and Blake who had their faces pressed up against the shop window. "You lost your brother, Melanie. There is no rulebook of how this should go. I just—" He hesitated, his voice cracking. "I just thought I was going to lose you."

"You won't lose me," Melanie said, letting out a deep breath. "I'm in love with you too, Calvin. I realize now that love isn't just about having the good moments, but also being there in the hard ones."

She brushed away his tears with her thumb. "And I want to be with you through them all."

He combed a hand through her hair, cupping the back

of her head as he pulled her mouth to his. He kissed her so earnestly, like he was out of breath and she was his oxygen. She was crying again as she kissed him back, reaching her arms around his shoulders and pulling his face even closer, savoring the taste of his lips, the feel of his hands, the rumbling of his voice.

Customers burst out in applause. She pulled away and chuckled, feeling embarrassed. He placed her down gently, but kept his arms wrapped tightly around her waist.

"There was so much I didn't know, so much my parents kept from me," Melanie admitted. "They told me he was bipolar, that he was on medication. They tried to get him help for his addiction."

He nodded, like this all made sense. He brushed his thumbs against her cheeks, his hands steady, catching the tears that wouldn't stop falling.

"I just wish there was something else I could have done," she said. "Something that could have saved him."

"Don't, Melanie. Don't do that. Addiction is a ruthless disease. It just takes and takes and takes. There's never any room for grace, it's just unrelenting and evil. And we're all powerless against it. The people it takes, and the people who have to watch. But Mel," he said, lifting her face as he rubbed his thumbs back and forth against her cheeks. "It was never your fault, and it was never something you would have been able to fix."

She just nodded, allowing herself to fall back into kissing him, Calvin's body firmly pressed against her own.

When they finally slowed, he dropped kisses on her lips, her nose, her cheeks, the lids of her eyes, mimicking the first time he touched her like this.

"I've spent so much of my life trying to hide the truth and just focus on school, that I feel like I sort of lost myself along the way," Melanie admitted. "And now, without him...I don't know who I am. And I don't know if I'm ready for what comes next."

"I know who you are," Calvin replied confidently. "You may not see it, but you are thoughtful and kind. You love people fiercely and care so deeply about their happiness."

He tucked a piece of hair behind her ear. "I know nothing makes sense right now, but I promise, you can always count on this. I love you, and I will always be here."

She nodded as he enveloped her in his arms, digging her face into his shirt. He kissed her forehead before resting his chin on the top of her head.

"Calvin?"

"Hmm?"

She pulled back, looking up into his sparkling blue eyes. "I'll have Strawberry. Waffle cone. Two scoops."

Calvin grinned. "On it, headband."

Even though she had no clue what the next chapters of her life would look like, at least Melanie was certain about one thing: Here, in Calvin's arms, she was truly safe. A safe harbor among the vast, unknown shores that lay ahead.

Epilogue

Eight months later

MELANIE SAT on the beach next to two sand castles that weren't half bad. She'd spent a lot of time out here over the past eight months, perfecting the art of packing damp sand into buckets for pristine-looking towers. They rarely toppled over anymore, but her castles were still far from anything like Duncan would create. But today, as she sat next to the twin set of castles, she had a feeling Dee would be proud of what she made.

Some days were certainly better than others. She would experience strings of good days, having enough energy to hang with Rory at school football games and participate in her classes at Haverport High. They weren't nearly as rigorous as her studies at Garrison Prep, but she liked the slower pace of it all—it just felt nice to breathe and take her time.

Then, as if it came out of nowhere, she would get pummeled with grief. It was always the little things that would remind her of him, like eating tacos or seeing cartons of chocolate milk at the grocery store. Sometimes the wave of grief would be unruly yet brief, causing her to sob uncontrollably. Other times it was longer, consuming her entire being, making it difficult to even get out of bed. On those days Calvin always showed up, bringing her a milkshake or a slice of blueberry coffee cake, and held her while she silently wept until she fell asleep.

She heard footsteps approaching from behind. Calvin plopped down next to her. "These came out great."

"He would've made fun of them still," Melanie said, twirling the scallop shell dangling around her neck. "But yeah, definitely better than my first."

"CAKE!"

She heard laughter on the porch behind them. She twisted her head and noticed the Scoopers were all crowded around the table on the porch. Jess was opening up a cake box as Rory and Tyler cracked up at something Blake just said. Jay just stood there and smiled, his arms crossed tightly at his chest. Ever since coming back from his first year at college, Jay was quieter and more reserved. He moved around Scoops like a ghost, his contagious laughter and constant banter completely leached out of him.

"Do you know what's going on with him?" Calvin asked.

Melanie did, in fact, know what was going on with him. She glanced at Rory, noticing how insanely happy she looked as she laughed at Blake's story, making some kind of witty remark at him. Her best friend trusted her with that secret, and even if Melanie did love Calvin with every fiber of her being, she knew it wasn't her story to tell.

"It's none of our business," Melanie answered him.

"Well, okay," Calvin responded. "But what *is* my business is how you're feeling about your big decision. Any regrets?"

Melanie sighed. It was this time last week that she sat down with her parents and told them she wouldn't be going to Yale.

It took her a while to feel comfortable with her parents again, and deep down, a part of her wondered if she would always feel hurt that they never told her the truth. And yet, despite how different everything felt between them, this particular shift in their relationship finally gave Melanie the freedom she needed to choose what *she* really wanted in life —instead of choosing something just to make them happy.

So even as she'd opened her acceptance letter earlier that year, the four of them celebrating with a bottle of sparkling apple cider Calvin brought over, Melanie knew she would be declining Yale's offer.

Ever since August 19, nothing in her life felt the same. And yet, somehow, over the past few months, her future had become quite clear.

Melanie knew Yale wasn't going to be an option—or any other college where she would live on campus, for that matter. Being around alcohol was the biggest trigger of all, enveloping Melanie in the darkest of nightmares as she relived the horrible storms of the lion. They were the memories she didn't want tied to her brother, and while she hoped someday being around alcohol wouldn't cause her to become completely crippled by anxiety, she knew heading off to college wasn't the best place for her right now.

Besides, Calvin was right. She had a talent for listening and caring for people. Instead, she enrolled at the University of Connecticut as a commuter student for that coming fall, with a plan to someday become a school counselor. She wanted to help teens like Duncan who struggled...and teens like herself who also struggled in the shadows.

"None," she answered him. "No regrets at all."

He nodded. "Good. I'm proud of you."

She planted a kiss on his cheek. "So...what cake flavor did Jess land on?"

"It's a double layer," Calvin said. "Strawberry on the bottom, and Birthday Cake on the top. Purple frosting lining the edges."

Melanie grinned, thinking about how the purple frosting would leave a mark for a few days. Just like another mark she now carried with her. "That's perfect."

She couldn't fathom having the purple cake without him this year, so Melanie requested they start a new tradition in his honor.

She watched as Mom and Dad pushed their way through the screen door of the house, followed by another guy holding a stack of paper plates and forks.

"Is that...Kevin?" Melanie asked.

"Yeah," Calvin said. "I brought him along, hope that's okay."

"Why?"

"Well...I think he's hoping for a miracle."

Melanie watched Kevin place the stack of plates down, his gaze lingering on Jess from across the table as she leaned over to carefully slice the cake.

"Interesting," she remarked, remembering their brief conversation in the bike shop last summer.

Calvin chuckled, sliding an arm around her waist as he pulled her closer. She tucked into him, now looking back out at the sea, the breeze feeling unusually warm for a late spring day.

He kissed her temple before pressing his face to hers. "Happy birthday," he whispered in her ear.

She smiled. "Thanks."

They sat there in comfortable silence, watching the waves slowly tumble back and forth on the shore.

Melanie exhaled as she glanced up at the wispy clouds in the sky. "Happy birthday, Dee."

READ THE BONUS CHAPTER

**Want to know Calvin's point of view on
the Fourth of July?**

Read the *Safe Harbor* bonus chapter for free by signing up
for my newsletter at the following link!

tinyurl.com/calvinchapter

Also by K.Sinko

Acknowledgments

First, I would like to thank you as the reader. Thank you for supporting my work, and I hope you enjoyed your summer in Haverport. I look forward to spending more time with you in my favorite little fictional beach town in books two and three.

To all the early readers and supporters of my work, I couldn't have been here without your encouragement and wisdom over the years: Genny Ryley, Alexis Wierenga, Samantha Boesch, Abby Hancock, Carleigh Stiehm-Wenik, Amber Strickland, Hannah Hickman, Anette Haylon, Lisa Sinko, and Grammy Sinko.

Thanks to Studio Ryley for the amazing artwork and cover for this book. Jonny, thank you for your dedication and vision that brought my first novel to life.

My editor Britt Tayler, the Paperback Proofreader. Thank you for making my words sparkle.

My social media whiz, Ann Marie Langrehr. You are the right amount of crazy and I absolutely love it. Thanks for always being my hype woman.

My New Yorkers, thank you for caring for me week after week. I'm pretty sure I owe my sanity to you: Andrew Koss, Taylor Arnold, Cheyenne Buckingham, and all of the Dear Ones.

Monica Spencer, for all the giggles and the storybook-worthy summers days on the beach. Thanks for always being the onion ring to my ketchup, and for teaching me what it means to truly disdain summer people.

The crew at the Niantic Dairy Queen, you know who you are. Thanks for making my summers extra sweet.

My family, both new and old. Thank you for always supporting my dreams and all of my crazy ideas.

Grandma Small, thanks for pointing at my journals and insisting that I "write that book." I did it, Grandma, here you go.

Mom and Dad, thanks for having faith in me, and for giving me room to spread my wings.

And of course, to my babe. You made a vow many years ago to always encourage me to be who I'm made to be. Thanks for never going back on that promise.

About the Author

K.Sinko is an indie published author with a deep love for love stories. She is the author of *Sunday Supper, Call Of The Loon, Please Be Mine,* and the Scoops Series—a trilogy of stand-alone romances featuring the of a fictional ice cream shop. Her debut novel *Safe Harbor* became an Amazon best seller for young adult contemporary romance and is the winner of two Indieverse Awards. Follow her on Instagram and sign up for her newsletter to get the latest book updates.

tinyurl.com/ksinkonewsletter

 instagram.com/authorksinko